Praise for the Gethsemane Brown Mystery Series

"The captivating southwestern Irish countryside adds a delightful element to this paranormal series launch. Gethsemane is an appealing protagonist who is doing the best she can against overwhelming odds."

– L̵

"Gordon strikes a harmonious chor̵ of a mystery."

– Susan M. Boyer,
USA Today Bestselling Author of *Lowcountry Book Club*

"Charming debut."

– *Kirkus Reviews*

"A fantastic story with a great ghost, with bad timing. There are parts that are extremely comical, and Gethsemane is a fantastic character that you root for as the pressure continually builds for her to succeed...in more ways than one."

– *Suspense Magazine*

"Just when you think you've seen everything, here comes Gethsemane Brown, baton in one hand, bourbon in the other...There's charm to spare in this highly original debut."

– Catriona McPherson,
Agatha Award-Winning Author of *The Reek of Red Herrings*

"Gethsemane Brown is a fast-thinking, fast-talking dynamic sleuth (with a great wardrobe) who is more than a match for the unraveling murders and cover-ups, aided by her various– handsome–allies and her irascible ghost."

– Chloe Green,
Author of the Dallas O'Connor Mysteries

"In Gordon's Exceptional third mystery...her ghosts operate under a set of limitations, allowing her earthly protagonists to shine as they cleverly solve crimes. Fans of paranormal cozies will be enthralled."

— *Publishers Weekly* (starred review)

"For any fan who has become completely enraptured by the character of Gethsemane Brown, you will not only love the 'spirit' in this one, but you will also be thrilled to join up with Gethsemane on her third adventure...an all-out, fun-filled story."

— *Suspense Magazine*

"Gethsemane Brown is everything an amateur sleuth should be: smart, sassy, talented, and witty even when her back is against the wall."

— Cate Holahan,
Silver Falchion Award-Nominated Author of *The Widower's Wife*

"Erstwhile ghost conjurer and gifted concert violinist Gethsemane Brown returns in this thoroughly enjoyable follow-up to last year's *Murder in G Major*...With the help of a spectral sea captain she accidentally summoned, Gethsemane tries to unravel the mystery as the murderer places her squarely in the crosshairs."

— Daniel J. Hale,
Agatha Award-Winning Author

"In the latest adventures with Gethsemane, murder is once again thrust upon her and with determination and a goal, she does what needs to be done...The author does a great job in keeping this multi-plot tale intriguing...I like that the narrative put me in the middle of all the action capturing the essence that is Ireland. The character of Eamon adds a touch that makes this engagingly appealing series more endearing."

— *Dru's Book Musings*

FATALITY IN F

The Gethsemane Brown Mystery Series
by Alexia Gordon

A Gethsemane Brown Mystery

FATALITY IN F

ALEXIA GORDON

HENERY PRESS

Copyright

FATALITY IN F
A Gethsemane Brown Mystery
Part of the Henery Press Mystery Collection

First Edition | February 2019

Henery Press, LLC
www.henerypress.com

Trade Paperback ISBN-13: 978-1-63511-459-1
Digital epub ISBN-13: 978-1-63511-460-7
Kindle ISBN-13: 978-1-63511-461-4
Hardcover ISBN-13: 978-1-63511-462-1

Printed in the United States of America

To my parents

ACKNOWLEDGMENTS

Thank you to:

My editors and the rest of the gang at the Hen House for making my books the best they can be;

Paula and Gina for their support and encouragement;

Kellye, Valerie, Abby, Cheryl, Tracy, and Rachel for the unicorn power;

Catriona McPherson and Hank Phillippi Ryan for letting me hang out with the cool kids;

My blog mates at *Miss Demeanors* and *Femme Fatales*;

My parents, Aunt Wilhelmina, and the rest of my family for their love and support;

Leslie Lipps for her graphic art skills;

Lifeworking Coworking for providing writing space;

The Deerpath Inn for letting me spend hours by their fireplace and for expanding my whiskey knowledge;

Missions Possible Bookstore at the Church of the Holy Spirit for shelving my books next to C.S. Lewis;

The Writer's Path at SMU for helping me grow from wanna-be writer to published author;

The entire crime fiction community for proving people who write about murder are fun at parties (and are awesome, caring, supportive, and friendly, too);

To the book reviewers/bloggers for taking the time to review my books;

To Kristine Hall for still inviting me to Lone Star Lit book blog tours years after I left Texas;

To my friends for being there for me;

To the readers for being the reason I do this.

One

The flower shop's heavy glass entrance door flew open.

"Ooph!" Gethsemane Brown flattened herself against the shop's wall just in time to avoid being smashed. She cradled a pot holding an ailing miniature rose bush, little more than a twig with a few sad leaves, to her chest. Someone, impossible to tell whether male or female, hunched beneath a floppy hat and an unseasonable, shapeless sweater, rushed past her. A sprig of small purple blossoms fluttered from the just visible bouquet clutched beneath the figure's arm. "Excuse me!"

The person ignored her and hurried away down the sidewalk. Gethsemane watched until they disappeared around a corner. "Have a nice day," she called after them.

"Welcome to Buds of May," a woman's voice said from inside the flower shop. "May I help you?"

Gethsemane gestured in the figure's direction as she navigated past tall, fluted bins overflowing with cheerful flower arrangements. "What's with him? Or her?" She set her flowerpot on the counter.

The woman behind the counter, a sweet-faced blonde about Gethsemane's age, shrugged. "Everyone's in a hurry these days, ain't they?" A brass plaque attached to a cache pot crowded with miniature succulents identified her as Alexandra Sexton, Florist.

She lifted the flowerpot and turned it back and forth to examine its sad resident. The dull, bloomless stems shed one of their few remaining leaves in response. "What's happened to this?"

"It's dead," a voice behind Gethsemane announced. She recognized Frankie Grennan, her friend and colleague at St. Brennan's School for Boys. "What've you done to it?"

"I didn't do anything to it." Gethsemane frowned at the copper-haired math teacher and amateur rosarian as she reclaimed the pot from the florist. The plant lost another curled leaf.

"There's your problem," Frankie said. "You do actually have to water and feed it."

"I watered it." Gethsemane ran a finger across the soil's surface. Dry. "Some. Maybe not as often as I should have but I did water it."

Frankie took the plant from her. "I know what you did. You let the poor thing get dry as the Sahara then unleashed a monsoon on it with a little watering pot you bought for three Euros at the grocer then let it get desert-dry again. That's no way to treat a rose."

"I didn't use a watering pot," Gethsemane mumbled. "I used a juice glass."

Alexandra frowned and clucked her tongue. "Tsk, tsk."

"I won't tell you what I think of your juice glass," Frankie said. "Poor rose. Why didn't you call me for help?"

"It's just a plant—" Gethsemane began.

Frankie cut her off. "Just a plant?" He addressed the florist, "Did you hear that, Alexandra? She said a rose is 'just a plant.'" He made a face at Gethsemane. "Up the yard with that. How'd you like me callin' that fancy violin of yours 'just an instrument?'"

Her Vuillaume "just an instrument?" No. She shuddered. Her nineteenth century masterpiece was a work of art. Frankie took roses as seriously as she took music. "Sorry. Plants are nice. I mean roses are nice. Beautiful. Magnificent." Her cheeks flushed. "I'll stop talking now."

Alexandra leaned her elbows on the counter and lowered her voice as if she shared a great secret. "Actually, the global floriculture market brings in tens of billions worldwide every year. People have killed for a lot less than billions."

Gethsemane lowered her tone to match Alexandra's. "Floriculture?"

"The flowering and ornamental plant business, including roses."

"Billions?" Why was she whispering? "Billions," she repeated in her normal voice, "As in dollars? Euros? For flowers?"

"Flowers," Frankie said. "Which you send to your Ma on Mother's Day and her birthday, bedeck the church with at weddings, send to your girlfriend when you're courting, your wife when you're apologizing—"

Gethsemane held up a hand. "Okay, I get it. That's a lot of flowers." But still...

"Don't forget the ones you plant in your garden," Alexandra reached over the counter and poked at the wan stems in Frankie's hand and frowned at Gethsemane, "or buy from the grocer. Did you know over 40 percent of the cut flowers you Americans import are roses? Maybe you should stick to the cut ones."

Gethsemane flushed and turned back to Frankie. "I wasn't belittling roses. I only meant I didn't think you'd have the energy to resuscitate my sad little plant. It's only been a minute since your, er, illness." Frankie, like the rest of Dunmullach's first-born males, had fallen victim to a wasting sickness unleashed by the curse of an angry spirit determined to avenge herself for the evil done to her centuries ago. If not for the actions of the ghosts of Eamon and Orla McCarthy, the late owners of Gethsemane's cottage, actions that exacted great sacrifice from the McCarthys, Frankie, and a good portion of the village's other males, would have died. "You've hardly had time to get back on your feet."

"It's been six months and I'm fine now." Frankie's tone left no doubt the reticent math teacher intended to stick to his practice of keeping his private life private. "St. B's staff gardener and some of the senior boys helped me keep up the garden." He caressed one of the miniature rose's more tenacious leaves with a finger. "And I'm never too busy for roses."

"Word at the pub pegs you as the odds-on favorite to win best garden this weekend," Alexandra said.

The International Rose Hybridizers' Association had selected Dunmullach to host the open competition portion, which pitted professional rosarians against skilled amateurs, of their Thirteenth Annual Rose and Garden Show. Gethsemane may have been as much of an expert in flower shows as she was in Sanskrit—which is to say, not at all—but she'd heard of the IRHA's annual show, which was almost as prestigious as the Chelsea Flower Show, even before she'd been asked to perform during the opening and closing ceremonies. A breeder who won a gold medal at the IRHA Annual Rose and Garden Show could sell or license their hybrid to one of the professional growers who scoured the event for promising cultivars to introduce to the market and potentially earn enough money to buy a small planet. Residents of the host city won the privilege of competing their gardens as well as cut flowers. Frankie had hybridized a rose, which almost no one, including her, had been allowed to see, and planned to enter it in both divisions.

Gethsemane sighed a mixture of guilt and resignation. A compost bin was the only place she'd be entering her rose. It wasn't boasting to say she had many talents: multi-instrumentalist, conductor, composer, and—three solved mysteries to her credit—amateur sleuth. However, gardening and cooking were two arenas not in her skill set. She tapped a finger against the neglected rose's pot. "Can you save it?" she asked Frankie.

"Well..." He bent one of the stems. It snapped off in his fingers. He bent another. It held. He offered Gethsemane a dimpled half-grin. "Maybe it's only mostly dead."

"Which is slightly alive." She returned the grin. She and Frankie shared a fondness for movie quotes. *Casablanca* was their go-to but *The Princess Bride* never disappointed as a source.

"No promises, mind you. I may be a handsome mathematical genius," he winked, "with a knack for flora, but I'm no Miracle Max."

"I have faith in you, Grennan. And speaking of handsome..." Gethsemane stepped back and gave him the once-over. "What's with the haircut and beard trim?" Frankie seldom paid much attention to his appearance. Although he never crossed the line into sloppy or unkempt, he wore his hair on the long side, his beard on the bushy side, and his clothes on the baggy side; a grownup version of Shaggy from the *Scooby-Doo* cartoon. In the almost-year she'd known him, the only time he'd polished his appearance without cajolement had been when the statuesque fashionista and true crime author, Venus James, came to the village. Most of the over-twenty-one men in Dunmullach had done the same, eager to impress the stylish American author. For a time, the pub had looked more like the scene of a men's magazine fashion shoot than the neighborhood watering hole. "Gotta date? It's not that new Latin teacher is it? The pretty blonde?"

Frankie adjusted his glasses. "No, I do not have a date and no, it isn't the Latin teacher. I am not dating the Latin teacher.

Whose name is Verna, by the way. We're friends. I have lots of friends."

"No, you don't. You're selective with your friendship and you don't suffer fools. Not that Verna's a fool. She likes you. In the romantic sense of the word. The chemistry teacher told me. He heard it from the French teacher."

"Who's a notorious gossip and slightly less reliable than the internet."

"A waitress at the Mad Rabbit verified it. Gossip from the Rabbit is more reliable than the BBC."

"I watch RTÉ." He turned to Alexandra. "I came in to pick up my boutonniere."

"A flower for your," Gethsemane brushed a thread from his shoulder. Several more threads framed his sport jacket collar like eyelashes, "somewhat frayed lapel and a twenty Euro trip to the barber. If not romance, what's the occasion?"

"It's picture day."

"Picture day? Not until the second week of school." St. Brennan's headmaster had texted the faculty a week ago warning them they'd be expected to pose for headshots for the new edition of the school's directory.

"Pictures for the *Dispatch*," Frankie said. "They're doing a feature on the competition."

The florist retrieved a single orange-red rose bud in a clamshell case from a cooler filled with a panoply of blooms and handed it to the math teacher. "We're all pulling for you, Frankie. You'll do the village proud."

"From your lips to the judge's ears." Frankie slipped the bud into the buttonhole of his wrinkled left lapel.

"You're not wearing *this* to a photo shoot?" Gethsemane asked. She pulled aside the jacket to reveal an ancient Newport News Jazz Festival t-shirt.

"What's wrong with this?"

She tugged at the pocket of his wrinkled khakis and rephrased her question as a statement. "You are *not* wearing that to a photo shoot. Do you even own an iron?"

Frankie sniffed. "It's a feature in the local paper about a garden show, not a fashion shoot for a men's magazine. No one cares what I wear."

"Never say that to a tailor's granddaughter." Her grandfather had been a high-end men's tailor in Washington, D.C. She'd gained an eye for, and an appreciation of, men's haberdashery from time spent with him. "Of course, people care. Haven't you heard the expressions, 'The clothes make the man'? 'It's better to look good than to feel good'? The *Dunmullach Dispatch* may not be *GQ* or *The Rake*, but your pictures will still be seen by hundreds—" The clerk snickered. Gethsemane ignored the interruption. "—dozens of people and will last far longer than your roses."

"The average rose bush lives for thirty-five years. Some have lived for hundreds. There's one in Germany—"

She cut him off. "The pictures will last longer than the rose and garden show, anyway. If you want people to believe you're a champion, you need to look like a champion."

"What do I look like now?"

"A math teacher on summer vacation." She looked at her watch. "What time's the photo shoot?"

"At half-past."

"Not much time but," she eyed him over again, "I'll manage. C'mon." She started for the door. "You're driving."

"Wait." Frankie stayed by the counter. "You're not planning to dress me up like a peacock, the way you did over in Ballytuam?"

"I did not dress you up like a peacock. Mr. Walsh did." Several months ago, she'd twisted Frankie's arm to let Mr. Walsh, of Walsh and Sons Tailoring, makeover Frankie's wardrobe as a distraction while she searched the tailor's office for evidence to clear her brother-in-law of theft and murder charges. Frankie's expression suggested he still held a grudge. "And it was in the interest of justice, a noble cause. We don't have time for Walsh and Sons today, anyway. I'll have to make do with items at hand. Too bad those suits you bought to impress Venus James were winter-weight."

"I took 'em to the charity shop."

Gethsemane shook her head. "Honestly, Frankie."

"You're making a holy show out of nothing."

"I'll trust you with my rose, you trust me with your image. Years of touring as a professional musician taught me a thing or ten about what to wear and what not to wear to a photo shoot." She tapped her watch. "Time's wasting. Pay the lady for your flower and let's go." She exited the store without giving Frankie another chance to protest. "Where's the photo session being held?" she asked him when he caught up with her.

"In my garden." Frankie lived in Erasmus Hall, the bachelor faculty quarters at St. Brennan's. "Where else?"

"We want an outfit that will complement your roses, not overshadow them."

"You can't overshadow roses." He held up her flower pot. "Well, you can't overshadow my roses."

Gethsemane ignored the gibe as she spotted Frankie's car in the parking lot across the village square. She headed for it then stopped suddenly. Frankie bumped into her.

Gethsemane pointed. "Someone's left you a present."

Two

Frankie handed Gethsemane her miniature rose and stepped around her to his car. He lifted the brown-paper bundle that had been tucked into the gap between the hood and the windshield.

"Flowers from an admirer?" she asked as he pulled the paper back to reveal a magnificent floral bouquet.

"This your doing?"

"Me? I was in the flower shop when you arrived and I left when you did. How could I have walked over here to leave flowers on your windshield without you seeing me?"

Frankie searched the bundle. "No card."

"I know who left them."

"Are you going to tell me?"

"No. I mean, I can't. I know who left them, at least I'm pretty sure I do, but I don't know who they are."

"Talk sense."

Gethsemane set her flower pot on the car's hood and examined the bouquet. She recognized tiny purple flowers and spiky green leaves identical to the sprig dropped by the person who'd almost knocked her down. She told Frankie about her near-collision.

"You didn't see this person leave the bouquet?" Frankie asked. "How can you be sure it was them?"

"I have to explain logic to a mathematician? Who else could it have been? The flowers are fresh, they match the ones the person carried, there's no other florist nearby, the wrapping paper is the same Buds of May uses for all their bouquets. And your secret admirer committed the cardinal sin of someone who doesn't want to be noticed. She or he wore a strange outfit bound to call attention to themselves and caused a commotion. That's two cardinal sins, actually."

"All right, Nancy Drew. You're sure you didn't get a look at their face or hear their voice or anything that would at least tell you if they were male or female?"

Gethsemane shook her head. "Sorry. But I know who must have."

Neither she nor Frankie spoke. Frankie broke the silence after a few seconds. "You're making me guess? Who?"

"Alexandra. Difficult to order a bouquet without speaking to the florist at least long enough to say what flowers to include." She examined the bundle again. "They're gorgeous. I don't recognize all the varieties. I know tulip." She pointed at the familiar red cup-shaped blossom and then at a frilly red bloom. "That's chrysanthemum. And these," she lowered her head to inhale the subtle sweetness of several perfect, red, urn-shaped buds, "Roses, of course. What's this one?" She pointed to a woody stem with tubular red-pink flowers.

"Honey flower, I think. And the one with the little purple flowers is motherwort."

"Sort of an odd collection. Unusual, I mean. Of course, commercial nurseries can supply just about any flower you want without regard to season or location, so maybe it's not so unusual."

"Not unusual for a commercial nursery, maybe. But for a local florist's shop? They don't stock flowers only ordered once in a great while on hand. They'd be wasted. They keep roses and carnations and tulips handy, maybe lilies and the odd orchid in the fancier places." Calla and daylilies had filled a section of the Buds of May's cooler and a corner display had been devoted to orchids. "The type of flowers a fella's likely to grab last-minute for a birthday or anniversary or half-arsed apology. If you want something non-standard, you have to order it."

"And if your secret admirer—"

"Stop calling them my secret admirer."

"I don't want to call them your stalker. Whatever you call them, if they placed a custom order at the florist, they left a name, address, and phone number."

Frankie turned back to the shop. "Let's go ask."

Gethsemane grabbed his arm. "Nope. No time. Photo shoot, remember? Once I get you ready for your closeup, I'll come back and talk to the clerk."

"Fine." Frankie tossed the bouquet onto the backseat of the car. "Let's be at it."

"You should take care of those." Gethsemane picked the bouquet up from where it had fallen to the floorboards. "Your admirer might turn out to be the woman of your dreams."

"You've met my ex." Frankie tossed the flowers onto the seat again. "You've seen what luck I've had. My admirer would turn out to be the stuff of nightmares."

"Let's go." Gethsemane retrieved her flower pot and opened the passenger door. "We don't have much time to fix," she waved a hand at his outfit, "this before the photographer arrives."

"What about your bike?" Frankie nodded toward the green Pashley Parabike chained to a nearby rack. An indefinite loan from the parish priest, Gethsemane employed it as her main source of transportation.

"We can tie it to the back." She excused herself to get the bike and walked it back to Frankie's car. "Don't you have some rope in your trunk?"

"It's a boot, not a trunk, and why would I have rope in it?"

"Because guys always have things that come in handy in a pinch, like rope and screwdrivers and pocket knives, in their trunks."

"What rulebook on manliness did you read that in?"

"No rulebook, just two brothers." She tapped the trunk lid. "Open up and take a look."

Frankie popped the lid release. A mishmash of old blankets, math textbooks, muck boots, and a faded mackintosh greeted her. Frankie plunged his arms into the mess and scrounged up a length of rope.

"I told you so." Gethsemane reached past him to fold the blankets and rain coat into a neat pile.

"Are you ever going to get a car?" he grumbled as he lashed the Pashley to the rear bumper, "or am I going to have to install a bicycle rack to keep chauffeuring you around?"

"Your Irish driver's licensing rules are ridiculous and your car insurance, usurious. I'll stick to the Pashley. Besides," she climbed into the car, "I'm riding with you to help you."

"And all the running to and fro', chasing after clues you've had me doing these past months? That was all for my benefit?"

"No, that was in the interest of justice." She balanced her flower pot next to Frankie's bouquet and tapped her watch. "Drive."

Half an hour later, Gethsemane sat on the porch at Erasmus Hall and watched as Frankie, transformed by the loan of an iron from the physics teacher and a blazer from the English teacher, posed in his rose garden. A *Dunmullach Dispatch* photographer, Max Something-or-other, snapped pictures of Frankie surrounded by rose bushes, some of them as tall as Gethsemane, exploding with blossoms in a kaleidoscope of pink, red, and orange. Frankie was certain to win grand prize in the garden competition. His roses rivaled those grown in the grand gardens of manor houses. If he ever tired of teaching math, he had a brilliant future as the Irish David Austin.

He lingered next to a rose bush set slightly apart from the others in the brightest corner of the garden. The photographer lined up a medium-distance shot then lowered his camera. "There's a watering can and a trimmer in frame. Can someone move those?"

Gethsemane grabbed the errant garden tools and set them next to her on the porch. "If you don't put away your toys, Frankie, you won't have nice things."

"They're not toys, they're precision instruments."

"All the more reason to put them away." The math teacher had a habit of leaving his garden tools lying about under bushes and at the bases of statues. "I put my precision instruments away properly in their cases when I'm done with them. That's why they last hundreds of years."

The photographer moved in to take some close-ups of the flawless blossoms that covered the compact shrub. How had Frankie described them to her? Orange-pink, full, with the globular form and heavy fragrance of an Old Garden rose. He'd hybridized the rose himself and christened it the 'Sandra Sechrest' in honor of the librarian who'd given him a biography of Pythagoras when he was seven and sparked his lifelong love of math. He'd entered the 'Sandra Sechrest' in the rose show. The local bookies pegged him odds on to win.

A shout interrupted the shoot. The photographer's head jerked up. Gethsemane and Frankie turned toward the voice. A man approached from the direction of St. Brennan's Shakespeare Garden, his arm raised in greeting. The July sun glinted off his blond hair. He wore cargo pants, brogans, and a multi-pocketed vest over a short-sleeved, collared shirt. He looked as if he'd just stepped out of a Nat Geo channel adventure show. As he came nearer, Gethsemane noted the lack of a suntan to match his outdoorsman attire. His pale, smooth complexion suggested he spent more time in the spa than in nature.

Frankie muttered. Gethsemane caught the words, "gobshite" and "wanker".

"Friend of yours?" she asked.

Frankie scowled.

The *Dispatch* photographer grasped the newcomer's outstretched hand in both of his and pumped his arms hard enough to make his camera dance at the end of the strap around his neck. It would probably leave a bruise. He appeared to have forgotten the 'Sandra Sechrest' blossoms. "Mr. Jacobi, such an incredible honor to meet you, sir, an honor. I watch your garden show all the time. I met my wife at one of the presentations you gave at the Chelsea Flower Show."

"How romantic." He spoke with a refined British accent. "Always a pleasure to meet a fan. Nothing compares to being out in the garden, does it?"

He extricated himself from the photographer's grip without waiting for an answer and bowed theatrically to Gethsemane. "Roderick Jacobi, author of *In a Rose Garden* and *Amazonia: A Horticulturalist Explores Culture*." He paused as if giving her a chance to fawn over him. She remained silent; she'd never heard of Jacobi or his books. He went on. "Pardon my bluntness in introducing myself but Mr. Grennan," he jerked his head toward Frankie, "is loath to speak my name."

"Granny warned me against speaking of the devil," Frankie said.

"Gethsemane Brown." She extended a hand, ignoring Roderick's showy gesture.

"The renowned musician," Roderick said. "Now I'm the one who's honored. I hope we can look forward to a performance or two during the week's festivities."

"I'll be conducting the Dunmullach Village Orchestra in Strauss's 'Roses from The South' for the opening ceremony and performing a Prokofiev solo at the awards ceremony. The Prologue from 'The Tale of the Stone Flower'," she said.

"Beautiful music befitting a beautiful occasion. I look forward to hearing you perform. Particularly the Prokofiev."

"A fan of Soviet music?" Roderick's palm felt sweaty.

He laughed a theatrical peal. "I'll be accepting the medal for best in show at the awards ceremony, so the Prokofiev will hold pleasant associations for me forever after."

She looked back and forth between Roderick and Frankie. "They haven't announced the winners of the rose show yet, have they?"

Frankie glared at Roderick. "Winners aren't chosen until the end of the week."

"But we both know who's going to win, old boy. Don't we?"

"I'm not your 'old boy'."

The photographer whispered to Gethsemane. "Roderick Jacobi's won every major rose trial he's entered. His hybrids are legend. And his cultivars?" He kissed his fingertips as if he were a chef describing the flavor of his signature dish.

Roderick leaned closer to Gethsemane and tightened his grasp on her hand. He lowered his voice. "Perhaps we could meet for a drink and discuss the inspiration behind your choice of music." He dropped his voice another decibel. "I find the creative process—stimulating. I'd love to hear the back story."

Gethsemane stepped back. "It's a short story. Flash fiction, really. You wouldn't have time to finish your drink before it ended. The president of the Dunmullach Amateur Rose Growers' Society selected them. They were her mother's favorites."

Frankie cleared his throat. As Roderick turned, Gethsemane used the distraction to free her hand from his grip. She balled both hands in her pockets against the urge to wipe her palm on her skirt.

"I'm sorry, Grennan." Roderick sounded anything but. "Didn't mean to step on your toes. You and the maestra are—"

"Friends," Frankie interjected. "We're friends. And friends don't let friends fall prey to womanizers with more ex-wives than Methuselah had years."

"Only four exes, old boy, and one current."

"I'm not your 'old boy,'" Frankie said, "I told you."

The *Dispatch* photographer produced a small notebook and pencil from a vest pocket and scribbled as he sidled closer to the two rosarians. Gethsemane glimpsed the word "feud" before he noticed her watching and shoved the notebook back into his pocket.

Gethsemane stepped between Frankie and Roderick as she addressed the photographer. "You've got both of the top contenders for 'Best in Show' standing here. What a perfect opportunity to get some shots of them together. I bet a photo of Mr. Grennan and Mr. Jacobi with the 'Sandra Sechrest' would look great on the front page of the *Dispatch*."

The photographer scowled at Gethsemane but agreed to the pictures. Roderick and Frankie arranged themselves on either side of the rose bush.

"Top *two* contenders?" The slickest politician would have envied Roderick's smile. "Are you being loyal, diplomatic, or are you actually following the competition?"

"I picked up the village scuttlebutt." She'd earned the story from the local bookie in exchange for a couple of pints of Guinness at the Mad Rabbit. "Frankie's 'Sandra Sechrest' and your 'Lucia di Lammermoor' have the best chance of winning the gold medal in the rose show. The only chance, really. None of the other entries come close. And odds are even on which of the two of you takes the prize."

"Alas," Roderick said, "only one of us can claim top spot."

"I'm sure Frankie will be a gracious winner." She winked at the math teacher. "Won't you?"

Anger—fueled by hatred?—distorted Roderick's face for an instant, replaced by a movie star smile as quickly as it appeared. "Loyalty is an admirable trait. But, then, you Americans do tend to favor the underdog, don't you?"

"Probably because we were the underdog back in the seventeen hundreds." An image of Captain Daniel Lochlan, an eighteenth-century sea captain whose ghost had helped clear her brother-in-law of murder and theft charges, popped into her head. Too bad the captain wasn't here to remind Roderick Jacobi what a bunch of colonial upstarts with the odds against them had done to the British way back in the day. She disliked Roderick. Not just out of loyalty to Frankie or his lothario routine. Instinct told her this man would throw a small child under a bus then throw his mother under the bus after the kid if he thought doing so would win him an advantage.

Roderick ignored the gibe. Instead he asked, "Does your interest in gardens extend beyond the thrill of the competition? Has Grennan turned you into a budding rosarian?" He chuckled. Frankie rolled his eyes.

"No," Gethsemane cringed at the memory of the defunct miniature rose, "I'm the grim reaper of the plant world. I limit my gardening to admiring those planted by others."

The photographer interrupted to set up the shot. Frankie and Roderick flanked Frankie's rose bush. Gethsemane sat on a garden bench and watched as the photographer snapped photos. Roderick, perfect teeth on full display in a smile that stopped just this side of cheesy, shifted poses with the grace of someone who lived in front of a camera. Poor Frankie. He looked almost as comfortable as a boy from the lower school standing in front of the classroom making his first public speech.

"What do you think about getting a few shots in front of those flowers over there?" the photographer pointed at an accent garden blooming with fuchsia and lilies.

The mention of the other flowers reminded Gethsemane she'd promised to go back to the village to find out who'd left the bouquet on Frankie's car.

She called to Frankie. "Hey, I've got to run. I'm going to—" She glimpsed Roderick from the corner of her eye. Something about his expression made her not want to tell him what she was up to. "I'll call you later." She excused herself and grabbed her bike.

Three

A ten-minute bike ride brought her back to the village square. She leaned the Pashley against a nearby tree and surveyed the parking lot and sidewalk near the Buds of May flower shop. People going about their business on a pleasant July afternoon. No oddly-dressed characters skulking around with bouquets.

"Boo."

She jumped before her brain registered who owned the familiar baritone. Inspector Niall O'Reilly of the Dunmullach Garda smiled a dimpled grin. "Not laughing," she said.

"Sorry. Didn't mean to startle you." Niall chuckled. "Well, yeah, I did. I waved to you from across the square but you didn't notice me. What're you so intent on? Lose an earring?"

Her hands flew reflexively to her earlobes. Both pearl studs, gifts from her late paternal grandfather when she graduated from Vassar, remained in place. "I was looking for Frankie's secret admirer." She described the incident with the flowers on Frankie's windshield and the strange customer who'd nearly run her over at the flower shop.

"Someone sweet on Frankie? Hope they know what they're getting after, Frankie being a temperamental fella." The math teacher had a reputation for blowing hot and cold, misanthrope one day, merry prankster the next. "You don't expect to find them hanging about the car park, do you, out in the open, waiting to be identified? You've snooped enough to know better than that."

"I don't snoop. I investigate." The darkening hue of Niall's storm gray eyes prompted amendment of her statement, "When the situation calls for it. Aren't you going to try to talk me out of it?"

Niall hesitated a moment before waving the question away. "Nah. 'T wouldn't do any good. I may be a dumb guard but I'm not so thick I'm incapable of figuring out that the words, 'no,' 'don't,' and 'can't,' fuel your determination. Besides, we're talking about flowers, not a dead body." He frowned. "We're not talking about a dead body, are we?"

"No one's been murdered." She ignored the "yet," accompanied by a few bars of "Pathétique," her internal early warning system, that popped into her head. "And congratulations on only taking," she counted on her fingers, "nine months to realize I don't follow orders."

"Please consider what I'm about to say as a suggestion. An investigative tip. Go talk to the florist. She'll remember who she sold the flowers to if you describe the bouquet."

"My next step. Want to tag along and watch me investigate?"

"Watch you snoop when there's no danger of burning, drowning, strangulation, or poisoning? Wouldn't miss it." He gestured toward the flower shop. "After you."

They crossed the street. Gethsemane paused on the threshold of the shop and studied Niall as he held the door. A healthy pink colored his cheeks and his salt-and-pepper hair glinted in the sun.

"What?" he asked

"Just glad to see you back to your old self. Thought I'd lost you and Frankie."

"Truth be told, I thought so, too. 'Twas a bad dose, that. Don't recall ever being brought so low, not even when I had the flu. Think the doctors will ever sort out what caused it?"

Would medical science ever figure out that the epidemic they attributed to, variously, a virus, a prion, a rare bacteria, and environmental contaminants had actually been caused by a supernatural agent bent on revenge? Doubtful. She shrugged. "I'll let you in on a secret my mother told me." Her psychiatrist mother often revealed medicine's "little secrets" to her. "Doctors never figure out what causes a lot of illnesses. Which doesn't stop them from labeling them with complex-sounding names that lend themselves to the formation of catchy acronyms." She stepped past him into the shop.

Alexandra looked up from a miniature topiary she'd been clipping into shape. "Hello, again. Brought another plant in need of resurrection?"

"No," Gethsemane said. "This time I brought a garda and some questions."

"Sounds serious." Alexandra laid her clippers on the counter and greeted Niall. "You're not here for your daisies then?"

"Daisies?" Gethsemane eyed the inspector. He'd never mentioned ordering flowers on a regular basis. Not that it was her business. "You don't look like a daisy man. I picture you more as an exotic succulent fan." Who was he sending flowers to? Asking directly might seem...She let the thought trail off. "Unless you're ordering them for your cat."

"If that's your way of asking if I have a secret girlfriend stashed somewhere, no, I don't," Niall said. "I send daisies to my baby sister once a month. Have for years. Ever since I left home for university. Dad had died and she was afraid I was going away and never coming back, either."

So much for subtle. She must remember she was talking to

a cop. "That's sweet."

Niall spoke to Alexandra. "This isn't a criminal investigation. Just a few questions about someone you sold some flowers to."

Gethsemane took over. "The person who almost knocked me down when I was here earlier. With the hat."

"Aye, a queer hawk, that one. Hardly spoke a word. Wouldn't look me in the eye."

"Could you tell if they were male or female?"

"A bure," Alexandra said.

"What was her name?" Gethsemane asked.

The florist shrugged. "Didn't give a name."

"She must've given a name when she placed her order. Frankie told me you don't keep bouquets with uncommon varieties ready-made in the shop." She took a better look at the bins filled with flower arrangements than she had earlier. Carnations, roses, and tulips predominated, just as Frankie'd said.

"The woman only picked up the order," Alexandra said. "It was placed online, through a business account. Pre-paid."

"But you're sure it was a woman?"

"Aye." Alexandra glanced back and forth between Gethsemane and Niall. "You're sure this isn't a criminal investigation?"

Gethsemane reassured her. "She left the bouquet on Frankie's car but didn't sign her name. He wants to thank her. The flowers were gorgeous."

"Well-chosen, too," Alexandra said. "Doesn't surprise me someone who speaks the language of flowers wouldn't reveal her name. 'T would spoil the fun."

"Language of flowers?" Gethsemane frowned. "I don't understand."

"Every flower has a symbolic meaning. Well, maybe not

every flower, but many do. Like in *Hamlet*, when Ophelia says, 'Here's rosemary, that's for'—"

"Remembrance," Niall cut in. His interruption earned a smile from the florist. He continued, "There's fennel for you, and columbines. There's rue for you and here's some for me."

"Fennel symbolizes infidelity; columbine, flattery and insincerity; and rue, regret. You can put several flowers together, based on their symbolic meanings, and spell out a coded message. If you gave someone a bouquet of rosemary, fennel, columbine, and rue, you'd be accusing them of insincere flattery and infidelity and telling them you regret knowing them, or you regret what's happened between you, and to remember you."

"Because you're about to drown yourself," Gethsemane said. "Charming."

"Shakespearean," Niall said.

Gethsemane pictured the flowers in the bouquet left on Frankie's car. "What do roses, tulips, chrysanthemums, honey flower, and motherwort spell out?"

"They spell 'odd taste in floral arrangements,'" Niall suggested.

"Your floral expertise extends beyond daisies?" Gethsemane asked.

"I've sent my fair share of flowers." The pink in Niall's cheeks deepened to red. "By way of apology, mostly."

Alexandra laughed. "Let's see if I can remember. Roses signify love, of course. Red roses mean passionate love, in particular. Tulips, red, perfect love. Honey flower and motherwort, both mean secret love and chrysanthemum signifies truth."

"Meaning our mystery woman harbors a true, perfect, passionate, secret love for Frankie," Gethsemane said. "Any ideas? What's the gossip from the Rabbit?" The Mad Rabbit, the village pub, served as much gossip as Guinness.

"You know as well as I do," Niall said, "that if you want to keep something secret you don't discuss it at the Rabbit. You don't even think about it too hard."

"True." Gethsemane pictured St. Brennan's female faculty. There weren't many—fewer than seven, in addition to herself and the Latin teacher. "No one at school seemed that far gone." Luckily, St. Brennan's only enrolled boys. A female student in love with Frankie wouldn't bode well. Not with a scandal-averse headmaster and conservative major donors.

"Maybe someone at Our Lady," Niall said. "Frankie's a regular." The math teacher attended mass at the parish church, Our Lady of Perpetual Sorrows, almost every Sunday and Wednesday. "He gives lectures on rose-growing to the church garden guild. Which is full of unattached females."

"Most of whom are old enough to be Frankie's grandmother. Not that older women can't have the hots for red-headed rosarians but the woman who rushed past me didn't seem elderly. Not the way she moved."

"If I had to guess," Alexandra said, "I'd put her in her late-twenties, early thirties."

"A younger woman," Gethsemane said. Frankie, like Niall, was past forty. As she would be in a couple of years. "Where would she have met Frankie? Church, or...hey, what about that jazz-lover's society he belongs to?"

"Wouldn't a fellow jazz lover leave music instead of flowers?" Niall asked.

"You come up with a theory, then."

Voices from the doorway intruded on the discussion. Two men, one tall and broad, the other short but equally broad, argued their way into the shop.

"Absurd!" the taller man shouted. "Absurd, I'm telling you. They'll never accept that."

"Calm down, Murdoch." The shorter man glanced at Gethsemane, Niall, and Alexandra. "We'll see what they say at the board meeting next week. You'd be surprised what people will agree to if you put the proper spin on it."

"May I help you?" Alexandra asked the newcomers.

The tall man, Murdoch, pushed between Gethsemane and Niall. He ran a meaty hand through mouse-brown hair then plopped his elbows on the counter. He peered over wire-rimmed glasses and boomed down at Alexandra, "Floral foam."

The florist stepped back. "Sir?"

"Floral foam. I ordered two cases." He spoke in a flat, Midwestern American accent. "Murdoch Collins."

"Oh, yes, Mr. Collins." Alexandra nodded recognition. "It's in the back." She excused herself and disappeared behind swinging doors that separated the showroom from the area of the shop not open to the public.

No one spoke. The shorter man roamed among the display stands, pausing occasionally to sneer at a bouquet. Murdoch drummed fat fingers on the counter; the random taps morphed into a rhythmic pattern. His immaculate fingernails—trimmed even and buffed smooth by a fifty-dollar manicure—seemed out of place with hair that protruded from his scalp at odd angles, a short-sleeved shirt patterned with geometric shapes borrowed from the 1980s, and khakis so wrinkled even Frankie would have been embarrassed. They also seemed out of place with an order for floral foam. Too perfect. Not one chipped nail, not a speck of dirt or fleck of green.

Murdoch stopped drumming. He frowned at Gethsemane and shoved his hand in his pocket.

"Here for the garden show?" she asked.

The three men started at the sudden break in silence.

"What?" Murdoch asked.

Gethsemane repeated her question. "I overheard you asking

for floral foam."

"Not for me," he said. "For Mr. Jacobi. Roderick Jacobi. You will, of course, have heard of him if you're following the rose show."

"I met him a little while ago. He crashed my friend, Frankie Grennan's, photoshoot. You'll, of course, have heard of Frankie Grennan if you're following the rose show."

Murdoch snorted. His companion sidled between him and Gethsemane and introduced himself in German-accented English. "Karl Dietrich. And you are Dr. Gethsemane Brown."

"Should I be flattered or frightened that you know my name?" She shook his hand. Calluses and chipped nails accompanied a firm grasp. Dirt stained the elbow of one shirt sleeve.

"Not frightened. I'm a long-time fan, ever since I heard you perform Stravinsky with the Cleveland Symphony."

"Definitely flattered," she said.

"Rumor has it, you gave up music after the—incident—in Dallas. Does your turning up in a," Karl paused to look out the window, "quaint village in the wilds of Ireland mean the rumors are true?"

"She's hardly in the back of beyond," Niall interjected. "We've got electricity, running water, and, next week, they're installing indoor plumbing."

Gethsemane bit her cheek to keep from laughing.

Karl bowed his head toward Niall. "Please don't take offense, Mr..."

"O'Reilly. Inspector O'Reilly."

"O'Reilly," Karl continued. "I'm sure your village is charm incarnate. However, it is an unusual spot for a world-class, African-American, classical musician to turn up."

He didn't know the half of it. "Dunmullach's an out of the way spot to run into a fan," she said aloud, "but I'm always happy to meet one. I haven't given up music." She'd given up plenty—home, family, fiancé, flashy career—but not music. "I've only given up touring. For now."

"Dr. Brown's the music director at our boys' school," Niall said. "Led the fellas to victory in the All-County Competition last fall."

Karl's expression suggested he thought that was also quaint. Niall's expression suggested he was not a fan of Karl's. Gethsemane jumped in. "You're here for the rose show."

"Yes," Karl said. "Partly, yes. I'm not so much here for myself as I am for Mr. Jacobi. I'm his chief botanist."

"Chief botanist?" Gethsemane raised an eyebrow. Frankie didn't have a botanist. "Is that allowed? Don't the competitors have to develop their own hybrids? Or cultivate them or whatever you call it?"

"Of course, they must do their own work," Karl said, "but they are allowed to consult others for advice and assistance. I'm sure your Mr. Grennan sought help once or twice."

Frankie had relied on the school gardener and some of the students to tend his garden while he recovered. Not the same as hiring a plant scientist. "He doesn't have a botanist on staff," she said aloud.

Karl chuckled. "You misunderstand. Mr. Jacobi didn't hire me for the competition. He's a skilled horticulturalist, himself. The few merit trial-related questions he had for me could have been managed with a phone call rather than a paycheck. I'm the chief botanist with Mr. Jacobi's pharmaceutical firm, Avar. I investigate the potential medical uses of a variety of plants. I specialize in the ethnobotany of indigenous rainforest populations, particularly in the Amazon basin region."

Murdoch clapped Karl on the shoulder. The shorter man staggered forward and grabbed the counter, just missing Gethsemane. "Karl does Jacobi's dirty work, don't you Karl?" He clapped him on the other shoulder.

Karl rubbed his arm and inched away from his companion. "Mr. Collins is attempting humor by making a very old and very bad gardening joke."

"What do you do for Mr. Jacobi, Mr. Collins?" Gethsemane noted the difference in the two men's manicures. Whatever Murdoch did, manual labor wasn't part of the job.

"I'm the Chief Operating Officer of Avar Pharmaceuticals."

"And chief errand boy," Niall muttered as Alexandra pushed through the swinging doors, arms full of boxes.

"Here's your foam."

A look from Karl to Murdoch cut off the tall man's retort. He paid Alexandra for the floral foam and headed for the door. He spoke without looking back. "C'mon Karl, we've got that conference call with Geneva."

Karl bobbed his head toward Niall and Alexandra and shook Gethsemane's hand again. "An honor to meet you. Will I have the good fortune to hear you perform while I'm in Dunmullach?"

"You will if you come to the opening or awards ceremonies." She told him her schedule.

"Karl!" Murdoch bellowed from outside.

"Please excuse me." Karl bobbed his head again and hurried out.

"You met this Jacobi character?" Niall asked Gethsemane as the door shut behind Karl.

"He didn't impress me. Came across as arrogant. And smarmy. And phony." She described the contrast between his outdoor adventure wardrobe and his never-sees-the-sun complexion. "Frankie despises him. Called him a gobshite."

"Grennan's not afraid of a little competition, is he?"

"I don't think the animosity has anything to do with the rose trials. I got the impression the hatred ran deep. Jacobi knows how Frankie feels about him. He made a joke of it."

"Never make light of a man's loathing," Alexandra said.

Gethsemane had forgotten the florist's presence. "I'm sorry. We've taken up a lot of your time. Can you tell us anything else about the woman who picked up the bouquet?"

Alexandra shook her head. "Sorry."

"Thanks, anyway." Gethsemane headed toward the door.

Niall caught up with her. "That's it? One dead end and you're giving up?"

"Of course not. I'm going to find a member of the jazz-lover's society and see if they can provide any leads. And I'll ask Father Tim if any younger women have joined the garden guild recently."

Music, Gounod's "Funeral March of a Marionette," sounded from Niall's pocket.

"The Alfred Hitchcock theme?" Gethsemane asked.

Niall shrugged and pulled out his phone. After a brief conversation to which his sole contribution was, "Yes, sir, I'm on my way," he excused himself. "Let me know what you find out about the flower lady," he called over his shoulder on his way to his car.

Gethsemane had just reclaimed her bike when a disembodied voice sounded in her ear. "The Flower Shop Killer."

Four

She dropped the Pashley. "Damn it, Eamon, I wish you wouldn't sneak up on me like that." A quick glance around the square as she righted the bike reassured her no one had noticed.

Eamon McCarthy's ghost materialized in front of her. Six feet, three inches of dark curls and green eyes appeared as solid as any human.

Gethsemane glanced around the square again. "You're going to do that here?"

He laughed, his aura an amused green. "No one can see me, except you."

"Then let's go someplace where we can talk without me looking like I'm talking to myself." She crossed the street to a garden alcove between Buds of May and a neighboring dress shop. "What do you mean, 'Flower Shop Killer'? What are you doing here? Why aren't you at the cottage?" Eamon seldom manifested outside the confines of Carraigfaire, the cottage they shared, or Carrick Point lighthouse, the ancient structure that stood sentry over Carrick Point, a few yards up the cliff from the cottage.

"Which of your rapid-fire questions would you like me to address first?"

"What are you doing here? Are you following me?"

"No, I'm not following you. Get over yourself. I wanted a change of scenery. I can go anywhere I went while I was alive, you know."

"If you weren't following me, how do you know about the flowers?"

"Okay, I was following you. But not in a creepy stalker kind of way. I like being near someone who can see and hear me and isn't afraid of me. Ever since Orla—" He de-materialized to near-transparency and his aura faded to a morose dull yellow. His late wife's ghost had returned to him, only to sacrifice herself to save the lives of the village's men.

"I'm sorry." Gethsemane reached for her friend's arm. A shock zipped through her fingers as her hand passed through him. "I haven't been good company lately, with all the rehearsals for the garden show performances."

The yellow brightened a little. "Unlike me, you have a life to live. I don't begrudge you that. I just hover on the periphery, soaking up a bit of vicarious vitality."

"Eamon McCarthy, dead or alive, is never on the periphery of anything. Which brings me back to my other question. What do you mean, 'Flower Shop Killer'? What killer? No one's been murdered, have they? Did you recognize the woman who left the bouquet on Frankie's car? Did you see her kill someone?"

"That's five questions. In reverse order: no, I didn't see her kill anyone; no, I didn't recognize her; no, no one's been murdered. At least not for the past several months."

Gethsemane winced. Dunmullach's murder rate had tripled after she arrived. Some villagers believed she'd brought bad luck with her.

"Sit down." Eamon gestured to a bench and sat next to her. The bench's wooden slats disappeared into his legs. "Back in the sixties, a married couple, the Coynes, were found murdered in their home. Someone, presumably the killer, had strewn flowers around their bodies. During the investigation, An Garda Síochána uncovered evidence Mr. Coyne had been receiving floral bouquets from an unknown admirer for three months before the murders. The killer was never found. The *Dispatch* nicknamed them the Flower Shop Killer."

"A serial killer in Dunmullach?"

"No, the Coynes were the only ones murdered. But no one could sort out why. They were lovely people. No one said a thing against them. The guards never identified a suspect. The only clue they had was the flowers. They came from Buds of May." He jerked his head toward the florist. "Wasn't called that, back then, but it was in the same building. No one at the flower shop could recall anyone buying the flowers, except for a young lad who said a lady paid him a few pence to pick up her order once or twice. The lad couldn't tell the guards anything useful about the woman's appearance."

"Someone who murdered a couple back in the sixties wouldn't be stalking Frankie now. Would they?" Her first murder case had involved a twenty-five-year-old grudge.

"Probably not. They'd be in their eighties or nineties if they were still alive."

"But a copycat—"

"Don't start." Eamon held up a hand enrobed in a mauve aura. "I apologize for mentioning it. I didn't mean to imply a crazed killer is stalking Frankie Grennan. It's probably a young woman with a crush and a flare for drama. Frankie's not a bad-looking fella, even if he does dress like a bogtrotter."

"But what if it's not an innocent crush? What if Frankie's in real danger? Maybe it's not a coincidence this secret admirer is using the same methods as the Flower Shop Killer."

"Maybe your imagination's working overtime. All this murder, it's getting to you. If you're not careful, you'll end up gone in the head, seeing a fiend behind every tree. Why don't you focus on something else? Something non-lethal? The garden show, how about? The opening ceremony is the day after tomorrow. Are you ready for your performances? Come back to the cottage and we'll work on the Prokofiev."

"My Prokofiev is fine and I'm not performing it until the awards ceremony on the last day, anyway." She looked at her watch. "I do have a rehearsal with the orchestra this evening. And I need to talk to Frankie about Jacobi, find out why he hates him."

"Will you please stop looking for trouble where there is none?"

"I'm not looking for trouble. I'm looking for explanations."

"Same difference with you."

"Don't be such an old woman. True, on occasion I've landed in some dangerous situations—"

"Near-drowning, near-shooting, near-immolation, near-poisoning, near-bludgeoning—"

"—But I didn't seek them out. They just sort of found me."

"*Rugadh tú faoi réalta an-ádh.*"

"Please don't tell me what that means." She stood. "Time for rehearsal. I'll catch up with Frankie afterward and find out what's going on with him and Jacobi. Maybe you can scare up—"

Eamon glowed an unamused mauve.

"Sorry." She smothered a grin. "Maybe you can find some information on the Flower Shop Killer in the meantime. An unsolved murder with ritualistic elements? Someone must have written about it—newspaper articles, magazine articles, a book—something our mystery woman might have come across. I'll be home late but I'll look at whatever you find before I go to bed."

"How'm I supposed to find information, if it exists? I'm a ghost, remember? I'm not a secretary nor a detective."

"Don't even. You helped Saoirse find the spell book she needed to fight Maja. You can move objects as well as I can. Just do your," she waggled her fingers, "levitation thing and float some books off shelves."

The mauve aura deepened and shades of blue flecked its edges. "My 'levitation thing' is not a parlor trick."

"No, it's an investigative tool. One you should use to help protect a friend."

"Where am I supposed to yield this investigative tool?"

"Start with the library. They've archived newspapers in the basement."

"Digitally archived. There's nothing to," he mimicked her finger wag, "float off shelves. You've been down there, you know that."

She'd forgotten. "And the *Dispatch* office has digitized their archives, too. Damn, technology." She snapped her fingers. "The cold case evidence room at the garda station. Niall said there are boxes and boxes and boxes of stuff. If the evidence from the Coynes's murders was preserved, maybe there'll be a suspect's or a witness's name, a name we can link to someone in the village."

"Why don't you ask your guard to let you look at the files? He's in charge of the cold case unit."

"He's not *my* guard. And the evidence room is off limits to civilians. I learned that when I investigated your murder. And if I ask Niall to get the evidence for me, he'll ask questions. I already told him I wasn't interested in any murders."

"He's known you more than five minutes; I doubt he believed you."

"Have I told you, lately, that snark is unbecoming to a ghost?"

Eamon blew her a kiss, then vanished.

She called after him to no avail. "I hate it when he does that."

"When who does what, dear?" An elderly woman poked her

head around the corner and peered around the alcove.

"Er, um..." Gethsemane fumbled in her pocket for her phone. She fished it out and pretended to text. "My fella. I hate it when my fella doesn't answer my messages."

The woman plunged an arm deep into a voluminous tote and withdrew a smartphone—a newer model than Gethsemane's. "That's why I installed *Buachaill* Stalk. You enter your fella's mobile number into the app and it uses GPS to track him. You should try it." She dropped the phone back into the bag and continued down the sidewalk.

"I take back what I said about not being an old woman." With a laugh and a headshake, Gethsemane headed in the opposite direction, toward the Athaneum Theater.

Five

Gethsemane arrived at the Athaneum to flurried activity. Musicians from the Village Orchestra came into the theater in twos and threes, instruments in arms. Others took their places on stage. Ebullient chatter filled the auditorium like the overture from "The Marriage of Figaro." No hint remained of the murder of corrupt music critic, Bernard Stoltz, or of the suffering and destruction caused by the vengeful spirit of Maja Zoltánfi. The theater felt safe again, a place dedicated to the sharing of beautiful music between musician and listener. Gethsemane waved and called out greetings as she turned toward the manager's office where she'd stored her score and baton.

An unfamiliar woman's voice answered her knock. "Come in."

"Excuse me," Gethsemane said to the stranger, a tall, elegant woman, dark hair pulled into a chignon, head bent over the manager's desk. "I'm looking for the manager."

The woman didn't look up from the papers she rifled. "He stepped away." Her accent screamed "posh."

"Do you know when he'll be—" Gethsemane crossed to the desk and put a hand on a stack of papers. "Should you be doing that?"

Annoyance creased the woman's brow as she raised her

head and stepped back from the desk.

"Who are you?" Gethsemane asked.

"Is that any of your business?" the woman countered.

"It's either mine or the gardaí's." Gethsemane pulled out her phone. "I'll be happy to call them and tell them I found you trespassing."

A practiced, corporate smile that ended at the corners of her mouth displaced the woman's annoyed expression. She extended a hand. "Ellen Jacobi, of Jacobi and Fortnum Gardens." Gethsemane's blank look prompted, "The principle sponsor of the International Rose Hybridizers' Association's Thirteenth Annual Rose and Garden Show."

"Oh, of course." Gethsemane shook Ellen's hand. "I'm Gethsemane Brown. I'm conducting 'Roses from the South' in the competition's opening ceremony. Rehearsal's getting ready to start."

"*You're* Gethsemane Brown?" Ellen raised sculpted eyebrows. "I pictured someone more..." She shrugged.

Was everyone named Jacobi a jerk? Gethsemane fought back her temper. "Jacobi's not a common name. You must be related to Roderick."

"Soon to be ex-wife number five. Which is why he's allowed to compete in a merit trial sponsored by me. Since I hate him, I can't be accused of influencing the judges in his favor."

Hating Roderick must be a national past time. "If he loses, won't he accuse you of influencing the judges against him?"

"He never loses. That's his problem. I've seen this year's entry, 'Lucia di Lammermoor.' Sadly, it's flawless. Roddy will take home another damned gold medal and become even more insufferable."

"I'm rooting for the 'Sandra Sechrest.' I'm no rose expert but I think it's gorgeous."

"Ah, yes, Francis Grennan's entry. Mr. Grennan will no

doubt win silver. As impressive a specimen as it is, the only way 'Sandra Sechrest' could take gold over 'Lucia di Lammermoor' would be if Roderick withdrew from the competition. Short of his dropping dead under the unbearable weight of his own ego, that's not likely to happen." Ellen eyed Gethsemane. "Have you met Roderick? He'd love to tell you how magnificent his specimens are. You're his type."

"I've met him and he's not my type, so…"

Ellen's smile reached her eyes, this time. "You're obviously a woman of discernment. Do stop by the judges' tent during the week. I'll introduce you to the judges and give you a behind-the-scenes peek at the thorny business of judging garden shows."

The manager appeared in the doorway. "You're still here, Mrs. Jacobi?"

"Yes, Mr. Greevy. Maestra Brown and I were discussing the musical program." Ellen looked at her watch, her arm angled so everyone could see she sported a Tag Heuer. "I have a meeting with the caterer. I won't keep you from your rehearsal any longer, Maestra." She left the office.

Gethsemane watched her go then turned to the manager. "I found her going through the papers on your desk."

Greevy examined the items on his desktop. "Nothing's missing. Not sure what she'd have been looking for. None of this has anything to do with the flower show."

"What was she doing here? She's not involved with the music. Is she?"

"She wanted to talk about signage for the floral arrangements we'll have in the lobby for the opening festivities." The manager shrugged. "Bit late to worry about the signs now. Everything's settled. Jacobi and Fortnum Gardens provided all of the flowers, so their name goes on the signs. We'll have two large signs on easels near the lobby entrance and smaller cards next to each individual arrangement."

"She came here in person to ask you that?"

"Yes. Well," Greevy sat on the edge of his desk and tapped his chin with a finger, "now you mention it, no, I don't think that's why she came here. Not really. She seemed to be after something but didn't want to ask. Not directly, anyway."

"Seemed to be after what?"

"Information, I think. She dropped Belles Fleurs Gardens' name several times. They're another of the show's sponsors but a much smaller one than Jacobi and Fortnum. Mrs. Jacobi kept trying to get me to describe Belles Fleurs' arrangements. They're providing the flowers for one of the lectures to be held here during the week."

"Why ask you? I mean why ask anyone? The flower arrangements are just decorations. They're not competing in the show. Are they?"

"Just decorations? Not into flowers then?"

Gethsemane shook her head.

"The flower arrangements are a big deal. Kept under wraps until the big reveal at whatever function they're gracing. Sometimes the flowers get more attention than the events." The manager blushed. "Not that a bunch of flowers could overshadow your performance."

She waved the comment away. "Maybe that's why she was searching your desk. Looking for details about her rival."

"Don't keep that kind of thing lying around in the open. I keep contracts locked up the same place I keep your music." He pointed to a large wall safe at the rear of the office.

"Did you tell Mrs. Jacobi anything about Belles Fleurs' flowers?"

"No." Greevy sat up straighter and puffed out his chest. "I'm a man of integrity. As charming as the lady was, I told her nothing. I kept mum, you could say." He chuckled at his joke. "Not that I could have told her what she wanted to know, anyway. I don't know, myself."

"You don't know what arrangements the gardens will be bringing?"

"Not down to the specific flowers. I know general sizes and shapes and I know the number of displays and where they'll be placed. But Mrs. Jacobi hinted about her husband's roses. I think she wanted to know if Belles Fleurs would be using any of them. That would be something, wouldn't it? Her husband's blooms in her rival's bouquets?"

The sound of violins drew Gethsemane's attention back to rehearsal. "That's my cue."

The manager retrieved her score and baton from the safe. She thanked him and returned to the stage. The other musicians had already taken their places. They tuned their instruments to the oboe's A-note then waited as Gethsemane ascended the conductor's podium. She raised her baton and led the orchestra in a nearly flawless performance of Strauss's energetic waltz.

"Nicely done," she said to the instrumentalists. "If we're half as good during the opening ceremony, no one will notice the flowers."

She made a few corrections—a trumpet came in too early; a contrabass came in too late—and led a few more run-throughs before calling it an evening. "We'll take tomorrow off," she announced, "but be here at seven, day after tomorrow for our final rehearsal before the performance."

She left the other musicians to pack up their instruments while she returned her score and baton to the manager's safe. Time to catch up with Frankie and find out the story behind his relationship with Roderick Jacobi. She rounded a corner on her way out and ran into something hard. Coarse fabric scented with pipe tobacco and sandalwood filled her nose.

A deep, English-accented voice spoke down at her. "Excuse me."

She pushed herself back and looked up at the speaker. A gray-haired man looked down at her with concern in his eyes.

"Are you all right?" he asked.

She smoothed the wrinkle her nose had made in his linen suit jacket. "I'm fine, thank you. And, please, excuse *me.*"

"Have you just come from the auditorium?"

She said that she had.

"Did you, by chance, see a tall woman, dark hair pulled back," he mimed pulling hair into a bun, "well-dressed?"

"Ellen Jacobi?" He'd described her spot-on. "Yes, I saw her a little while ago in the manager's office. I don't know where she went."

"She didn't mention Gerrit Byrnes?"

"No. We didn't talk much. She was going out as I was coming in." No reason to tell him about Ellen's snooping, especially since she didn't know who he was—Gerrit Byrnes? Someone looking for Gerrit Byrnes?—nor why he wanted Ellen.

"Thank you. And my apologies, again, for running into you." He hurried past Gethsemane.

She stared after him. Should she follow and pry for answers to her questions? Or was she making too much out of an innocent accidental encounter?

A commotion at the opposite end of the hall decided for her. Murdoch and Karl argued with a third man as they burst through the doors leading to the parking lot.

"No, Gerrit, absolutely not." Karl stepped in front of the third man.

He stopped just in time to avoid tripping over Karl. "Be reasonable, Dietrich. You won't get a better offer."

This must be Gerrit Byrnes. What offer? Gethsemane pressed flat against the wall and tried to make herself small enough to go unnoticed. She wished she could fade into the wall, like Eamon.

"Reasonable?" Murdoch asked. "For the risk we'd be taking? Your offer's an insult. Look who we're dealing with."

"What's life without risk, Big Man?" Perhaps it was the English accent, but the sobriquet sounded more like an insult than an endearment.

"Forget it, Murdoch. You'll get nowhere with this one. He's—Oh!" Karl's eyes widened as he noticed Gethsemane. "Hello, Dr. Brown."

"Hello." She nodded at Karl and Murdoch and tried to play off her eavesdropping. "Just on my way out."

Gerrit stepped in her path. "What's your opinion on risk?" His glacier-blue eyes challenged her.

She didn't flinch. Instead, she pulled herself up to her full five three and held her hand an inch from Gerrit's nose. "I'm Gethsemane Brown. I don't believe we've met."

He stared at her for another moment, then smiled and shook her hand. "Gerrit Byrnes. Fan of bold risk-takers."

"Gerrit Byrnes," she repeated. "I just ran into someone asking about you. Gray-haired gentleman. Linen suit. Bespoke. I didn't catch his name."

The smile dimmed. "Which way did my brother go?"

"Toward the auditorium." Gethsemane jerked a thumb over her shoulder.

Gerrit turned to Murdoch and Karl. "If you change your mind..." He shook Gethsemane's hand again. "I bet you'd accept the offer."

She watched until he'd disappeared around a corner in the direction his brother had gone. "Offer?" she asked the other two men.

"Ridiculous speculation. Pay him no mind," Karl said.

"Speculation like the stock market?" Gerrit hadn't struck her as a stockbroker but Karl hadn't struck her as a botanist, nor Murdoch as an executive.

"Nah," Murdoch said. "Some so-called surefire money-maker. Not worth the time to explain it."

She didn't believe Murdoch's glib answer. But with no reason to press him for a fuller explanation, she let it go.

"Gerrit and his brother, Glendon, are co-owners of Belles Fleurs Gardens," Karl said.

Gethsemane tried not to show she'd heard the name.

Karl went on. "They're one of the show's sponsors. Not a major sponsor but large enough to only have to share a tent with two others."

"Tent?" she asked.

"At the show grounds. The sponsors are in tents. The more significant the contribution, the fewer sponsors per tent. Jacobi and Fortnum have a tent to themselves."

"And don't think for a minute that doesn't tick ol' Gerrit off," Murdoch said. "He'd love to knock J and F off their rose-covered perch."

She remembered something Mr. Greevy said. "Bet the Byrnes brothers would be able to afford their own tent if they licensed some of Mr. Jacobi's rose varieties."

Karl went pale and Murdoch blushed. Karl made a show of consulting his watch. "If you'll excuse us, Dr. Brown, we have to meet with a potter about some custom flowerpots we ordered. Come on, Murdoch." The two men excused themselves and scurried away as fast as their bulk allowed.

"Sure-fire money-maker." She smiled after them. "Selling your boss's roses to his wife's competitor is a sure way to get fired."

She reached St. Brennan's at dinnertime. A smattering of people roamed the campus's dignified grounds. Few students boarded at the school during the summer; their reduced numbers created a bucolic atmosphere within St. Brennan's walls. Faculty members who lived on campus year-round relaxed with picnic baskets in courtyards or with books on benches lining paths leading to Georgian classroom buildings, devoid of boys for the next few months. Several people she passed on the way to Erasmus Hall wore badges suspended from colorful lanyards around their necks. They paused by various flowers and trees to point or snap photos or scribble notes in pocket-sized notebooks. Early arrivals for the garden show, Gethsemane assumed. Several gardens on St. Brennan's campus, including Frankie's and the Shakespeare Garden, were stops on the program's itinerary.

No one answered her knock on Frankie's door. She stopped the English teacher as he passed in the hall. He hadn't seen Frankie since he'd returned his blazer after the photo shoot. She texted Frankie but received no response. She searched in her bag for paper to leave him a note when a scream from outside behind the building ripped down the corridor. Gethsemane's stomach dropped and her heart leapt. She stared dumbly for a moment at the pen and scrap of paper she held in her hand, as the ridiculous thought that the scream had been aimed at her flashed through her head. She chided herself for foolishness then ran in the direction of the horrible noise. She rushed out the back door but froze at the foot of the steps, a few feet from Frankie's rose garden. A group of people clustered around something—someone—lying on the ground. All Gethsemane could see were the handles of hedge pruning shears protruding from what she judged to be the someone's back.

Six

She crept up to the onlookers, breath held, forbidding herself to think who might be—who she feared it was—lying in their midst. She checked her phone again. Why didn't Frankie answer his damned text? She noticed the roses, perversely, looked exceptionally spectacular this evening, each blossom full and round, with inner petals seeming to burst forth like arils from a ripe pomegranate. Their heady fragrance suffused the air to the point of becoming cloying. She tried not to vomit. A man turned aside as she reached the group, enough so she saw—blond hair. Roderick Jacobi lay face down at the foot of Frankie's most beautiful 'Sandra Sechrest' hedge rose with a pair of hedge shears buried to the hilt in the center of his back like a flag atop a sand castle.

She sighed relief, then closed her eyes in a quick prayer of thanksgiving that Frankie wasn't the one who'd met his untimely end, followed by a quick prayer for forgiveness for feeling more joy that Frankie had been spared than horror at the sight of Jacobi. He hadn't been her friend—hadn't even been likeable—but he didn't deserve murder. No one did.

Murdered. Gethsemane looked away from the body and looked around at the scene. Murdered in Frankie's garden. She inched close enough to Jacobi, without touching anything, to make out the letters "FG" on one of the shears' handles. Murdered with Frankie's hedge trimmers. She moved to the rear of the cluster and pulled out her phone. Damn and double damn. Why didn't Frankie answer his text?

"I've already called 999," a woman next to her said.

"What?" Gethsemane started and nearly dropped her phone.

The woman nodded at it. "I've already called the guards. They're on the way."

Law enforcement on the way. She knew how the gardaí who answered the call would react when they saw her at yet another murder scene. She looked toward Erasmus Hall. Why not leave the garden, come out when the gardaí arrived, pretend she'd been inside all along? Or not come back to the garden at all? She could slip out the front door and be back at Carraigfaire before the guards had taken their first statement. She looked back at the other witnesses. They'd already noticed her. They'd tell the guards if she left. How would she explain that?

She spied a familiar face approaching, Inspector Bill Sutton from the homicide unit. Too late to leave now. "Good evening, Inspector."

The garda's lithic features morphed into a scowl. He muttered several angry words in Gaeilge. She didn't need them translated to know they weren't compliments.

"Not you again," he greeted her.

The woman who'd called 999 interrupted. "It's Roderick Jacobi, Inspector, the horticulturist. He's been murdered. Stabbed." She pulled at the Inspector's sleeve as she pointed toward the corpse. "He's right over there. Stone cold."

Sutton shook the woman's hand off. "Did you touch him?"

"'Course not." The woman bristled. "What do you think I am, a ghoul?"

"Then how'd you know he's cold?"

"It's an expression, Inspector. Any fool can see he's dead and I'm no fool. Lying prone with his face in the dirt, stiller than the summer air. And you don't survive being run through with hedge shears, do you?"

"No, ma'am." Sutton's shoulders drooped in wearied resignation. "I don't suppose you do."

"But you have to verify it, don't you? Check his pulse and see if he's breathing, like they do on television."

"No, ma'am, I don't." He pointed to a gray-haired woman approaching with three uniformed gardaí. "She does. She's with the coroner's office."

"You'd think I'd have met her before now," Gethsemane said. "Considering."

"She's based in Cork. Happened to be in Dunmullach for the flower show." He pulled a notebook and ballpoint pen from his jacket pocket. "What do you know about this?"

The other woman grabbed Sutton's sleeve again. "I'm the one who called you. I got here before she did."

Gethsemane silently thanked the woman.

Sutton narrowed his eyes at Gethsemane then turned to the eager witness. "All right, Ms..."

"Heaney, with two e's." She spelled it out. "H-E-A-N-E-Y. Ms. Moira Heaney. I'm one of the judges." Her cheeks reddened and she stammered. "F-for the junior trials, you understand. The under-eighteen group. I'm not cheating since I'm not judging the main competition."

"Cheating?" Sutton asked.

"By viewing the gardens too early. The juniors don't compete in the garden division, only cut flowers. Mind you, some of those young rosarians grow roses every bit as fine as the adults."

"I'm sure they do, Ms. Heaney." Sutton closed his eyes for a moment and tapped his pen on his notebook. "How did you happen to come upon the deceased?"

"I came around the corner and there he was. Just lying there. Good thing students aren't around this time of year. I'd hate for one of them to have seen him. Such a shock could be quite traumatizing for a young lad. I have a strong constitution, myself. Grew up on a farm and was married to a butcher."

A muscle in Sutton's jaw tightened. Gethsemane almost pitied him. Dealing with the garrulous junior judge seemed to pain him as much as seeing her at the scene every time a dead body turned up.

"I meant, what were you doing here, on school grounds," Sutton said.

"Mr. Grennan's rose garden is a highlight of the show." The judge, defying the Inspector's efforts to free his sleeve from her grasp, leaned toward him and lowered her voice. "Word in the judge's tent is that he's the man to beat for Best in Show in the garden division." She straightened up and released his arm. "Not that I have any influence in the matter, of course."

Sutton appeared to have aged years since he'd arrived at Erasmus Hall. "Because you're judging the under-eighteen."

Ms. Heaney nodded and went on. "And I'm only judging the cut flower specimens, not the gardens, so I didn't see any harm in getting a peek at Mr. Grennan's roses ahead of schedule."

"As you said. Because it's not cheating." Sutton turned to Gethsemane. "What about you? Here for a surreptitious gander at the posies?"

Gethsemane chewed her lip as she looked over at the other witnesses, either clustered around the coroner's assistant as she completed her grim examination or being interviewed individually by gardaí. Did she admit she came to find Frankie? That would lead to questions about his whereabouts—unknown—which would lead to questions about alibis and motives and whether he had one or both. She knew Frankie would never kill anyone, but Inspector Sutton didn't and wasn't likely to take her word for it.

"Well?" Sutton clicked his ballpoint so fast, he risked a repetitive motion injury.

"Um..." She hesitated, trying to think of an answer that wouldn't throw suspicion on Frankie but wouldn't require lying to law enforcement, either. "I borrowed an iron."

"An iron?"

"For clothes." Not her clothes but why nitpick?

"Yes, I know what an iron's for." The creases in Sutton's trousers and crispness of his shirt endorsed his statement. The inspector may have been a thorn to Gethsemane but he was a well-dressed thorn. He eyed her slacks. "You wear linen but don't own an iron?"

She dodged a direct answer. "Nothing takes the wrinkles out of linen like the dry cleaners."

Sutton didn't challenge her. She tried to read his stone face but couldn't tell if he believed her or had just decided the line of questioning wasn't worth pursuing for the moment.

"Do you have any idea what Jacobi was doing in Grennan's garden?" he asked.

Gethsemane shrugged. "Spying on the competition?"

Ms. Heaney cleared her throat.

Sutton pinched the bridge of his nose, a gesture Niall often made when irritated. Must be something they taught in Garda school. "You have something to add, Ms. Heaney?"

The woman plucked at Sutton's sleeve again. "Nothing certain, you understand? Nothing I'd testify to in court, if it came to that. Only a rumor."

"Any information you have, Ms. Heaney, that might help the investigat—"

She cut in. "Rumor on the garden show circuit has it that Jacobi isn't," she glanced at the corpse, "wasn't above sabotage."

"Sabotage?" Sutton wrote in his notebook. "You mean like stealing flowers to enter in shows under his own name?"

"No, Inspector, that would be theft. Besides, it wouldn't work. Judges at this level are world-class experts. They'd spot it straight away if someone attempted to pass off another breeder's flowers as their own." Ms. Heaney shook her head. "No. Jacobi was, supposedly, no one could ever prove anything. He'd damage competitor's rose bushes. You lose points for anything less than perfection. Even minor damage, an errant footprint, a broken stem, can cost you the gold medal."

Had Jacobi come back to damage the 'Sandra Sechrest'? Gethsemane forced herself to peer past the coroner's assistant at the shears protruding from Jacobi's back. The handles looked like the handles of Frankie's shears. But Frankie didn't keep his garden tools locked up. Anyone, Jacobi included, could have grabbed them. She scanned the roses for signs of damaged. As she did so, she spied something lying at the base of a birdbath. A bouquet of purple and white flowers. She pointed. "What's that?"

Sutton and Mrs. Heaney turned to look. Mrs. Heaney started toward the bouquet; this time, Sutton did the arm grabbing. "Please, allow me."

He led the way to the birdbath and squatted near the flowers. Gethsemane peered over his shoulder. The wrapping paper matched the paper wrapped around the bouquet left on Frankie's windshield, the paper used by Buds of May.

"Flowers for the dead," Sutton said. "A message for Jacobi."

Or for Frankie. A warning? He's next? Or a promise to eliminate anyone who stood between Frankie and a gold medal? How far would Frankie's admirer go to give him what he wanted? To put him in her debt?

Mrs. Heaney recited the names of the flowers. "Ox-eye daisy, pansy, purple columbine, carnations. Odd funerary arrangement."

"I've seen this before," Gethsemane said. "Not this exact bouquet but one similar. This morning in the village square, someone left a floral bouquet on Frankie Grennan's car. It was wrapped in the same paper, from the village florist."

"Who left it?" the inspector asked.

"A woman who didn't want anyone to see her face." Gethsemane described the mystery woman and shared the information she'd gathered at the flower shop.

"O'Reilly was with you, eh?" Sutton rose and motioned to one of the uniformed gardaí. "I'll catch him at the station and see what he has to say about this." He scribbled in his notebook and added, "And remind him he's cold case, not homicide," in a voice so low Gethsemane wasn't sure she'd really heard it.

She resisted the impulse to tell Inspector Sutton that Niall couldn't give him any more than she had. At least he wasn't asking where Frankie was. Sutton stepped aside to whisper to the uniformed garda. Mrs. Heaney crept away from the birdbath to eavesdrop. Unnoticed, Gethsemane slipped her phone from her bag and snapped a picture of the bouquet.

Sutton turned as she slipped the phone back into her bag. She answered his raised eyebrow. "A text from my, um, dinner date, wondering where I am. May I go?"

The inspector looked at his watch, then at the coroner's assistant, who made her way toward him. "Go on," he said to Gethsemane. "I know where to find you. I'll expect a formal statement tomorrow."

"*I* know where to find *you*. I'll come to the station." That would give her time to find Frankie and find out more about the Flower Shop Killer and maybe uncover a clue leading to Frankie's admirer. Or stalker. If the mystery woman had stabbed Jacobi and left the flowers as a signature, she had definitely graduated from admirer to stalker. Had she caught up to Frankie? Had Frankie caught her in the act of killing Jacobi? Had she kidnapped Frankie? Or worse? Gethsemane went for her bike before the inspector could change his mind. She detoured through the Erasmus Hall parking lot on her way to the main road. Frankie's car wasn't there. She told the Tchaikovsky playing in her head to shut up and forced herself to think of anything other than flowers and missing math teachers all the way back to Carrick Point.

"Eamon!" Gethsemane burst into the cottage. "Eamon, where are you?" She looked into the music room. No auras, no disembodied voices, no leather-and-soap smell to signal the composer's ghost's imminent appearance. She ran to the study. "Eamon!"

A scrapbook flew from a shelf and landed on her foot.

"Stop shoutin'." A blast of men's cologne, with prominent leather, pepper, and hay notes, hit her nose. "I'm not deaf." Eamon materialized near the bookshelf. "And there's your Flower Shop Killer." He pointed at the scrapbook. It levitated from Gethsemane's foot to her hand.

Puzzlement, and a throb in her toes where the book had landed, derailed her initial thoughts. She stared at the faded pink cover of the old, post-bound album, thick with newspaper clippings, their yellowed edges curled beyond the borders of the album's pages. "What's this?" She opened the book to the first article, headlined, "Six Women Disappear from Dublin Hotel."

"Orla's sister was a true crime fanatic. She collected all sorts of macabre clippings, must've filled a couple dozen albums like that one. I found 'em in some boxes up at the lighthouse."

"Why were Orla's sister's books in your lighthouse?"

"She eloped with a man her parents couldn't stand. Ran off to Canada with him. Her parents planned to chuck all her belongings in the bin, but Orla brought them here. Just in case her sister ever sent for them. Which she didn't. Which doesn't matter." Eamon glowed an impatient turquoise and pointed at the book again.

Gethsemane held it tighter as it fluttered open. Pages flipped to an article from the *Dispatch* pasted about a third of the way in. She read aloud, "Local couple found dead in home. Early on the morning of May ninth, Liam and Radha Coyne were discovered deceased in the parlor of their home by a neighbor, who declined to give her name. The neighbor became concerned when Mrs. Coyne did not keep an appointment with her to go shopping in Cork. The gardaí have not released an official statement but a source, speaking on condition of anonymity, at the coroner's office estimates the Coynes had been dead for about eight hours before they were discovered, and foul play is suspected."

Pages flipped and she continued reading. "Authorities have now revealed details of the Coynes's murders. Both victims were stabbed in the back—" She paused.

"What's wrong?" Eamon asked.

"N-nothing."

"Liar. I can see your aura as well as you can see mine. But I'll leave it for the moment. Keep reading."

Her mouth felt dry. She swallowed and read. "Stabbed in the back. Assorted flowers lay strewn around the bodies and a floral bouquet stood in a vase near Mr. Coyne's feet." She slammed the album shut.

"There's one more article." Eamon pointed. The book leapt from Gethsemane's hands and hovered in the air. It opened to another page.

Gethsemane stepped closer and read. "Local florist, Mrs. Rosemary Finney, said a lad, about twelve, came into the shop on several occasions to pick up the flowers. He paid cash. Gardaí interviewed the lad who said a veiled woman gave him money to get the flowers from the florist and deliver them to the Coyne residence. The woman never told the lad her name nor was he able to provide a description. Gardaí have no other leads. Anyone with information, please contact..." She broke off and sank onto the sofa. "I think Frankie's in trouble. Serious trouble. What are we going to do?"

Seven

Eamon vanished then reappeared next to her on the sofa. "Aren't you getting carried away over a few old newspaper clippings? That's not like you."

"Roderick Jacobi's dead. Murdered in Frankie's rose garden. Stabbed in the back with a bouquet from Buds of May lying nearby. And Frankie's missing. He's not home, his car's not in the parking lot, he hasn't been seen since the photo shoot, and he isn't answering texts."

"I take back what I said about 'carried away.' Your landing in the middle of a murder mystery is typical you. Rugadh—"

She held up a hand. "Don't start spouting Gale-gee at me."

"Do me a favor. Call it Irish. Your pronunciation's as bad as your brogue."

"Gale-gee, Gaeilge, Irish, whatever. I don't care. I just—" She stood and ran a hand through her hair as she paced near the windows. "How are we going to find Frankie? What if...?" She couldn't say it. She couldn't think it.

Eamon disappeared from the sofa and rematerialized in the way of her pacing. She walked through him. The electric jolt of the full body contact forced her to stop and catch her breath.

"Deep breath, that's right," Eamon said. "Now, recite some batting averages."

"I don't need to recite batting averages," she said, rejecting the suggestion she resort to her ritual of reciting Negro League baseball statistics to regain calm and focus.

"You need to do something other than panic. Put your beautiful brain to work and come up with a plan. Panicking won't help Frankie."

"I am not panicking." She added a silent, *Josh Gibson, 1930, three thirty-eight, 1931, two eighty-eight, 1922, three twenty-six.* "But you're right, we do need a plan."

"Would that be the royal 'we'?"

"No, that would be the you and me 'we.' I don't know what we're going to do yet, but you're going to help do it."

"I'm a ghost, lacking a corporeal body. How can I help?"

She threw her hands in the air. "I don't know. How about as usual, by making snarky remarks and aggravating me to the point of forcing me to act just to prove you wrong?"

Eamon bristled umber. "I do not aggravate you."

Gethsemane's argument devolved into laughter. "You do aggravate me but only because you bring up valid points and rein me in when I'm about to rush into some ill-conceived scheme. And don't sulk. Umber is not a becoming color for you. And don't give me that 'I'm just a ghost, what can I do?' nonsense. Six months ago, you saved half the village."

The umber faded and a dimpled smile took control of Eamon's lips. "What are you—we—going to do?"

"First, find Frankie."

"Call the guards. Finding missing people connected to murder investigations is what they're paid for, rightly or not."

"Call the gardaí and tell them I think my friend, who, by the way, hated the murder victim and owned the murder weapon, may have been kidnapped by his secret admirer because she brought him flowers and I read a decades-old newspaper article that mentioned a couple being stabbed in the back and some flowers being left behind and concluded from that there must be a copycat killer on the loose?" She snorted. "If they didn't hang up on me right away, they'd thank me for offering up Frankie as a murder suspect and *then* they'd hang up on me. No, I take that back. They wouldn't thank me. Guards cringe when they hear my name. Seriously. Inspector Sutton actually cringed. And swore."

Eamon made a rude gesture. "That's to Inspector Sutton. But you've got to come up with something better than pedaling your bike 'round the village yelling, 'Frankie, Frankie Grennan.'"

She smacked her forehead. "Duh. Niall. He's Frankie's friend, too, and he doesn't cringe when I call; he only slightly frowns. He listens to me. Most of the time."

"He works cold cases, not homicide or missing persons."

"He's still law enforcement. And if someone—Frankie—was in imminent danger—" There, she'd said it out loud. "—it would be all hands on deck, never mind your usual duty station. Right?" She headed for the entryway where she'd left her bag with her phone.

"What can I do while you're marshaling forces?" Eamon called after her.

"Don't 'spose you can pop over to the flower shop and ask Alexandra Sexton who picked up the second bouquet?"

"I don't 'pop,' I translocate. But no, I can't. Ask her, I mean. Sorry. She can't see or hear me. However, I could go over to the Rabbit..." He vanished.

Gethsemane stared at the spot where he'd been. "Eamon?"

He reappeared. "Miss me?"

"Why do you do that?"

"Because I can. Being a ghost has some advantages. And he's not there."

"Who's not where?"

"Grennan's not at the pub. Cop on. In case, O'Reilly asks if you checked."

She stuck out her tongue and dialed. O'Reilly answered on the third ring.

"Don't hang up on me," she said.

"Don't hang up—" A pause. When Niall's baritone returned to the line, suspicion coated every word. "Sissy, what have you done?"

She hated that nickname. Granted, Gethsemane was a mouthful, but "Sissy" was a ridiculous nickname for a grown woman. Someday, she might forgive her brother-in-law for using it outside the confines of family. She also hated the presumption she'd made trouble. "I haven't done anything." She took a breath and fought the annoyance rising in her throat. "I need you—I can't find Frankie."

Another pause. Niall's voice came back minus the accusatory tone. "Where have you looked?"

"Erasmus Hall." She glanced at Eamon hovering nearby. "And the pub."

"You tried calling?"

"I texted. He didn't answer."

Niall swore.

"You're not telling me I'm overreacting or not the full shilling or stirring up trouble. Which worries me. You know about Roderick Jacobi?"

"I know. I also know Frankie's the number one suspect."

"Suspect? Not, um, victim?"

Eamon whispered, "He doesn't know about the Flower Shop Killer."

"You don't have to whisper. Niall can't hear you."

"Who's that you're talking to?" Niall asked.

"But he can hear you," Eamon reminded her.

"Um, no one," she said to Niall. "Myself. Why's Frankie a suspect?"

"A *Dispatch* photographer reported witnessing Frankie eat Jacobi's head off at the photoshoot."

"Must have happened after I left."

"According to the photographer, they almost came to blows."

"Did Inspector Sutton tell you about the flowers?"

"The bouquet you found by the birdbath? Yeah, I heard about them."

"You don't think that's significant, given the bouquet left on his car this morning?"

"His secret admirer was in the area but—"

"She could have killed Jacobi and kidnapped Frankie."

"Kidnapped. *Now* I think you're sounding a bit out there. Unless...What haven't you told me?"

She recounted the details of the Flower Shop Killer.

Niall sighed. Gethsemane imagined him massaging his temples. "If anyone other than you tried to sell me on a connection between an unsolved double homicide in the sixties and a murder this afternoon, I'd tell them—never mind. Half the department's on the lookout for Frankie. If he's in or around the village, one of the uniforms will find him. I'll head down to the evidence room and dig through the files on this flower shop business, see if I can find a clue as to where a copycat might have taken a victim away from the village."

"Thank you. While you're doing that, I'll—"

"Stay put?" Niall's tone sounded hopeful.

"Try Frankie again."

"Let me know if you hear from him." Niall rang off.

"We both know you're going to do more than try Frankie again," Eamon said after the call ended.

"I'm also going to speak to Alexandra Sexton. If the gardaí have focused on Frankie's relationship with Jacobi as a motive for murder, they probably haven't given much thought to those flowers yet. Maybe I can find out who claimed them from the shop before Ms. Sexton realizes she should be talking to law enforcement instead of me."

"There's the snoop I've come to love."

"Why does everyone keep calling me snoop?"

"You prefer Sissy?"

"You know I hate that name. How about calling me an amateur investigator?"

"Too stuffy. Miss Marple-ish. You're more Nancy Drew."

She rolled her eyes and sent Frankie a text: *Where are you? Urgent. 911.*

Eamon read over her shoulder. "Wrong country."

"What? Damn." She resent the text: *999.*

Seconds later, the opening notes of Beethoven's Fifth Symphony alerted her to an incoming text: *Where's the fire?*

"Frankie!" She dialed his number. "Where the hell are you?" she asked before he could speak. "I texted you over an hour ago. Why didn't you answer me? Where've you been? Are you okay? Are you safe?"

"You texted me fifteen seconds ago and I answered you right away. Are *you* all right?" he asked. "Stranded on a cliff with a sprained ankle? Fallen down a well? Being held hostage by an ax murderer? Strike that last suggestion. Knowing you, that's entirely possible. You're not are you? Being held hostage? And if you're not, would you mind telling me what you're on about? My mother didn't make this much fuss over my whereabouts when I was ten."

"Francis William Rowan Grennan, be happy you're not in arm's reach because I'm not sure if I'd hug you or slug you."

"Did someone slug *you*? Have you got another head injury? Because you're not making much sense."

Eamon tapped his finger through her shoulder, sending a shock down her arm. "He doesn't know about Jacobi."

"Which means he wasn't on campus when the murder occurred," she said. "Which proves he didn't do it. Not that I thought he did."

Frankie's voice came over the phone. "Who are you talking to? What murder? Please make sense."

Gethsemane explained. "Roderick Jacobi was found dead in your rose garden with your hedge shears sticking out of his back. A bouquet of flowers similar to the one left on your car this morning was found near his body. So, naturally, I deduced your secret admirer was a homicidal stalker who'd been inspired by the still-unsolved crimes of the Flower Shop Killer to murder your rival and kidnap you."

Silence. Then, "How many shots of Waddell and Dobb have you had so far?"

"I'm serious, Frankie, and I'm sober. I thought you were dead or chained up in some dank basement or something."

"I'm fine. You mean it about Jacobi? He's dead? In my garden?"

"Quite dead. Right in front of the 'Sandra Sechrest'. And, Frankie?"

"Yeah?"

"Since you're not a victim, you're the prime suspect. That loser photographer told the guards you and Jacobi had a fight this morning. They're on the lookout for you."

"Shite."

"Can you tell me where you are?" She hesitated. "What's her name?"

"What's her—Wait, you think I—Jaysus, Sissy." Frankie laughed. "I supposed I should take that as a compliment."

Three "Sissys" in under an hour. Had to be a record. "If you're not on a date, where are you? Where've you been all this time? On walkabout?"

"In my garden."

"No, you haven't."

"Not at Erasmus Hall. My secret garden."

"Secret garden?" She'd fallen into a Frances Hodgson Burnett story. "At Our Lady?"

"The church garden's hardly secret. I'm up at Carnock."

"Golgotha?" Gethsemane shuddered. The grim nickname suited the dismal outcropping south of the village. "There's no garden there. Just overgrown brush and the burned out remains of St. D's." St. Dymphna's, the abandoned insane asylum, perched on Carnock. Her head throbbed with the memory of the attack she'd endured in the hospital's basement.

"Brush, remains, and a wee plot I cultivated where the hospital's garden used to be. I found a few rosebushes that had reverted to rootstock. Turns out, the rootstock roses were a rare heirloom variety. I decided to try my luck, see what I could do with them. They're quite lovely."

"How did you find roses up there in the first place?"

Frankie stammered. "Well, I, um, you see, we, it was no one you know, she was just, I mean she wanted, we went up, well, we—"

"Never mind. I can hear you blushing over the phone. Just stay there, I'm coming to get you."

"Out here, on your bike, at this hour? With a murderer running 'round?"

"It doesn't get dark until almost ten. But I get your point."

"I have my car, I'll drive to the garda station."

"To make it easy for them to arrest you?"

"Arrest me for what? I argued with Jacobi, I didn't kill him."

"You own the murder weapon and you have an unconfirmable alibi. Trust me when I say don't trust the gardaí to take your word for it that you're innocent."

"Call Niall. He's at the station looking for a link between the cold case and Jacobi's murder. A) He'll be delighted to hear you're safe and well, b) he'll be an ally. He can keep Inspector Sutton from feeding you to the wolves."

"Fine, I'll call him before I do anything. But please don't come out here. I know you don't like men fussing over you and telling you what to do—"

"No, I don't. But I'll listen to you this once." She said her goodbyes and ended the call. "Because I have something else I need to do."

"Flower shop?" Eamon asked.

"Flower shop."

Eight

Gethsemane and Eamon arrived at Buds of May just before closing.

"You didn't have to come with me," Gethsemane said as she leaned her bicycle against the flower shop's wall.

"If *we're* investigating then *we* ought to interview witnesses together."

"You said the florist can't see or hear you."

"She can't. But I can see and hear her. You talk, I'll take notes. Go on in, before she locks up."

A quick glance around the square confirmed the absence of gardaí. She pushed open the shop door and stepped inside.

Alexandra looked up from sweeping. "Dr. Brown. Your handsome friend's not with you?"

"Told you she couldn't see me," Eamon said. "If she could, she'd know your handsome friend stood right beside you."

Gethsemane ignored him. "Inspector O'Reilly's busy with something right now. He didn't come by to see you earlier this evening? Or call?"

"No." Alexandra frowned. "Any reason he should have?"

She must not have heard about Jacobi's murder. Or at least not the details. "We found another bouquet." Gethsemane pulled up the photo she'd taken on her phone. "Daisies and pansies."

Alexandra enlarged the picture on the screen. "I remember this one. A young girl came in for it a couple of hours after you left."

"Young, meaning...?"

"About ten, eleven years old."

Just like the boy who picked up the killer's flowers. "Wasn't it strange, an eleven-year-old buying flowers?"

"She didn't buy them, she only picked them up. They were ordered online. And, no, the girl didn't say who sent her to get them. She came in with the order number written on a slip of paper. They were pre-paid so I just handed the girl the flowers."

"Did you know the girl?"

"I did."

"Well, why the bloody hell don't you tell her the girl's name instead of making her drag it out of you?" Eamon asked, his aura bright blue.

Gethsemane dropped her gaze to the floor and covered a smile with her hand.

Alexandra went on, oblivious to the angry outburst. "'Know' might be too strong a word. Recognize is more like it. I don't know her name but I see her around the square. Her ma works at the laundry down the way. The girl goes with her sometimes when she picks up and delivers laundry from the restaurants. The girl's sweet. I gave her a peppermint from the stash I keep behind the counter. She thanked me pretty as you please."

Gethsemane thanked her as well. "One more question." She showed Alexandra the picture of the flowers again. "Do you know what these mean?"

Alexandra took a moment to answer. "Let's see, ox-eyed daisies stand for perseverance, pansies mean think of me, purple columbine means resolve to win, and carnations are for boldness. Wait a minute." She ducked behind the counter. When she came up, she held a small, tattered book. "I dug this out after your visit this morning. *The Language of Flowers*. Why don't you loan it to your friend so he'll be able to read his crush's messages?"

"Thank you again." Gethsemane spied a uniformed garda walking across the square. He wasn't looking toward the flower shop but no point in taking chances. "We, er, I won't keep you any longer. You've been a help."

"Always willing to lend a hand in the service of romance. That's why I'm in this business."

Gethsemane huddled in the shop's doorway until the garda went into the pizza parlor. Then she grabbed her bike and wheeled it around the corner into the alcove. "Can you think of a cover story," she asked Eamon, "to give me a reason to track down and interrogate an eleven-year-old that doesn't make me seem creepy?"

"Not off the top of my head, no. Do you think the same person's behind both bouquets?"

"Two stalkers, each acting on their own?" Gethsemane shook her head.

"Why pick up the first bouquet in person but send a kid to get the second?"

"Because the stalker couldn't go back to the Buds of May herself. Too risky. She knew she'd been noticed picking up the first bouquet by someone other than the florist." Gethsemane jerked a thumb toward her chest. "Noticed by someone connected to the object of her obsession. She wouldn't repeat her mistake. Besides, having a kid pick up the flowers follows the original crime more closely. If you're going to be a copycat, you have to copy. Unless you think the similarities between the Flower Shop Killer and our stalker are coincidence?"

"No. As much as it pains me to say it, I think you're right. Whoever left the bouquets for Frankie is a copycat. Except they didn't kill Frankie, they killed his rival in the rose show."

"Right after Frankie and Jacobi had a witnessed fight and during a time when Frankie has no alibi. Thanks, copycat. No better way to show a guy you love him than setting him up to take the fall for murder."

"Now what do you want to do?"

"Call Niall." Gethsemane dialed the inspector but the call went to voicemail. "Or Frankie." Her call to the math teacher went unanswered as well. "Or worry. Rudolph Ash, one sixty, Bingo DeMoss, three oh-one, Dink Mothell, one fifty-two..."

"We can go to the station, see what's happening. Or I can take the spectral express route while you wait here. I'm only half-ashamed to admit that I saw the inside of the Dunmullach garda station more than once while I was alive."

"I appreciate your offer to pop—translocate—over to the station but I can't just wait here. I've got to try to find the little girl. If—when—the gardaí realize the bouquet isn't just a red herring, they'll track the kid down. And if they get to her before I do, I'll never be able to talk to her."

"All right, I'll go with you to the laundry. At least I can keep an eye on you. Since telling you to be careful never seems to do any good."

"A spectral bodyguard. Just what I wanted for Christmas."

"Hey, I'm pretty handy with a fireball." A blue orb sizzled past her and exploded against the wall. A black smudge marked the place where it struck.

"Show off." She looked around to see if anyone had noticed. "Stop it before you accidentally burn down a building or something. C'mon."

Gethsemane stopped her bike a block away from the laundry. She knelt and scooped up a handful of dirt and grass.

"What are you doing?" Eamon asked.

"Making a sacrifice to the cause of justice." She smeared the dirt on the knee of her robin's egg-blue linen pants. "You don't have a pocket knife, do you?"

"Since I don't actually have pockets, no, I don't."

"Never mind." She rooted through her bag until she found nail clippers. She used the attached file to rip a hole in the center of the dirt stain. "Aren't you going to tell me I'm not the full shilling for tearing up a pair of perfectly good pants?"

"No, because I think I know what you're up to."

She put the clippers away and headed for the laundry on foot.

"It'll be more convincing if you limp," Eamon called after her.

The laundry appeared deserted. She limped up to the counter. A faded card next to an old-fashioned hotel desk bell read, "Ring for service." She tapped the bell's plunger.

"Excuse me." She craned her neck to peer past bags of clothes hanging from overhead racks. "Anyone here?"

Plastic rustled. The clerk, a frazzled woman with several dark hairs escaping from her untidy pony tail that framed her face like an exasperated halo and lines drawing down the corner of her eyes and mouth, appeared from behind the clothes. "Help you?" she asked in a tone that suggested she wanted to do anything but.

"I hope so." Gethsemane balanced on one leg and tried to hold her knee high enough for the woman to see the dirt and the tear. "I had a bike accident. Landed in the dirt."

The woman leaned forward to examine the tear. "No blood."

"I didn't damage anything but my pants, luckily, but they're my favorite pants and I don't know what to use to get the dirt stain out."

"Any decent laundry detergent. Borax might work. Or Oxy. White vinegar. Rubbing alcohol. You'll have to rub it in to the stain before the stain sets."

"Do you have anything here you could sell me?"

The woman turned and disappeared behind the clothes. Gethsemane tried to see where she went, then looked around for any sign of a little girl. She spotted Eamon gesturing through the window toward the washing machines at the rear of the store.

She poked her head out the door. "Why don't you come in?"

"I can't. Laundry's only been here a few years. Don't remember what was here while I was alive. Never mind all that, the girl's at a table in the corner. Hurry up."

She pulled her head in. Before she could make it to the back of the store, the clerk reappeared at the counter. She held a small bottle in her hand. "Got this."

Gethsemane examined the bottle. A long, chemical name assured her grass stains were no match for the contents. She pulled out her wallet. "May I put some on here? I've got a ways to go before I get home. I want to treat it before it sets, like you suggested."

The woman shrugged and disappeared behind the clothes again. Gethsemane took the bottle and headed for the washing machines. She peered around a bank of the heavy-duty cleaners and saw a thin, preteen girl sitting at a table, reading.

She sat in the chair opposite. "Hello."

The girl didn't look up from her book. "Hello."

"My name's Gethsemane." She pressed on when the girl didn't reply. "Do you mind if I sit here while I treat my pants?"

"No," the girl said, still not looking up.

Gethsemane squirted clear liquid on the stain. Silence filled the laundry as she dabbed at the stain with her fingers.

"That would be easier with a cloth," the girl said. "You can use one from that basket in the corner."

"Thanks." Gethsemane retrieved a white rag and returned to the table. "What are you reading?"

"*Alice's Adventures in Wonderland.*"

"That's one of my favorites. Why is a raven like a writing desk?"

"Because it can produce a few notes, though they are very flat; and it is never put with the wrong end in front." The girl put the book down and smiled.

"I like the garden of live flowers, especially the rose and tiger-lily."

"I wish real flowers could talk."

"They can." Gethsemane pulled out the *Language of Flowers*. "You can use flowers to send secret messages."

The girl slid the book over and turned pages.

"Pretty cool, huh?"

The girl nodded.

"Has anyone ever sent you flowers?"

The girl made a face. "I'm only eleven, who'd send me flowers?"

"Have you ever sent flowers to anyone? I sent my mother flowers for Mother's Day when I was about your age."

"I gave flowers to someone. Sort of. A lady gave me five euros to get some flowers for her. I didn't pick them out, though. If I had, I would have picked these." Her finger rested on a picture of a gardenia. "It's pretty."

"It's beautiful. And the smell's divine."

"You've seen them for real?"

Gethsemane smiled. "My grandma had a garden full of gardenias, back in Virginia. What kind of flowers did the lady have you get?"

The girl turned a few pages in the book. "Some were like this." She pointed to a pansy.

"Did the woman tell you her name?"

The girl shook her head.

"What did the woman look like?"

The girl shrugged. "She had on a funny hat. I couldn't see her face."

"How tall was she?"

"Taller than you."

"What did she sound like? Like she was from around here?"

"Yeah. She sounded regular. Not funny, like you."

The clerk appeared around the corner. "Oona, finish the chapter you're reading then help me close up. It's getting late."

"Sure, Ma." The girl gave the flower book back to Gethsemane and went back to *Alice's Adventures in Wonderland.*

"We're closing," the clerk said to Gethsemane.

Gethsemane stood. "Thanks for the stain treatment. I think it's working. I'll apply some more when I get home. You may have saved my pants."

The woman nodded and headed back to the front of the store.

Gethsemane turned to say goodbye to Oona. The girl stared out the window.

"Who's that man?" she asked.

"What man?" Gethsemane faced the window. Eamon stared back at them.

"That man. With the curly hair." Oona waved.

Eamon turned a surprised brown and waved back.

"You see a man with curly hair and green eyes standing by the window?" Gethsemane asked.

Oona looked at Gethsemane as if she was thick. "Is he your husband?"

"Um, no. He's a friend. My roommate."

"Why didn't he come in with you?"

"He's, uh, allergic to laundry detergent."

"Oona," the clerk called from the front of the store.

"Coming, Ma."

Gethsemane followed the girl to the front of the store but walked out before Oona could tell her mother about the curly haired man with the detergent allergy.

As soon as they'd moved out of sight of the laundry, Gethsemane asked Eamon, "Why could Oona see you?"

"Why can you see me?"

"Good luck and clean living? I don't know."

"Nor do I. Some can see me, some can hear me, and some haven't got a clue."

"And then there are the fortunate ones like me who get the multi-sensory Eamon McCarthy spectral experience." Touched or gifted—or cursed—her grandma would have called someone with the ability to see the "haints" who frequented the stories she used to tell Gethsemane when Gethsemane was a little girl sitting on her rickety porch at her rickety house in the middle of nowhere on sultry Virginia summer evenings. Stories Gethsemane's citified mother forbade her grandma to repeat when she found out. Stories Gethsemane rejected as superstition—until she moved to Ireland and into Carraigfaire Cottage and met Eamon.

Eamon's umber aura mirrored his hurt look. "Are you being sarcastic or do you really wish you were shed of me? Sometimes it's hard to tell with you."

"I'm sorry. That was sarcastic. I'm worried and angry and had to let it out somewhere and you happened to be in the line of fire. You know I don't want you to go away again. You went away and I was miserable until you came back." Eamon had been banished to limbo for a while. She'd been lost and lonely without him. "I'll try to keep the snark in check."

"Apology accepted. And as a fellow devotee of snark, I don't mind when you deploy it. Just aim it in a different direction.

Like toward the gardaí. They deserve it."

"Some of them, anyway. I'd feel more confident about letting the ones that deserve it have it if I had something to back it up with. Like the identity of Frankie's admirer." She picked up her bike.

"Where to now?" Eamon asked.

"Home." She looked toward the garda station. "I guess. I want to read through *The Language of Flowers* again. Maybe I missed something. Some alternate floral message that will give us a clue."

Eamon jerked his head in the opposite direction. "Home's that way, darlin'."

She kept her gaze fixed on the gothic structure where she'd spent more time in interrogation rooms in the past several months than she'd ever before spent in her life. "I know."

"You're wondering if Grennan took your advice and called O'Reilly."

"Kind of." She gripped the Pashley's handlebars and rolled the bike back and forth in front of her.

"You're worried and you want to know if he's in custody."

"Sort of." She climbed onto the bike.

"You want to ride over to the station to see what you can find out because not knowing is driving you mad."

"Exactly." Gethsemane pedaled toward the garda station. "Coming?" she called over her shoulder.

"You take the high road, I'll take the low road, and I'll be in the car park before you." Eamon winked out. He re-materialized in the station's parking lot as Gethsemane pedaled up. "What took you so long?"

She ignored the question and laid the Pashley on the ground. A survey of the lot revealed only a couple of uniformed gardaí going to their cars. No red-haired math teachers.

"There's your boy," Eamon said behind her.

"Frankie? Where?" She craned her neck to scan the lot's periphery.

"Your other boy. The garda." Eamon pointed toward the building's entrance. "I'll let you handle this." He vanished.

Niall walked out of the station, several file folders tucked under his arm. He saw Gethsemane, readjusted his fedora, and changed course in her direction.

"What are you doing here at the station?" he asked when he reached her. "And what happened to your pants?" He pointed at her torn knee.

She'd forgotten about the tear. "Oh, nothing. Minor, uh—" It hadn't really been an accident. "—incident. What's that you've got?" She pointed at the folders. She hesitated to ask about Frankie. If he hadn't called Niall yet, she didn't want to give him away. Niall's expression, reserved with a hint of careful-where-you-go-poking-your-nose warning, betrayed nothing.

Niall shifted the folders. "Evidence from the Flower Shop Killer investigation. Witness statements. I thought I'd go over them again and see if there's anything that could help Frankie."

Had Frankie called? She chewed her lip for a moment then pushed aside the urge to ask. Instead she said, "Those are slim folders." None was over an inch thick. "Not much in them."

"Not much in the way of witnesses."

"O'Reilly!" The angry shout echoed off the station's stone walls and carried across the parking lot. Gethsemane and Niall turned toward the source. Inspector Sutton loomed, arms crossed, feet planted wide, in the entrance way. Even from a distance, Gethsemane felt anger radiating from Sutton like heat shimmering on a road on a hot, Virginia summer's day.

Niall swore. "Something eatin' ya, Bill?"

Sutton stomped over. "Is the Superintendent merging the cold case unit with homicide?"

"Not that I know of," Niall said.

"Then why are you sticking your damned nose into my murder case?" A flush spread up Sutton's neck and along his jawline. He jerked a thumb toward Gethsemane. "She put you up to this?"

"No one put me up to anything," Niall said. "And I'm not buttin' in." He held up the folders. "The Flower Shop Killer case is mine."

"Your nineteen sixties flower shop killer has eff all to do with Jacobi's murder. Unless you suspect a geriatric, garden shear-wielding maniac. Maybe I should send some uniforms over to the old folks' home, round up a few shuffleboard players, and bring 'em in for questioning?"

"Maybe you should get your head out—" Niall closed his eyes and held his breath for a three-count. "Maybe you should consider all of the possibilities before your laser focus railroads an innocent man."

"You know for certain he's innocent, do you? 'Cuz he's your friend or because you have some evidence that will stand up in court?"

"I have evidence that adds up to reasonable doubt you'll be able to pin anything on Frankie and make it stick. I have evidence that a disturbed woman borrowed elements from a notorious unsolved murder, stalked Frankie, and may have killed a man who represented a threat to the object of her obsession."

"Why? As a love offering? Like that cat of yours leaving dead mice in your fancy shoes?" Sutton eyed Niall's monkstraps.

Niall shifted his weight and hitched up a pant leg to give Sutton a better view of his designer shoes. "Nero leaves me mice because he thinks he's earning his keep. Maybe you should try it. Do some actual detective work instead of settling on the first idea that pops into your head."

Sutton advanced. He held his face inches from Niall's and

lowered his voice to a growl. "Okay, O'Reilly," he loosened his necktie, "let's take this—"

Gethsemane stepped between them. "Inspector Sutton, do you have any evidence that refutes Inspector O'Reilly's theory? Anything that proves a disturbed woman with knowledge of an infamous cold case couldn't have killed Jacobi?"

Sutton turned his glare on her but stepped back. "You keep out of this. Maybe your boyfriend doesn't mind you meddling in his moribund cases but this is an active investigation and there's no tolerance for civilian interference."

"Inspector O'Reilly isn't my boyfriend and I'm not interfering in the investigation," Gethsemane said. "I'm merely pointing out the flaws in your investigative logic in your rush to wrap up this case by pinning it on the first—"

Niall interrupted. His expression suggested pity for the target of Gethsemane's wrath outweighed his personal animosity toward him. "Why don't we take it up with Superintendent Feeney?"

"Fine. We'll take it up with her. I'm sure she'll see it my way. She's no fan of goose chases. She likes results."

"Don't be too sure the Super will support ignoring leads. She doesn't like to be made fool of in court."

Sutton grunted and headed for the station. Niall winked at Gethsemane and followed Sutton.

Eamon rematerialized next to Gethsemane. "How long are you going to wait here?"

"Until they come back."

"They might be a while. I don't imagine their chat with their boss will be pleasant or easy. You're going to stay here all night?"

She kicked the spokes of her bike wheel. "What am I supposed to do? Go home and fiddle? Bake a cake?"

"Oh, please, no baking. You're a brilliant woman and your

skills are legion, but cooking doesn't number among them." Eamon pointed at the bike and levitated it to lean against a tree. "And don't take it out on the Pashley. What'd she ever do to you?"

A small laugh defied Gethsemane's effort to stifle it. "I'm sorry. I'm just—I hate this. Waiting. Not knowing where Frankie is, if he's okay, wondering if he's going to be arrested for murder or if some nut is going to do to him what they did to Jacobi." She leaned against a tree and pressed the heels of her hands against her eyes. "You know me, I'm a doer, a fixer. Waiting patiently to see what happens is another skill that's not in my skill set." She stepped toward the station. "Maybe I should go in—"

Eamon moved in front of her. She passed through him, then stopped short as a charge buzzed through her. She shivered. Eamon paled, leaving the cars in the lot visible through his chest.

"Nothing good ever happens when you go into the garda station," Eamon said. "I may hate myself later for suggesting this, but why don't we go look for Grennan? You're less likely to land in trouble searching for a murder suspect than taking on the guards on their own turf."

Gethsemane stared through him to the street at a car approaching from the road. "Ask and ye shall receive. That's Frankie's car."

"He's decided to turn himself in, then."

"Don't say it like that. You make it sound like he's under arrest."

"He will be if he goes in there. Flower Shop Killer copy cat or no, Sutton'll have his man."

"Damn. I hate it when you're right."

"Which is always."

Gethsemane raised an eyebrow.

"Almost," Eamon added.

Frankie's car turned into the lot. "I've got to stop him," Gethsemane said.

"Stop him? You told him to call O'Reilly."

"Call. On the phone. Not show up in person. Besides, I didn't know how much of a bulldog Sutton was going to be about laying Jacobi's murder on Frankie when I said that." She started toward Frankie's car, parked at the far end of the row farthest from the station building. "C'mon."

Eamon shook his head. "I want no part of you interfering in a garda investigation."

"I'm not interfering. I'm preventing a miscarriage of justice. And since when did you get so prissy?"

Eamon sighed and dematerialized.

Gethsemane reached Frankie's car as he opened the door. It slammed shut. Eamon materialized next to the car with a grin.

Frankie rattled the handle. The door didn't budge. He rolled down the window. "What the—? Feckin' piece of junk."

Gethsemane leaned against the door, elbows rested in the open window, forcing Frankie back. She cast a glance at Eamon as she spoke to Frankie. "Mechanical malfunction. You need to leave."

"I just got here." Frankie rattled the handle again. "Why won't this open?"

"Humidity. Makes the door stick. Really, you should leave."

Frankie frowned. "Have you lost the plot? There's no humidity. Humidity doesn't make car doors stick shut. And you're the one who told me to come here."

"No," she said, "I told you to call Niall. Call, not come in. And now I'm telling you to leave."

"What's happened?" Frankie let go of the door handle. "And don't tell me nothing. I've known you long enough to know better."

"Sutton has decided you're it. He's pretty hell-bent on

locking you up for murder."

"I didn't murder anyone. I won't pretend I didn't hate Jacobi or that I'm sorry he's dead. But I didn't make him dead. I'm a curmudgeon, not a murderer."

"I know you didn't kill Jacobi, Frankie. Niall knows it, too. But it's Sutton's case and Sutton doesn't want to do any work and you're the easiest to fix up for the crime. So you should leave. Go hide."

"Damn, Sutton." Frankie smacked his steering wheel.

"Why do people take out their frustrations on innocent vehicles?" Eamon asked.

"This from a man who once trashed an innocent hotel room because the chef cooked his eggs wrong," Gethsemane muttered.

"What?" Frankie frowned up at her.

"Nothing. Talking to myself." Sometimes she wished more people could see and hear Eamon. "Trying to figure out how to convince you to drive away."

"Why's Sutton so sure I did Jacobi?"

"You mean besides his body being found in your garden with your hedge shears sticking out of his back and your obvious dislike of the man?"

"Yeah, besides that." Frankie slumped in his seat. "I can see it from Sutton's point of view. Jacobi a renowned horticulturist and pharmaceutical titan, me a humble maths teacher who grows roses for a hobby, robbed of my dreams for a medal by a charismatic egomaniac backed by money and prestige."

"'Speaks to motive,' as they say on the cop shows."

He seemed lost, as if his thoughts were someplace far away from the present situation. "And then there's Yseult..."

Yseult? How did his ex-wife figure into this? Gethsemane leaned farther in the window. "Frankie?"

He didn't answer.

"Frankie?" She snapped her fingers. "Hey, come back."

Frankie shook his head and returned his attention to Gethsemane. "Sorry."

"What about Yseult?"

He shook his head again, as if trying to clear it of bad memories. "I'll tell you later. I'm in a bad way, aren't I?"

"Yes."

"I can always count on you to tell it to me plain." He stared past her, his gaze on the horizon. "I could drive out of here, away from Dunmullach, keep driving to Cork, get a plane ticket—"

"I said, 'hide,' Frankie, not flee. If you run, you'll only make yourself look guilty. More fuel for Sutton's fire."

"If I go to ground, how long am I supposed to stay there?"

"Not long," she hesitated, "hopefully. Niall and Sutton are talking to their boss now. Niall is trying to sell her on his alternate suspect."

"Alternate suspect?"

"The Flower Shop Killer."

"Flower Shop Killer? From back in the sixties? The killer wouldn't still be alive, would they? Or is Niall counting the killer's ghost as a suspect?"

Eamon made a noise. Gethsemane ignored it. "Not the actual Flower Shop Killer," she explained. "A copycat. The person who's been leaving you the flowers."

Frankie looked doubtful.

Gethsemane persisted. "A copycat killer is more likely than you as the killer. Niall sees that. Sutton would see it, too, if he wasn't digging in his heels. If Niall can convince the Superintendent to see it, you'll stay out of jail."

"Copycat killer." Frankie massaged his temple. "Forgive me for being a pessimist as well as a curmudgeon. Maybe I should find a solicitor."

"An excellent idea. You should leave now, get yourself a

solicitor, and call Niall later to find out if it's okay to come out of hiding. Call, as in, on the phone. Not drive unarmed into the lions' den."

"All right, all right, I'll do as you ask." Frankie started his car. "And, Sissy?"

That name. She bit back her retort. Being under suspicion for murder warranted a pass for using that stupid nickname. "Yes?"

"Thanks. It's nice to have you in my corner."

She stood away from the car as he pulled out of the parking space. She watched until he reached the parking lot's exit then turned her back. "In case anyone finds out he was here," she said in response to Eamon's raised eyebrow, "If they ask me which way he went, I can honestly say I don't know."

"If you go home and stay there, no one will think to ask you."

She spied Niall coming out of the station. She risked a look over her shoulder. Frankie's car was out of sight. She turned back toward Niall. "Maybe there's an update."

She headed for the building and met Niall mid-parking lot. "Well? What happened? How'd it go with your boss?"

"Two things. Superintendent Feeney agreed with me about expanding the investigation to include other suspects, such as your stalker." He fell silent.

"Frankie may be the math teacher but even I can count to two. You only listed one thing. What's the second."

Niall sighed. "Second thing. Superintendent Feeney agreed with Sutton that I crossed the line by making a bags of his case without proper authorization. She sentenced me to desk duty for the rest of the week. And warned—or promised—me that further transgression would result in suspension."

"I'm sorry, Niall. As grateful as I am that you kept Frankie out of a cell, I don't want you to lose your job."

Niall waved the concern away with a wan smile. "What's the point in having friends if you won't risk getting sacked for them?"

"Really, Niall, I—"

"No more about it. Now, we just need to find Frankie." Niall raised an eyebrow. "Don't suppose you know where he is?"

Gethsemane looked past Niall's shoulder. If she looked him in the eye, he'd know she wasn't being a hundred percent straight with him. "Nope. No idea where he's gone." Which was, technically, true. She ignored Eamon's laughter. "Maybe he'll call."

"We'll find him. I've got a couple of uniforms I trust, and who are no fans of Sutton's, keeping an eye out for him. Why don't you go home?" Niall grinned. "In case he turns up at the cottage or the lighthouse."

"Why would he?"

"Why would someone in trouble turn to the fearless Gethsemane Brown, notorious amateur sleuth with a knack for getting people out of trouble and a habit of defying the gardaí? Hmm, I wonder."

"Leave the sarcasm to me, Niall."

"Go home. If Frankie turns up or calls you, call me right away. Meanwhile, I'll see if I can't track down some clues to the identity of your flower girl and leave them under Sutton's nose like breadcrumbs."

"Your boss told you to back off."

"Gethsemane Brown's not the only hardhead in this village. Desk duty doesn't mean I can't sneak in a bit of snooping. Investigating."

"You're starting to sound like me."

Niall's smile spread to his eyes. "If you repeat this, I'll deny it, but I'll take that as a compliment."

Nine

"One more parallel between the Flower Shop Killer and Frankie's admirer. But nothing that puts us closer to figuring out who she is." Gethsemane slammed *The Language of Flowers* on the coffee table.

"We know she's local," Eamon said.

"How many women are in Dunmullach? We can't investigate every one of them." She pulled her phone out. "I should try Niall again. Maybe he found something useful in the files."

"Maybe you should get some sleep and look at things with fresh eyes in the morning."

"I don't know. I—" Her ringtone interrupted her. She didn't recognize the number. "Hello?" she answered.

"Dr. Brown?"

She did, however, recognize the caller's voice. She pictured the speaker, a tall, undernourished specimen on the high side of seventy, who lived well-enough off her late husband's inheritance to devote her time to high-profile prestige events and charitable causes. Like the International Rose Hybridizers' Association's Thirteenth Annual Rose and Garden Show.

The caller confirmed her suspicion. "This is Jane McLaren, the president of the Dunmullach Amateur Rose Grower's

Society. How are you holding up during this dreadful tragedy?"

"Okay, I guess. I didn't know the victim well."

"I know you're close to Mr. Grennan and I know the guards have taken him to the station to question him."

"Mr. Grennan didn't kill anyone so there's nothing to worry about. I'm sure the questions are just routine." No way would she let this woman see past her game face.

"Yes, yes, well, I'm sure we're all doing the best we can, under the circumstances. You may have been wondering about the status of the rose and garden show, in light of Mr. Jacobi's tragic demise."

She hadn't been, but..."The show's been canceled?"

"Oh, heavens no," Jane said. Gethsemane imagined her clutching her pearls in horror. "Quite the opposite. The society's board of governors met this evening and decided the show would go on as planned."

"Not exactly as planned." Unless the plan had included the death of a major competitor.

"Well, no," Jane conceded, "not exactly as planned. But go on, it will. In Roderick Jacobi's honor, of course. We'll dedicate the events to him. The board felt everyone had invested so much effort into their roses, denying them the chance to compete would compound the tragedy."

Compound it for the Rose Growers' Society by forcing them to refund entry fees and reimburse sponsors. "What about Jacobi's entry? Will it be pulled from the rose show?"

"We thought allowing 'Lucia di Lammermoor' to remain in the trials would form a fitting tribute to Mr. Jacobi's contributions to rose growing. His wife will accept the award in his place. Should he win, of course."

Should he win? Gethsemane laughed to herself. Jacobi's death guaranteed his win on the sentimental vote. How could the judges vote against a top competitor murdered days before the competition without seeming ghoulish? Jacobi winning gold posthumously was a given.

Jane was speaking about music. "So, I hope you'll still be up to conducting. The opening ceremony is one of the highlights of the event."

"What? Yes, yes, sure."

"Wonderful. We've written a moving tribute to Mr. Jacobi. I'll present it immediately after your performance. It will be beautiful." She made the outcome seem as certain as Jacobi's win. "I'm so glad you're game to continue." She ended the call.

Gethsemane leaned back on the sofa and stared at her now-silent phone for a moment before looking up at Eamon. "That's convenient."

"What's convenient for whom?"

"Not canceling the rose show and not pulling Jacobi's entry are convenient for Mrs. Ellen Jacobi, now the grieving widow instead of the bitter, soon-to-be ex-wife. Her garden company is a major sponsor. She'd have lost a fortune if the competition had been canceled."

"And she'll earn a fortune if her late husband's rose wins. Which it will. Who'll vote against a dead guy?"

"I've met Ellen Jacobi. No doubt she'll translate her widow's weeds into free publicity and sympathy sales. Plus, she gets the prize money from Jacobi's win and marketing rights to his rose. Plus, no messy divorce. Mrs. Jacobi has more motive to kill Roderick than Frankie and the Flower Shop copycat combined."

"May I suggest something?"

"That I leave this to the gardaí?"

"No, that you leave it until morning. Go to bed, sleep, wake up bright and early, and corner O'Reilly before he knows what hit him. I'll even have coffee ready for ya."

"Do you keep a journal or a diary or some sort of calendar?"

"Where, with my pocket knife in my non-existent pocket?"

"Then you'll just have to memorize this date and time. Because for the first time in the history of our relationship, I'm not going to argue with you. Goodnight."

Ten

Gethsemane awoke early the next morning, well before bright, to pounding on her door. She tried to reconcile the noise with the time on her alarm clock—four thirty a.m.—but couldn't reason why anyone in their right mind would be knocking at such a ridiculous hour nor why she'd get out of bed to admit anyone who wasn't in their right mind.

Unseen hands snatched her pillow and her covers. "It's Grennan," boomed an unseen Eamon. "Get up."

She tried to grab her covers, but they dangled out of reach. "You let him in."

"Fella's been through enough without having to deal with the paranormal before coffee."

Her robe landed on her head.

"Okay, okay, I'm up." She shrugged on the robe and stumbled downstairs. She opened the door to a haggard Frankie. Dark circles engulfed his green eyes and his copper hair stood out in tufts as though he'd run both hands through it more than once. His khaki's wrinkles had wrinkles and sported dirt stains on both knees.

He leaned his head against the door frame. "May I come in?"

"Before you fall in." Gethsemane stepped aside so he could

pass. "Let me guess, Inspector Sutton." Memories of her own all-night interrogations at the garda station came back to her. She'd looked as bad afterwards.

Frankie nodded. "I called Niall after we talked. He convinced me to come into the station. They let me go."

"Did you get to see Niall?"

"Yeah. He's the reason I'm not locked up without bail on homicide charges." Frankie recapped what Niall had told her the day before. "He convinced his and Sutton's boss that Sutton's decision to limit his investigation to me was premature. Niall made a solid case for the mystery woman, the flower girl, killing Jacobi because of her deviant devotion to me. Whatever he said convinced the Superintendent of enough reasonable doubt to overrule Sutton and release me. Niall didn't win any friends in homicide, though. Sutton hated having to spring me. Now he'll have to do some actual work. And the Superintendent reprimanded Niall for straying out of his lane and interfering in Sutton's case without authorization. She stuck him on desk duty and threatened to sack him if he did it again." Frankie stifled a yawn.

"Poor Niall. Poor you. I have to ask..." Ask what? Questions flooded her mind and competed for answers. Had Niall found something in the cold case files to conclusively link Frankie's stalker to the Flower Shop Killer? Why had Frankie mentioned Yseult? Did she figure into the bad blood between Frankie and Jacobi led to their fight? Had the gardaí questioned Mrs. Jacobi? Did they know the Jacobi's were headed for divorce? She looked at her friend slumped on the entry way bench, head in hands. Questions could wait. Except one. "Do you want the sofa or the spare bedroom?"

"Any chance of a hot shower first? I must smell as special as I look."

"No, you look worse. Bathroom's upstairs. Help yourself."

"Thanks. I apologize for showing up unannounced at this ungodly hour. I couldn't face the thought of Erasmus Hall after a night at the garda station."

"Don't apologize. I've been where you are more than once." She held out her hand. "Loan me your keys and I'll run over to your place for a change of clothes."

"Don't trouble yourself. It's four thirty."

"It's the least I can do for a guy who's smuggled me out of a hospital, broken and entered into a dead man's apartment with me, and feigned an interest in fashion for me. Keys."

Frankie handed her his ring.

"I'll be right back. Make yourself at home. Oh, and if you hear any strange noises—"

"What kind of strange noises?"

Gethsemane shrugged. "Knocks, bangs, creaks, groans, disembodied voices, phantom footsteps, remember it's an old house. It's just settling." She glimpsed Eamon from the corner of her eye. "Just kidding about the voices and footsteps. It's not like the place is haunted."

"You're going out like that?" Frankie asked as she reached the door. "In your kerchief and robe?"

Oops. Her hand flew to the silk scarf covering her hair. She shrugged. "It's dark. No one will see me."

Eleven

The night sky had lightened with the first hints of sunrise but the campus still slept when Gethsemane pulled up in front of Erasmus Hall. She crept along the hallway to Frankie's rooms, careful not to make noise. She'd never live it down if someone caught her in her colleague's apartment in her pajamas. Working in darkness, she located a duffel bag and stuffed it with clothes and a dopp kit. She searched for anything else Frankie might need when her gaze landed on the view through Frankie's window. Crime scene tape cordoned off his garden. The shapes of individual plants became more distinct in the early morning light. She squinted. Had one of the shapes—she went closer to the window—moved? She dropped the bag and pressed her forehead against the window. There it was again. Definite movement. Not one of the plants, a person. Gethsemane rushed out of the apartment, not caring who she woke up. By the time she arrived in the garden, it lay still again. Whoever she saw had gone. She ran to the parking lot but saw only cars. She returned to the garden. A quick search under rose bushes and the bird bath failed to turn up any bouquets. She spied something protruding from underneath the base of a small statue of Copernicus. She tipped the statue to get a better look. A card with a colored pencil drawing of a floral arrangement peered up at her. She reached for her phone then cursed herself for having left it on her bedside table. She hesitated, then slipped the card into her pocket. She ran back to Frankie's apartment, grabbed the bag she'd packed, and rushed back to Carraigfaire.

"Tampering with evidence?" Eamon pointed at the coffee pot. It levitated to the kitchen table and poured steaming, rich, dark liquid into Gethsemane's cup.

She added cream and sugar. "What was I supposed to do? Leave the card? I couldn't take a picture and I knew I wouldn't be able to reproduce the drawing."

"I'm not criticizing. I'm impressed. Why do I bother to make coffee if you insist on adulterating it?"

"I like cream and sugar. You do coffee your way, I'll do it mine." She took a long sip. "Frankie's still asleep?"

"Like the dead."

"Which gives me time to decipher the flower message on that card before I call Niall to find out what he told Sutton's team about the flower lady."

"And tell him you removed evidence from a crime scene?"

"I'll assume that was rhetorical. Hand me *The Language of Flowers*, please." She lay the card on the table next to the book. "This would be easier if I knew one flower from another." She pointed to drawings of a cheerful blossom whose white petals surrounded its yellow center like a lion's mane and similarly shaped flower with yellow petals and black center. "I do recognize daisy and black-eyed Susan. According to the book they symbolize innocence and justice."

The chair across from her slid back from the kitchen table. Eamon sat, the woven pattern of the chair's cane back barely visible through his chest. He tapped a finger through the card. "That's mullein, the one with the cluster of tiny yellow flowers and thick green leaves. My grandmother used it to treat coughs and fever."

"Mullein, mullein..." Gethsemane turned pages. "Mullein. 'Take courage.' Nothing to do with coughs or fever."

"I don't know. Back in the day, if you had a cough and fever, courage was about the only thing you could take."

"What are these tiny white flowers on a branch? They remind me of a van Gogh painting."

"Almond blossoms."

"Hope. And this last one? The perky red? It's not a poppy."

The answer came from over her shoulder. "It's an anemone."

Gethsemane jumped at the sound of Frankie's voice, nearly upsetting her coffee cup. Eamon erupted in a throaty laugh. Gethsemane remembered Frankie couldn't see or hear ghosts just in time to bite back her retort. She hid her expression in the book. "Anemone symbolizes truth."

Frankie walked around the table and sat in the chair opposite her—right through Eamon. Eamon sputtered and swore. Gethsemane pretended to drop her spoon and dove under the table to hide her silent laughter. When she sat upright, Frankie was studying the card. Eamon had translocated to the kitchen counter where he leaned into the sink.

"What's this?" he asked. "Did you draw it?"

"Nope. Found it in your garden when I went to pick up your clothes. Tucked under Copernicus."

He tugged at the John Coltrane t-shirt. "Thanks for doing that, by the way. I know you're not a morning person. Packing a bag for a fella at oh-dark-thirty before you've had so much as a cup of coffee is a sign of true friendship."

Gethsemane waved the remark away. "How're you feeling?"

"Better than last night. The guards were relentless. A dog with a bone would be no match. Mind if I help myself to coffee?"

"Drink up. Do I have to wait until after your first cup to ask about your fight with Jacobi?"

"Why don't you tell me how you happened to find a picture of posies underneath a statue? By that time, I'll have finished this." He raised his cup.

"I looked out the window in your apartment and saw a figure moving around in your garden. I ran outside but by the time I got there, the figure was gone and the card was there."

"You presumed this figure was my secret admirer."

"I upgraded her to stalker."

"You convinced a garda inspector to upgrade her to murderer. And you ran after her in the dark in your bathrobe. Did you at least grab something you could use to defend yourself with? In the event you'd actually caught up with her?"

"Of course she didn't," Eamon said.

Gethsemane glared at him. Frankie turned to see what she was looking at.

"Nothing. Thought I saw a rat scurry by." Eamon made a face. Gethsemane continued. "I didn't have time to come up with a carefully crafted plan or hunt for defensive weapons. I wanted to at least get a glimpse of the flower lady. I've had no luck finding a clue to her identity."

Frankie reversed the card to its plain white back then turned it over to the flower drawing again. "Is this a clue?"

"The flowers, daisy, black-eyed Susan, mullein, almond blossom, and anemone, mean innocence, justice, take courage, hope, and truth. Which suggests the flower lady believes in you."

"Because she killed Jacobi herself."

"Which means she's not likely to go to the guards and tell them why she knows our man didn't do it," Eamon said. "We'll have to find some other way to clear him."

Gethsemane peered into Frankie's coffee cup. Only a trace of brown liquid remained. "Your turn. Why do you hate—did you hate—Roderick Jacobi?"

"Present tense is fine. I still hate him, I don't care if he is dead." Frankie poured a second cup and sipped it before continuing. "I hate Roderick Jacobi because he slept with my wife."

"With Yseult?"

"Fortunately, I have only had one wife. He and Yseult had an affair. Yseult was in Manaus, authenticating some documents for the Museum of Natural Sciences. Jacobi was meeting with doctors at the university hospital, trying to sell them on participating in clinical trials for one of the drugs he'd developed from a medicinal plant he'd discovered in the rainforest." Frankie sipped more coffee. "Discovered is the wrong word. Stole from a traditional healer whose ancestors had been using it for eons is more accurate. The affair continued after they left Brazil. They were at it for almost a year before I wised up."

"Is that what led to your divorce? The affair?"

"It didn't help matters. But I might have forgiven Yseult, I could have forgiven her for cheating on me, if she'd left it at that. If she'd cheated out of boredom or anger, we could have worked through it. Even if she'd cheated because she'd fallen in love with Jacobi. I would've understood and forgiven her and tried to win her back. But she betrayed me because she was greedy. She didn't feel for Jacobi any more than she felt for me. The only thing she loved, the only thing she's capable of loving, is money."

Having dealt with Yseult, Gethsemane didn't doubt Frankie's assertion. "What'd she do?"

"She stole two of my roses, hybrids I'd spent three years developing. She stole the roses, rootstock and all, as well as the notes and photographs that proved I developed them, and gave everything to Jacobi for a promise of a share of the profits if he commercialized them. Which he did. Without the notes and the photos, I had no way to fight back. I hadn't entered the roses in any shows, so they had no public association with my name."

"I'm so sorry, Frankie. That must have cost you a fortune."

"I developed the plants out of a love for roses, not a desire for profit. Which is why I couldn't forgive Yseult. She was the love of my life, my everything, but I was nothing more to her than a get rich scheme. Not that Jacobi represented anything more, either. A chance for Yseult to cash in. It's ironic Yseult's scheme introduced Jacobi to Ellen, née Lowery. Yseult and Jacobi needed her. Ellen inherited her garden business from her father so she had the resources and the facilities to turn my hobby roses into Jacobi's commercial success."

"Why ironic?"

"Because Jacobi dumped Yseult for Ellen. Ellen is as greedy and ruthless as Yseult. She saw the opportunity to revitalize and expand her business and turn Jacobi into a brand. And she was smart enough to get a marriage certificate before she cut Jacobi in on any deals. Yseult, on the other hand, wasn't quick enough to get a divorce from me before handing over the roses to Jacobi. Once he and Ellen had control of the plants and the documentation, Yseult found herself out in the cold."

"So Jacobi cost you a wife and a fortune. That does give you a motive to kill him," Gethsemane said. "Not that I believe for a second you did it. But I can understand why Inspector Sutton might not be so charitable."

"Especially after that wanker photographer told Sutton about the fight I had with Jacobi. I may have actually used the words, 'I'll kill you' once or twice during the course of the discussion."

"Frankie..."

"I know, I know. The likelihood someone will overhear you threaten another man's life is directly proportional to the likelihood that man will actually end up murdered at a time when you have no alibi."

"No one saw you up at Golgotha?"

"Nary a soul. That's kind of the point of growing roses way out there. One thing I learned from Yseult is the value of keeping things secret."

Gethsemane picked up the card. "Our best chance of clearing you is throwing Sutton the flower lady as a bone. Ellen Jacobi has motive, too, but I don't know if we can tie her to the crime scene. We have proof the flower lady was there."

"Tie her to the crime scene?" Frankie and Eamon said simultaneously. "Don't you sound the right Nancy Drew?"

Frankie's raised hand stopped her rejoinder. "I know, I know. You're trying to help. You're a good and loyal friend who can't stand to see anyone railroaded. But please be careful. Between poisonings and stabbings and strangulations and epidemics, we don't need to add another tragedy to the roster."

"I'll be careful." Eamon rolled his eyes. She ignored him and stood. "Make yourself at home," she told Frankie.

"Where are you off to?"

"The garda station to see Niall." She pushed the flower card toward Frankie. "I won't tell him about that, since, number one, my fingerprints are all over it and, number two, removing evidence is probably a crime—"

"Definitely a crime," mathematician and ghost said together.

"But I'll tell him about seeing the figure in the garden and find out if he discovered any link between anyone in the village now and anyone involved in the Flower Shop Killer investigation back in the sixties. I also have to do a run through of Prokofiev at the Athaneum. Since the show is going to go on, I want to be prepared. I won't be back for a while."

Frankie tossed her his keys. "Make life easy, take my car."

"How will you get around?"

"If you don't mind, I'm going to take you up on your offer of hospitality and lay low out here for a while. I'll spruce up your garden for ya."

"I don't have a garden," she said.

"You used to. I can see from the upstairs window where the plot was laid out. If you've got some half-decent garden tools around—"

"In the lighthouse," Eamon said.

"In the lighthouse," Gethsemane repeated for Frankie's hearing.

"I'll see if I can begin to restore her to something of her former glory. It'll keep my mind off of...things."

"Have at. And thanks for the car."

Gethsemane turned into the parking lot next to the sign announcing "Dunmullach Garda" and navigated Frankie's car into the space farthest away from the grim building that housed the village's law enforcement. She took out her phone and re-read the text from Niall: *Car park. Fifteen minutes.* She looked at her watch. Two minutes to wait. She hummed the melody from The Police's "Every Breath You Take." She spotted the inspector walking toward her from the station, a large envelope clasped under his arm. He opened the passenger door of Frankie's car and climbed in beside her.

"Here." He handed her the envelope. "Sorry about the cloak and dagger bit. I'm supposed to be chained to a desk."

"Frankie told me what you did for him. I'm sorry you got into trouble for helping a friend." She held up the envelope. "What's this?"

"The Flower Shop Killer files."

She tore open the envelope and peered inside. "That's it?" The entire contents consisted of a stack of documents a few inches thick and several photographs.

"There wasn't much. That and a few dried flowers, which I left in the evidence room. How's Frankie?"

"Worried. Angry. Depressed. Happy not to be locked up. The same way I felt after being released on the numerous occasions I was hauled into that place," she pointed at the station, "for questioning."

"Have to admit, it's odd seeing someone other than you in one of our interrogation rooms in connection with a murder case. Your name's written on one of the chairs."

She hit his arm with the envelope.

"Hey," he laughed. "Assaulting an officer's a crime. And I'm not kidding about your name. Some wiseacre wrote it on one of the chairs with a black marker. Spelled 'Gethsemane' wrong, though."

"Police humor." She rolled her eyes. "Hysterical." She sorted through the photos. Exterior shots of an unassuming house on an unremarkable street in an average neighborhood. Flowers in planters flanked the front door, a squat car with rounded edges sat in the drive. She held up the photo and looked closely at the car. "Is that a Ford?"

Niall took the photo. "A Cortina. Ford had a motor plant in Cork until the 1980s."

Gethsemane looked through more photos. One made her wince—a woman lay face-down, the blood-stained tears in her dress made it clear she'd been stabbed. "I've seen more than my share of dead bodies by now but seeing her lying there..." Gethsemane shook her head and went onto the next photo.

A man in shirt sleeves lay in a similar pose with similar wounds in his back. Most of the rest of the photos featured the unfortunate couple pictured from a variety of angles. They lay in their parlor, she near the fireplace, he near the door. Dozens of flower blossoms, all stemless, surrounded each body as if some maniacal flower girl had gotten carried away at a wedding. A lush bouquet filled a vase near the man's foot.

"The names of the flowers are written on the back." Niall reached and turned the photo over.

"Camellia, cherry blossom, carnation, chrysanthemum."

"We need Ms. Sexton here to translate."

"No, we don't." She pulled *The Language of Flowers* from her bag. "I've got her book." She opened it to camellia. "My destiny is in your hands."

"A profound statement for such a delicate flower."

"Cherry blossom—impermanence. Carnation. Hmm. Carnations mean a lot of things. Depends on the color."

"The ones in the photo have pink stripes."

"So they mean 'let me go, I cannot live without you.'"

"The chrysanthemums are yellow. Does that matter?"

Gethsemane turned to chrysanthemum. "Yes. According to the book, yellow chrysanthemums stand for slighted love."

"Impermanence, slighted love, my destiny is in your hands, let me go, I cannot live without you. Does sound a bit Shakespearean, doesn't it?"

"Sounds like a message an obsessed, psychotic murderer might leave." She traded the photos for the papers. "Anything in these?"

"Crime scene reports, witness statements. Not many of those. The neighbor, the florist, the lad who picked up the flowers."

"Speaking of which." Gethsemane told him about Oona at the laundry. "She couldn't tell me any more about the woman who paid her to pick up the flowers—" She sorted through papers until she found the boy's statement that was only two paragraphs. "—than the boy could say about the woman who paid him. Oona got a better deal. Five euros."

"Oona, a juvenile, at the laundry may be a material witness

in a murder case. As soon as you discovered this lead you did the responsible thing and informed one of the investigating officers, of course."

"Sarcasm doesn't suit you, Niall."

"Sutton and the other fellas working Jacobi's case need to know about the girl."

"I'm not talking to Sutton even if he ties me to that chair with my name on it. Besides, I've already shared the information with law enforcement. You're a garda and I told you. I've done my civic duty. You tell Sutton."

"I'm persona non grata with the homicide unit right now. They can be a bit territorial—more than a bit—and Sutton, especially, didn't appreciate me bollixing their case against Frankie by offering up an equally viable suspect. He put on a holy show when Superintendent Feeney agreed with me." Niall chuckled. "It helped that I let the Super win at poker last week."

"Her poker winnings didn't keep her from threatening to fire you for—what? Doing your colleague's job for him?"

"For overstepping my bounds without clearing it with her first. Superintendent Feeney doesn't like dissention in the ranks and she doesn't like to be the last one to know what's going on. Don't worry, I'll let her win next week's poker game again."

Movement near the station caught Gethsemane's attention. "Hey, I know those two." She pointed at a Mutt-and-Jeff duo standing by the station's main entrance. "Murdoch Collins and Karl Dietrich. They work for Jacobi's pharmaceutical company. What are they arguing about?" Karl waggled his finger under Murdoch's nose while the taller man waved his arms over Karl's head.

She'd climbed halfway out of the car before Niall finished saying, "You're going to find out, aren't you?"

"C'mon." She motioned to him to hurry. "Maybe you'll learn something else you can offer up to your poker buddy."

Twelve

Gethsemane wove through the station parking lot, keeping vehicles between herself and the arguing men. Not that they'd have noticed her. The intensity of their debate consumed their focus.

"Jacobi's death changes nothing!" Karl shouted.

"The board may feel otherwise. In fact, I'm confident they'll see this my way."

"What have you done, Murdoch?" Karl drew himself up on his tiptoes and brought his face even with the taller man's. "Don't make the mistake of thinking I'll let this drop!"

"Keep your voice down." Murdoch glanced around the parking lot. Gethsemane ducked behind a panel truck. "Do you want the whole world to know our business?"

"Whole world? We're stuck in an Irish backwater waiting for some pompous garden enthusiasts," Karl sneered when he said the word, "to pin a ribbon on some amateur hybrids and hobby gardens. No one out here has the capacity to understand the significance of what I'm saying even if they overheard me."

"Amateur hybrids and hobby gardens." Murdoch smirked. "Your true nature emerges. Botany snob."

Karl balled his hands into fists. "You fat, greedy, cheating—"

Niall motioned to Gethsemane to stay put behind the panel

truck and stepped between the two men. "Is anything the matter, sir?" he asked Karl.

Murdoch reached around Niall and clapped Karl on the shoulder. "Nothing at all, nothing at all. Just discussing a few business matters, right, Karl?"

Karl mumbled something Gethsemane couldn't hear. She leaned around the panel truck.

"I'm sorry if we caused a disturbance, sir," Murdoch continued.

Gethsemane joined Niall. "Mr. Dietrich, Mr. Collins. How are you? All right, I hope, considering you're heading into the garda station."

"We were summoned by someone named Sutton," Karl said, "to answer questions about Mr. Jacobi."

"Inspector Sutton is in charge of the investigation into Roderick Jacobi's passing," Niall said.

"You mean his murder," Murdoch corrected.

"And you, Doctor Brown? You're here to answer the Inspector's questions, too?" Karl asked.

She had promised Sutton a formal statement. But, seeing as he attempted to pin the crime on her friend, she'd let him wait. Or wait until he came after her. "I'm here to see Inspector O'Reilly."

"Not about another murder, I hope," Karl said.

"No, at least not a recent one. Inspector O'Reilly specializes in cold cases."

"You gentlemen should go inside now. Inspector Sutton's not the most patient garda on the force."

"We apologize, again, for creating a disturbance," Murdoch said.

Niall pointed up the stairs. "Homicide's on the second floor."

Murdoch and Karl disappeared inside the building.

"I wouldn't recommend going after them," Niall said.

"Don't worry, I'm not that foolhardy."

"Have you given Sutton a statement?"

"Not yet. I'm going to make him work for it." She looked at Niall and facepalmed. "I shouldn't be telling you this. You're on his team."

"Just this once, I'll pretend I'm not. I'll even do you a favor." He flashed his notebook. "You can give me your statement and I'll pass it on to Sutton."

"You'll be doing me and Sutton a favor. He doesn't want to see me anymore than I want to see him."

"That's probably true." Niall jerked his head toward Roasted, the coffee shop across the street. "Had breakfast?"

"I had coffee with Frankie."

"So the answer is no."

"Coffee's breakfast."

Niall cringed. "Only in America and you're not in America. C'mon."

They crossed the street to the popular coffee spot and joined the line at the counter. Morning rush had started, about half the tables were already occupied. People chatted, read, or tapped on phone screens as steam rose from oversized coffee mugs and the smell of cinnamon muffins filled the air.

"Any idea what you're having?" Niall asked.

"Large caramel latte."

"There are, like, fifty drinks on that menu." He gestured toward the over-sized chalkboard hung on the wall behind the counter. "How do you decide what to get so quickly?"

"I know what I like."

"I like tea, but they refuse to serve Bewley's." Niall wrinkled his nose. "Who wants tapioca pearls in their tea, anyway?"

A commotion outside caught Gethsemane's eye through the window. Two women shoved each other. Gethsemane nudged

Niall's arm. "Déjà vu."

"What the bloody..." Niall muttered as he headed outside. Gethsemane and several other patrons followed. Niall stepped between the two women. One stumbled into him. "May I assist you, ladies?" he asked.

"You can assist her straight to hell." The woman farthest from Niall jerked her head toward her antagonist as she bent to pick up a catalog. She smoothed the cover. A rip ran through a photo of a rose.

The other woman started forward but Niall grabbed her arm. "Ma'am," he asked, "everything all right?"

The woman strained against Niall's grip then relaxed into resignation. Niall released her. She smoothed her hair and dress. "Would you call an officer of the law?" she asked with a Spanish accent.

"I'm a garda," Niall said. "An officer of the law," he added in response to her blank look.

"Then I demand that you arrest this woman." She pointed. "She stole my catalog."

"It's mine." The other woman clutched the damaged book to her chest.

"You stole it from me." The Spanish woman lunged. Niall caught her arm again.

"I'm sure you can pick up another catalog from the ticket office or guest services," Gethsemane said.

"Not one signed by Roderick Jacobi."

"No," Gethsemane said, "I don't suppose you can get another of those."

"And signed by Ellen Jacobi, too. It'll be worth a fortune once she's convicted of killing him." The woman with the catalog smoothed its cover. "At least it would have been worth a fortune. Before you ruined it."

The Spanish woman made a face. "I didn't rip my catalog,

you did. Give it back."

"I won't."

"Excuse me," Gethsemane said. "I hate to interrupt this important debate but you said Ellen Jacobi murdered her husband. You sounded certain."

"Well, she did, didn't she? Everybody knows it. Who else? Dozens of people heard her say she'd kill him often enough. 'Better for me if Roddy dropped dead.' 'I could hire someone to kill him and solve all our problems.'"

"Did you see her kill him?"

"Of course not. Ellen Jacobi's not thick. She wouldn't do it in front of witnesses. Probably wouldn't do it herself. Pull the trigger, I mean. She'd hire someone to do the dirty work, like she always does. She's done it all the same. She's still guilty, everybody knows."

Niall held his hand out for the book. "If you'll give that to me, I'll take it to the station and you can both come there to sort out who owns what."

The woman with the catalog clutched it tighter. "How do I know you're a guard? Maybe you just want this for yourself."

Niall showed her his identification. "I can take both of you in with the catalog, if you prefer."

The woman let him take it.

"I suggest you both walk about for a while before coming to the station," he said. "And walk in opposite directions."

With a final glare, the women departed. The coffee shop onlookers filtered back inside.

"May I?" Gethsemane took the catalog. Photos and descriptions of roses and gardens shared pages with glossy advertisements for garden supply companies, florists, and commercial gardens. An ad for Jacobi and Fortnum claimed a two-page spread. Several page margins bore names scribbled in ink.

"All this fuss over flowers," Niall said. "I don't get it."

"Don't say that in front of Frankie. You know, judging by the ads in this catalog, flowers are a big business."

"Worth killing for?"

"Money's a prime motivator for homicide."

"True." Niall reclaimed the book. "But flowers seem so genteel and delicate. Hard to associate them with killing or with mercenary autograph hounds. I'd dismissed the rose and garden show as a dry-as-shite, academic, horticultural exercise. I'm beginning to think they're akin to fan conventions."

"I'm trying to picture you at a fan convention."

"I've been to one or two. Mystery-themed, not floral." He sighed.

"You're going to offer me a rain check on breakfast, aren't you?"

He hoisted the catalog. "I better get this thing back to the station before those two show up and start acting the maggot in the lobby. I'll hand it over to Sutton as a peace offering. You stay and eat something. Eat means solid food, not coffee."

Gethsemane gave a mock salute and watched him head back across the street. She waited until he disappeared inside the station building then crossed back to Frankie's car. Murder took precedence over breakfast.

Thirteen

The Dunmullach Amateur Rose Growers' Society had set up for the rose show on the grounds of Dunmullach's former girls' school. When the school located to more modern facilities on the other side of the village, it left behind several athletic fields and gothic buildings. The village rented them out for a variety of festivals and exhibitions.

Gethsemane parked and walked to a field dotted with white canvas tents. Their peaked roofs reminded her of circus tents minus the red stripes. She guessed the largest and fanciest tent—the one that stretched the entire length of the field and had windows cut into the canvas walls—must be for the sponsors. A small map posted near the edge of the field proved her guess correct. She ignored a security guard who lounged near the entrance flap and breezed in as if she was expected. A sign in the hallway emblazoned "Jacobi and Fortnum" spared her having to ask directions. The interior of the tent had been divided into rooms. She entered the one closest to the sign and approached a receptionist stationed at a desk.

"Gethsemane Brown here to see Ms. Jacobi."

"Do you have an appointment?" the receptionist asked in a tone of voice that clearly indicated she already knew the answer to her question.

Gethsemane spotted Ellen over the receptionist's shoulder, seated at a desk in an adjacent room. "Oh, I see her. No need to get up, I'll show myself in."

Gethsemane brushed past the woman, ignoring her "Hey, wait, no, you can't go in there."

Ellen looked up. Her expression signaled surprise mixed with annoyance bordering on anger.

The receptionist arrived in the doorway. "I'm sorry, Mrs. Jacobi, she burst in. I'll call security."

Gethsemane stuck her hand under Ellen's nose. "Gethsemane Brown, we met at the theater. I'm sorry for your loss. I wondered if you'd like me to play something special, as a tribute to your late husband, during the awards ceremony. I'd planned to play Prokofiev, but I have time to substitute something else."

Ellen's shoulders relaxed and she waved away the receptionist. "Please, have a seat, Dr. Brown." One hand gestured toward a chair. The other slid a magazine over top of the papers she'd been reading. "What did you have in mind?"

"Did Mr. Jacobi have a favorite piece of music? Or can you suggest a piece that would mirror the character of the man he was?"

Ellen let loose a sardonic laugh. "Is there a piece of music titled, 'Pig of a Man?' Or 'Back-stabbing Wanker?'" She laughed again. "Back-stabbing. Poor choice of words?"

"Forgive my presumption," Gethsemane said, "but I assume you won't be donning widow's weeds?"

"You know how I feel—felt—about Roderick. I told you we were getting divorced and I hated him."

"I assumed that was hyperbole. The kind you drop after the object of it dies a violent death."

"I'm a lot of things, Dr. Brown, few of them nice. One thing I am not, is a hypocrite. I had no kind words for Roderick while he lived, I have none now that he's dead. I'm rather happy about that last bit, truth be told. Saves me the expense of a divorce."

"And lets you inherit everything instead of settling for half?"

"I certainly hope so. If the bastard didn't have time to change his will."

"You must have loved Roderick at some point. Or at least liked him a lot. You married him."

"Dr. Brown, you're not as naïve as you're pretending to be. People marry for a variety of reasons. I doubt love even makes the top ten."

"How about a gardening empire and a controlling interest in a pharmaceutical company? Where do those rank?"

Ellen touched her nose then pointed to Gethsemane. "Slightly ahead of a patent on a hybrid rose."

Gethsemane stood. "I'll stick with the Prokofiev."

Ellen shrugged and pulled the papers out from under the magazine.

"One more question. Did you hate Roderick enough to kill him?"

Ellen's smile spoke more malice than her words. "Of course, I did. What you meant to ask was, 'Did I kill him?' Would I tell you if I had?"

"You might, but then you'd slip me tea laced with weed killer or something to keep me from telling anyone."

"I wouldn't bother. If I had killed him, I'd have done it in a way that no one could prove I did it. Without evidence, accusations of murder are just gossip. And if I killed every gossip who swore I did in my not-so-dearly departed husband, I'd soon run out of weed killer." She turned her back to Gethsemane and reached for her desk phone.

Gethsemane paused by the receptionist's desk on the way out. "I've been dismissed."

The receptionist made "Hmph" sound like "good riddance."

"A word of advice? Keep the weed killer away from your boss."

Ellen Jacobi's words lingered in Gethsemane's mind as she departed the sponsors' tent. *Could* Ellen have hired someone to kill her husband? She seemed to hate him enough. And she seemed arrogant enough to admit it. She had a point—without proof, accusations were just gossip. What if the mysterious flower girl wasn't an obsessed stalker? What if she was a hired assassin? Women could be hitmen, too. What if the bouquets were red herrings, ruses to hide the real reason for the murders? Did Ellen Jacobi know about the flower shop murders? Would she have heard about the unsolved crimes as the head of a garden empire?

She climbed into Frankie's car and drove as far as the old school grounds' main gate. Without warning, a red sports coupe rounded a curve into her path. She swerved just in time to avoid a collision. She swore as two wheels left the roadway and a tree loomed into view. She jerked the wheel and lurched back onto the paved surface. The car veered toward the opposite edge. Gethsemane jerked the wheel again, slammed the breaks, and skidded to a stop just short of a ditch. The coupe didn't stop. It didn't even slow down. Determined to give the driver the piece of her mind he deserved, she raced back to the show grounds.

The sportscar glided into a parking space near the sponsors' tents as she arrived back at the field. She idled the car near the lot's entrance and stared as the driver's door opened and Glendon Byrnes unfolded himself from the car's interior. How could a man who'd been so solicitous when he bumped into her in a hallway be so cavalier after he'd run her off the road? She'd ask him when she caught up to him. She eased into the lot as she watched where Glendon headed. He started toward Belles Fleurs' shared tent then veered to one side and doubled back toward Jacobi and Fortnum. He disappeared behind the end of the tent where Ellen had her desk.

Gethsemane steered the car into the neares parking space and crept after Byrnes. She crouched behind the corner of Jacobi and Fortnum's tent in time to see Ellen step out through a tent flap in the rear and embrace Glendon in a passionate kiss. She watched as Ellen pulled Glendon into the tent, letting the tent flap fall closed behind them. She clamped a hand over her mouth to keep from exclaiming out loud and stood and spun in a smooth motion—right into the burly chest of the security guard she'd ignored earlier.

"Lost, are you?" His frown said she'd better be lost, or else.

Hand still over her mouth, her brain fought to think what to do. No good running. The security guard would catch her without half trying. No good saying she was here to see Ellen; he'd already seen her go through the front door to meet Ellen a short while ago. She silently borrowed one of Eamon's Irish swear words and wished she could borrow his vanishing skills.

Desperate, she bit the inside of her cheek to make her eyes tear up and put on her best overwrought stammer. "I, I, I knew it. I knew it. I didn't want to believe it. I'm such a fool." She grabbed the security guard by the lapels of his uniform jacket and buried her face against his chest.

"Hey, now!" He grabbed her by the shoulders and pushed her away. "What's all this?"

"Gl-Gl-Gl-Glennie." She nixed a wail for fear of attracting attention. Instead, she covered her face with her hands and let out a few fake sobs. Another cheek bite produced fresh tears.

"Mr. Byrnes?" the security guard asked. "What about him?"

"He's, he's..." Her hands flew back to her face and muffled her "Oh, no, it's too terrible."

"I didn't hear you, Miss. What about Mr. Byrnes has you putting on a holy show?"

She donned her best pathetic expression and looked up at the guard through tear-damp lashes. "Gl-Glendon Byrnes is, is, my—" Dramatic pause then lower the gaze and turn away in mock shame. "Baby daddy."

The security guard gaped. He looked from Gethsemane to the tent then back to Gethsemane. "Didn't know ol' Byrnes had it in him. The younger one, maybe, but…"

"Our dear, sweet, little girl sits at home pining for her daddy while he runs around with that, that—"

"Ain't she, though?" The security guard nodded in response to his own question.

Gethsemane sniffled and tried to look noble. "At least now I know."

"Do you want me to drag him out here so you can eat his head off?"

"No, no." She held up a hand. "Whatever else he is, he's still my daughter's father. I'll let the lawyers handle this."

"Maybe I can help." The security guard pulled out his phone. "I worked security for a corporate party in New York a few months ago, some fancy Avar shindig to celebrate the FDA approval of a new gene therapy they developed." He pulled up a photo and held the screen so she could see it.

Murdoch Collins, a suit jacket hiding most of the hideous pattern on his shirt, posed center frame. Four people crowded around him, heads close together, arms around shoulders. All of them, Murdoch and the four she didn't recognize, smiled. Karl stood slightly to the side of the group, his expression neutral, his eyes fixed on the camera.

"Look in the background," the security guard said, "near the drinks table." He pinched the photo to enlarge it.

Ellen and Glendon huddled near a table filled with wine

glasses. Glendon held a drink in one hand and Ellen's rear end in the other. Her smile suggested she didn't mind.

"I can text the photo to you," the security guard said, "for the lawyers. Don't care much for deadbeat dads. Had one myself."

Gethsemane thanked him and gave him her number. A moment later, her text alert sounded.

"You're sure you don't want me to get him? Won't take but a moment."

"Please, no. You've already done enough. You've been such a help. And, please, don't say anything to anyone about seeing me."

The security guard raised an eyebrow.

"If he knows I've tracked him down, he may run again. It's taken me eight months to find him. I don't want to lose him."

Rehearsal would wait for a while. She detoured to Frankie's rose garden. The crime scene tape had vanished but the garden still bore an air of malevolence. A blood-stained depression marred the grass in front of the 'Sandra Sechrest' rose. Several of the bush's lower branches lay bent and broken, stripped of their leaves. The soil around its base bore a partial foot print. Frankie would be heartbroken when he saw it. Bad enough a man died in his garden and the murder weapon pointed the finger of suspicion at him; the damage to his prize rose rubbed salt in the wound. Like Jacobi claimed the last laugh.

Gethsemane checked beneath the birdbath and under Copernicus and in every other place where someone might have hidden a message spelled out either with actual flowers or a drawing. Nothing. Not surprising. If the flower girl hadn't killed Jacobi but only stalked Frankie, she'd know he wasn't at the hall. She wouldn't leave a message he wouldn't find and wouldn't risk the gardaí catching her. If the flower girl murdered Jacobi, either on her own or for a paycheck, she'd be on the run. If Ellen hired her, she'd have run a lot farther—a one-way ticket to a country without extradition treaties probably accompanied the paycheck. If she killed independently, she might not have had the funds to get far. But it didn't take much to get as far as Cork. The average school boy could manage a bus ticket with his allowance. A murderer could get lost in a city the size of Cork.

Convinced the garden held no more clues, Gethsemane returned to the parking lot. A woman waved to her from the opposite end—the new Latin teacher, Gethsemane's initial candidate for Frankie's secret admirer.

"Excuse me," the pretty blonde called.

Gethsemane waited by Frankie's car. "Hello, Verna," she said when the woman caught up to her.

"That's Frankie's car, isn't it? Have you seen him? Is he all right?"

"He's fine. He's, uh, gone to ground for a while."

"Can't say's I blame him. That dreadful Inspector Sutton suspecting him of murder. I know Frankie's mercurial but he'd never stab someone in the back, figuratively or literally."

"Sutton talked to you?"

"Yeah. Wanted to know if I sent Frankie flowers. Practically accused us of having an affair." Verna blushed. "We aren't, regardless of the faculty lounge gossip. The odd lunch at the Rabbit hardly equals an affair."

So, the Latin teacher knew what people said about her and Frankie. Rumor spread through the St. Brennan's faculty lounge almost as fast as it spread through the pub.

"Would you tell Frankie I asked about him?" Verna asked. "And tell him I know he didn't do it."

"Of course." Gethsemane moved to get in the car when she caught sight of the *Dunmullach Dispatch* folded under Verna's arm.

Verna noticed her gaze. "Have you seen it? I swear the *Dispatch* is getting to be more and more of a rag every day." She unfolded the paper.

Roderick Jacobi's face stared up from the front page. The headline read, "Murder! Pharma CEO and Amateur Horticulturalist Stabbed. Gardaí Question Local Teacher."

"Can you believe it?" Verna asked. "They've practically convicted poor Frankie."

"I wouldn't make too much of it. Newspapers print outrageous headlines to convince people to buy the paper. The print equivalent of click bait."

"Frankie's photo shoot was supposed to be on today's front page. Pushed aside by this rubbish. I'd much rather have read about him and his rose."

"May I borrow that?" Gethsemane asked. "If you've finished with it."

Verna handed her the paper.

"Thanks," Gethsemane said. "I'll give Frankie your regards."

Rehearsal would have to wait a bit longer. She had a newspaper photographer to talk to.

Fourteen

Gethsemane sat parked across from the *Dispatch* office and tried to concoct a ruse to get inside to see the photographer. He saved her the trouble by bounding down the steps, camera slung over his shoulder. Gethsemane waylaid him at the end of the sidewalk.

"You." She shook the paper Verna had given her in the photographer's face.

He stepped back and looked around as though searching for an escape or an ally.

Gethsemane persisted. "Explain this."

"Explain what?" He took the paper. "Self-explanatory. Man murdered, teacher suspected." He squinted at her. "Do I know you?"

"We met at Frankie Grennan's photo shoot. You remember, the one that was supposed to be today's front-page news?"

"Oh, yeah, the musician. You're codding, right? You don't really think an uninteresting human-interest story about some flowers would send the story of a vicious murder to page six, do you? Do you read newspapers much?"

"I read enough to understand 'if it bleeds, it leads.' But I hesitate to call the *Dispatch* a newspaper. I've read better written articles in church newsletters."

"Yeah, well, I don't write the articles, do I? I just shoot the photos." He stabbed his finger at the byline. "See there, photos by Max Barnaby. That's me."

"Photos aren't the only things you shoot. You also shoot your mouth off to the gardaí. You told them Frankie and Jacobi had a fight."

"Is that what this is about? They did have it out, didn't they? After you left. Couldn't keep quiet about it, could I? That'd be withholding evidence."

"A photographer *and* a legal expert. Did you make a deal with the gardaí for exclusive photos of the arrest, if there was one? Or maybe you just couldn't wait to rat on Frankie. I saw the way you fawned over Jacobi at the photo shoot, shaking his hand." She mimicked him. "'I watch your show all the time, Mr. Jacobi.' 'Met my wife at your lecture, Mr. Jacobi.' I expected you to drool on him. His number one fanboy."

Max lowered the paper. "I'm Roderick Jacobi's fan because he saved my sister's life."

"Saved her life?" Jacobi didn't come across as the noble type. "Saved her how?"

"With the drugs Avar Pharmaceuticals developed. One drug in particular, Theravin. Derived from *Vinca jacovensi*, a plant he discovered in the Amazon. It's the only known treatment for Marquette-Kruchko Syndrome. You'll agree keeping a girl alive past her twelfth birthday is more important than growing pretty flowers to put in vases on the mantle." He handed the paper back. "If you'll excuse me, I'm on my way to Ó Muireadhaigh's farm to shoot some photos of a sheep that's just had triplets." He snapped a picture of Gethsemane and went on.

Point taken. Life-saving drugs trumped ornamental plants. She'd never heard of Marquette-Kruchko Syndrome. She texted her brother, Zeb, a physician.

He'd answered her text by the time she got back to the car:

Rare metabolic disease. 1 in 500K US births. Fatal by teens. Why?

She replied: *Explain later. Theravin?*

Older drug. Expensive. Only treatment now. Gene therapy in pipeline.

Gene therapy. The security guard had taken his photo at a party celebrating a new gene therapy. She recalled something on the news about a new gene therapy for a rare inherited eye disease costing nearly five hundred thousand dollars per eye. Even if only half-a-million people had the disorder, at a million dollars per patient, some drug company would earn five hundred billion dollars. People have killed for a lot less. Ellen Jacobi would kill for less. Ellen Jacobi might kill for looking at her cross-eyed.

If she inherited. Jacobi might have changed his will. Or Avar's board of directors might do some legal maneuvering to keep her from getting Jacobi's shares. Murdoch and Karl had been arguing about "spin" and "deals" and the board "seeing things" a certain way. Maybe they didn't like the idea of Ellen Jacobi calling the shots on the pharmaceutical side of the house. Maybe they'd hatched a plan to convince the board to agree with them. Which one of them could she convince to tell her about it?

Rehearsal pushed its way to the top of the priority list. Murdoch and Karl would have to wait for Prokofiev. She drove to the Athaneum.

People milled about the auditorium when she arrived, carrying signs and clipboards and pushing carts loaded with flower arrangements. The stage sat empty, except for a chair and music stand. She peered into the orchestra pit on her way to the stage entrance. Now dark and deserted, the image from six months ago of a body, another stabbing victim, lying in the pit by the piano, seemed as if it belonged to a grim graphic novel or slasher film. She shook her head to clear it of the memory and went on stage.

A few moments later, she sat with her Vuillaume violin poised on her shoulder and sheet music for "The Tale of the Stone Flower, Op. 118: Prologue: The Mistress of the Copper Mountain" open on the music stand. A deep breath and then she drew her bow across her strings. Eerie, yet majestic, notes meant to evoke the Russian mountain spirit who protected the mines and their underground treasures welled up from the violin and spilled over onto the stage and into the auditorium. All activity stopped and all eyes locked on Gethsemane until, four minutes and fifteen seconds later, she lowered her bow. Applause erupted. She acknowledged the crowd with a bow.

She turned back to the sheet music, intending to run through a section where she heard herself fall behind an eighth of a beat, when she saw Karl Dietrich waving to her from the first row. She put her violin and bow back in their case and went to greet him.

"Dr. Brown, a fantastic performance. I felt myself transported to the Ural Mountains. If you play this well at rehearsal, I know you will be the essence of perfection at the awards ceremony."

"Thank you, is it *Doktor* Dietrich or *Herr*? Or Herr Doktor? I apologize, my German etiquette is marginal."

"Herr Doktor is correct. But how did you know?"

"You said you're a botanist. Botany's usually an advanced degree. Since you work for a pharmaceutical company, I figured you must hold a doctorate."

"As perceptive as you are talented. And, please, call me Karl."

"You may call me Gethsemane, if you can say it with a straight face."

"You have no pet name, er, nickname, I believe you Americans call it?"

She imagined Eamon standing next to her shouting, "Sissy!" "No," she said to Karl. "Couldn't come up with a good one."

"'Karl' does not lend itself to nicknames, either. But, please," he gestured toward her chair, "do not let me keep you from your work."

"May I ask you a question? I planned to find you later but since you're here..."

"Of course. Shall we sit?" He waited until she sank into one of the blue velvet auditorium seats then sat next to her.

"I'm sure you're busy, getting ready for the rose show. With Mr. Jacobi's..." She waved a hand, searching for the right word.

"Death," Karl offered.

"Death, you must have a lot of extra work to do. By, the way, what are you doing here? In the theater, I mean."

"As you say, extra work. Roderick's widow is determined everything proceed as planned. Murdoch and I are here seeing to the flower arrangements for the opening. Rather, Murdoch is ordering people about and I am checking behind him to make sure he doesn't ruin anything. But that was not your question."

"No. My question deals with Avar Pharmaceuticals. My brother, a physician, told me about some new gene therapies being developed to treat rare diseases. I confess I didn't grasp all the scientific details but I gathered these novel therapies may revolutionize medical care but at a significant cost."

Karl nodded. "New drugs, especially those as radical as gene therapy, are expensive to research and develop. And with no guarantee they'll win approval."

"My brother is thinking of investing in some companies that are developing gene therapies. Avar Pharma came up. Word in the doctors' lounge is, new gene therapies are in the pipeline for some diseases whose more traditional treatments are already patented by Avar. My brother wondered, given what happened to poor Mr. Jacobi," she lowered her gaze for a moment, "if Avar intended to go ahead with those research and development plans."

"I'm afraid you've put me in an uncomfortable spot." Karl shifted in his seat. "I don't like to refuse to answer your question but I can't talk about sensitive internal matters."

"I don't want any insider trading-type information. It's just that Zeb, my brother, is a family physician who divides his time between community health centers and medical missions. He doesn't have money to spare and I'd hate to see him lose it all on a wrong investment. I guess I'm concerned what will happen if Mrs. Jacobi inherits Roderick's interest in the company. I'm sure she's a competent saleswoman but, at the end of the day, she's a glorified florist. What's she know about medicine?"

"Many of the drugs we use to live better and longer lives are derived from plants: colchicine, digoxin, ephedrine, atropine..."

Gethsemane tensed with an involuntary shiver. She'd gained more familiarity with digoxin and its plant parent, foxglove, than she'd ever hoped to. Eamon had been poisoned to death with the pills. Her investigation of his murder led to her own near-poisoning with the plant. The phrase "digitalis glycosides" had seared into her brain. She'd never look at clusters of bell-shaped purple flowers again without remembering.

"Are you all right?"

"Fine, just a cold chill down my back. Doesn't that mean someone's walking over my grave?"

"I confess to a limited knowledge of, and no belief in, folk tales and superstition."

She used to say the same. Until life in Dunmullach proved folk tales were often less fake than the news and skepticism wasn't always healthy. "You were telling me about plant-derived drugs."

"Ah, yes. There are thousands, perhaps tens of thousands, of species of as-yet-unknown, at least to Western medicine, plants with medicinal properties waiting to be discovered."

"In places like the Amazon."

"Tropical climates have yielded more than their fair share of medicinal herbs."

"Travel to remote places to identify, harvest, study, and commercialize these plants must be expensive."

"True. However, compared to the cost of gene therapy, which is targeted to specific genes and, therefore, has a much narrower application and will benefit fewer people?" Karl shrugged.

"So, Mrs. Jacobi, being a plant-person, might be more inclined to fund botanical research than genetic research. If she takes an active role in Avar."

Karl leaned closer and lowered his voice in a conspiratorial fashion. "Between you, me, and, what is the saying, the lamppost, I am no fan of Ellen Jacobi. She frightens me. I don't trust her half as far as I can push, no, throw her. However, I must give her credit for being more than a 'plant-person' or 'glorified florist.' She has degrees in both botany and horticulture. At the master's level."

"So, she'd definitely be more inclined to fund plant-finding expeditions than reverse engineering viruses or whatever they do to alter the genes."

Another shrug. "Mrs. Jacobi is an astute business woman. Whatever her background, she is well aware of the direction in which the future demands medicine proceeds."

"So, she's pro-gene therapy?"

"Ellen Jacobi is as inscrutable as a cat. And it's to be seen whether she takes on a significant, or any, role in Avar

Pharmaceuticals. She has her garden empire to attend to. If Roderick's hybrid does as well in the rose show as expected, a patent will generate sizeable income. The global floral trade is worth more than one hundred billion dollars."

"Less than the genetic modulation industry but not chump change. Guess I'll tell Zeb to look into a Roth IRA instead."

A scream, a nerve-shattering shriek—Male? Female? Inhuman?—from the direction of the lobby filled the auditorium with terror and dread.

"Not another one," Gethsemane said as she, Karl, and the others ran to investigate.

They found Murdoch Collins in the lobby, tears down both jowly cheeks, cradling the withered remains of a rose bush.

"They're dead," he blubbered. "They're all dead."

Fifteen

"Murdoch," Karl rushed to his colleague, "what's happened?"

"This!" Murdoch held up his plant. Curled leaves marred with scorched, yellow-brown edges hung limp on brown canes. Only dried, broken petals remained of once-vibrant red blooms. "The 'Lucia di Lammermoor,' They're all like this. They're all dead."

"My god," someone said, "It's sabotage."

Several people ran toward the area where flowers were stored before going on display.

"What did that?" Gethsemane pointed at the destroyed rose, a twin of the sickly plant she'd given Frankie to save.

Karl examined the leaves. "Sabotage is an accurate assessment. Weed killer did this. Someone's sprayed weed killer on this rose. A highly concentrated dose, judging by the damage."

"Not just this one, Karl. All. Of. Them. Here and over at the show grounds. 'Lucia di Lammermoor' is no more."

"You're sure about the show grounds?" Karl asked.

Murdoch nodded. "I called as soon as I discovered the damage here to have some new plants rushed over. Pinky went to check on them and, and,..." Tears flowed.

"Pinky?" Gethsemane asked.

"One of the garden assistants," Karl said.

"What are we going to do, Karl?" Murdoch wiped his nose on his sleeve.

Karl, red-faced, muttered in German and paced the lobby. "What can we do? What can we do? We can do nothing!" He pounded his fist against his palm. "Who could have done this to us?"

Murdoch tore at his hair, leaving mouse-brown tufts sticking out at odd angles. "The money we've lost. Lucia was practically guaranteed a gold medal. Garden centers would have crawled on their bellies over broken glass to beg for a chance to bring her to market. We could have sold her patent for millions. How are we going to tell Ellen?"

"From a great distance," Karl said. "Although if the 'Lucias' in the show tent look the same as this, she already knows. Poor Pinky."

Karl's and Murdoch's phones rang simultaneously.

"I don't need caller ID to know who that is." Karl pulled his phone from his pocket and spoke without waiting for the person on the other end to speak. "Right away, Mrs. Jacobi. We'll be there right away."

Karl and Murdoch left the theater. Murdoch still sniffled and cradled the dead plant. Gethsemane hurried after those who'd gone to check their plants. She entered a space normally used for pre-concert lectures. Riotous color greeted her. Long, folding tables sporting rose-centric floral arrangements of various shapes and sizes filled the room. Flowers that had lost the competition for any inch of available table space settled for a spot on the floor. Folding chairs displaced from their ordinary places in the center of the room leaned stacked against walls in corners. She wandered along the narrow aisles, admiring blooms ranging from pale, almost luminescent white to the deepest, almost-black crimson. Rose growers chattered with relief their flowers had been spared the fate of Jacobi's and whispered about who could have done such a vile thing. However dreadful Jacobi may have been, his roses had never hurt anyone.

She stopped in front of a table that stood off to one side by itself. A Jacobi and Fortnum sign marked it as their exclusive territory. An empty pot, its soil disturbed as if someone had yanked a plant out by its roots, sat at the table's front edge. Three other pots, filled with scorched, wilted, yellow-brown leaves and the bedraggled remains of blossoms, sat behind it.

"Shame, ain't it?"

Gethsemane turned to see an elderly woman in an old-fashioned, but still stylish, green linen suit with a pale pink rose pinned to her lapel. "I guess someone decided to level the competition. With Frankie Grennan out—"

"The 'Sandra Sechrest'? What happened? Not more weed killer?"

"No, gardaí feet." Gethsemane described the appearance of the rose bush in Frankie's garden.

"Oh, that would only take Grennan out of the running in the garden show. The entries in the rose show are judged separately and required submission of plants not in the garden. He still has a chance there."

"Maybe Grennan poisoned the 'Lucia di Lammermoor,'" a man in an old-fashioned, and no-longer stylish, suit said. "Knocking off ol' Jacobi didn't work to knock his rose out of the competition so Grennan went in for the direct kill."

Gethsemane opened her mouth to speak but the elderly woman beat her to it. "I know Francis Grennan and he is not a killer. Even if he were to strike out at another human in anger, he'd never harm a rose."

Gethsemane wanted to hug her.

The man continued, unmoved. "You think you know

someone but when the stakes are high enough...He doesn't have an alibi for Jacobi's murder, from what I hear. Does he have an alibi for this?" He jerked a finger at the dead roses.

"You know Grennan as well as I do," the woman said. "Have you seen him?"

"No," the man said, "but people are in and out of here all the time. Easy enough for someone to slip in—"

"With a gallon of Round Up?" Gethsemane asked.

The man hesitated. "Well..."

"And attractive young men with bright red hair are so easy to miss in a crowd," the woman added. "I'm sure Prince Harry is hardly ever noticed when he goes out in public."

The man shoved his hands in his pockets and skulked away.

"This is the kind of thing I'd expect from Roderick Jacobi, not from Frankie Grennan," the woman said. "Roderick cared about winning, not about fair play."

"You knew him, too? Roderick? I admit I'd never heard of him before this competition."

"I know him from the amateur competition circuit. It's rather like Peyton Place. Everyone gets to know everyone else. You're not a fan of gardening shows? Roderick made a name for himself on one of those DIY channels, on the basis of his looks, not his botanical talent. The behind the scenes people did the work and Roderick grabbed the glory. He did have an uncanny knack for winning competitions, though. I don't know how he managed to get his hands on so many prize-winning hybrids and cultivars. I can't imagine him putting in sweat equity. But no one ever found any proof he cheated. And accusations without proof—"

"Are just gossip. It helps being married to a woman who owns a commercial garden empire."

The woman laughed.

Gethsemane looked around. "Doesn't this event have

security? These flowers must be worth a fortune. I remember how much the flowers cost at my sisters' weddings and those weren't prize-winning displays."

"Security of a sort. A few rental guards supplied by Jacobi and Fortnum. My three-year-old great-granddaughter could probably slip by them with little trouble. Security tightens up a bit when the show officially opens. Mostly for crowd control. We grow roses. We don't race monster trucks or cage fight. People expect us to behave."

The woman moved off. With a final look at the remnants of 'Lucia di Lammermoor,' Gethsemane returned to the auditorium to pack up her violin. She noticed something white sticking up from beneath the Vuillaume's body. A card. A card with a colored pencil drawing of flowers. Gethsemane whipped around. The stage was deserted. A janitor passed through the rear of the otherwise empty auditorium.

Gethsemane called to him. "Excuse me, sir. Did you see anyone near my violin a few moments ago?"

He shook his head. "No, ma'am."

Gethsemane turned, slowly, and looked around three hundred sixty degrees. No one. She'd been within, possibly, arm's reach of Frankie's admirer—or Jacobi's killer—and hadn't known it. Damn.

Still mad at herself for missing the flower girl, Gethsemane sent gravel flying as she skidded to a stop in front of Carraigfaire. She grabbed her violin and got as far as the porch, then stopped. She sniffed. What did she smell? She took a deep breath. Bread? Not some otherworldly harbinger of spectral visitation scent. She smelled actual bread. Eamon didn't cook? Did he?

"Hello," she called from the entry way.

"We're in the kitchen," Frankie answered.

"Who's we?" She detoured by the music room to deposit her violin then stepped into the kitchen. Frankie, Colm and Saoirse Nolan, and Father Tim Keating sat around the table laden with dishes of ham, potato salad, cheese, and fresh-baked Irish soda bread.

"Hello, Miss," Colm and Saoirse greeted her.

Gethsemane hadn't expected to see her student or his younger sister until the next school term began. "What are you guys doing here?"

"Father Tim took me hiking to find wild flowers to sketch." Saoirse picked up her sketchbook from the floor by her chair and showed it to Gethsemane. Saoirse, a certifiable genius, was homeschooled and Father Tim tutored her in several subjects. "We saw Mr. Grennan in your garden and asked if we could help. He said yes, so we called Colm to bring us some tools from the church. He stayed because he's bored at home so he's into mischief and Ma's threatening to send him to stay with Grandma for the rest of the summer."

"I am not into mischief," the green-eyed blond said. "I'm experimenting. It's science. I'm keeping my mind active over the summer so I'll be ready to go when school starts up again."

"Colm Nolan," Gethsemane said, "I've never been a sixteen-year-old boy but both of my brothers were. I'm not buying that 'getting ready for school' story."

Frankie laughed. "Colm found out what happens when you mix hydrogen peroxide, dish soap, warm water, and yeast. Lads find it hysterical. Their mothers, not so much."

"Especially when they find out what happens all over the kitchen counter," Saoirse said.

"And how are you, Father Tim?" Gethsemane asked.

"Well, thank you. Trying to keep up with this one," he nodded at Saoirse. "Keeps me young. I hope you don't mind us helping ourselves to your kitchen."

"Of course I don't. Especially since I didn't cook."

"Seat yourself," Frankie said. "There's plenty. We'd have waited but I didn't know when you'd be back."

"Sit by me, Miss." Saoirse moved her sketchbook from the chair where she'd set it.

Gethsemane took the thick notebook. "Where did you get this, Saoirse?" The heavy-weight paper looked and felt like the cards the flower girl used.

"From the art supply store on the village square. It's really watercolor paper but I like to draw on it because the paper doesn't tear so easily."

"Is that the only place in town where you can get it?"

"Are you thinking of taking up watercolor as a hobby?" Father Tim asked.

"Um, no, I was thinking this would be a good weight to use for flashcards for the lower school boys in my intro to music class next term." She disliked lying to Tim but she didn't want to discuss a homicidal stalker in front of Colm and Saoirse. She put the book next to Saoirse's chair and sat. "Pass the potato salad?"

She worked to keep the dinner conversation light and dodged questions about the specifics of her day. She listened to the others describe the work they'd done in the cottage garden.

"We haven't set any plants out yet," Frankie said, "but the weeds are gone and the ground is tilled."

"Help yourself to some cuttings from the church gardens, Frankie," Father Tim said.

"By the way," Frankie asked, "do you have a radio going somewhere in the cottage?"

"A radio? No. Why do you ask?"

"I was working in the garden before Father and Saoirse arrived and I swear I heard music. Classical music. Don't know who by. I'm not good with composers if they didn't compose jazz." He tugged at his John Coltrane t-shirt. "But it sounded modern. I mean, modern compared to Bach or Beethoven. It reminded me of something I heard you play by that Irish composer who used to live here, McCarthy."

Father Tim and Saoirse, who knew about Eamon's ghost, fixed their gaze on their plates. Colm, who didn't, reached for more ham.

Frankie went on. "Sounded like the music came from the music room. When I went inside, the music stopped. I looked for a radio but I couldn't find one."

Gethsemane hoped her shrug was nonchalant. "Probably the wind. It sounds strange coming off the cliffs. Voices, music, you name it."

"It's July. It's a fine, sunny day. What wind?"

Saoirse chimed in. "There's a rare bird in the northeastern United States whose call sounds just like Leonard Bernstein's 'Chichester Psalms.'"

"We're in Ireland," Colm said.

"Well, wouldn't you expect an Irish bird call to sound like an Irish composer?" Saoirse asked her brother.

He replied by sticking his tongue out at her.

"On that note," Father Tim rose from his chair, "I think I'd better get these two home. Many thanks for the fine meal, Frankie. And for the hospitality, Gethsemane."

"Any time, Tim," Gethsemane said. Frankie echoed her sentiment.

Gethsemane escorted her guests to the door then returned to the kitchen to help Frankie clean up.

"Are you going to tell me what really happened today?" he asked. "Or, are you going to stick to the sanitized for the sake of the children version?"

"Well, let's see." She counted on her dish soap-covered fingers. "I looked at gruesome, fifty year old crime scene photos, watched Niall break up an argument between Murdoch Collins and Karl Dietrich, eavesdropped on enough of the argument to guess it had something to do with Avar Pharmaceuticals' board of directors, watched Niall break up a shoving match between two women fighting over a show catalog signed by a dead man, learned at least two people think Ellen Jacobi killed her husband, crashed Ellen Jacobi's tent and discovered she's a terrifying woman who makes Yseult seem like a pussy cat and who hated her now-dead husband." She paused to rub an itch on her nose.

"You left soap." Frankie wiped it off with a dish towel. "Is that all you did? No rehearsal? You took your violin."

"I'm getting to that. I scoped out your garden but didn't find anything. I ran into Verna—she sends her regards, by the way—who is ashamed of the way you're being treated in the press. Meaning the *Dispatch*. I tracked down the *Dispatch* photographer and ate his head off for running photos of Jacobi on the front page instead of the pictures he took at your photo shoot—Yes, I know the editor decides what goes on the front page, not the photographer, but I wanted to yell at someone and he was convenient. Then I learned he doesn't really care any more about flowers than he does about sheep birthing triplets but he's got a man crush on Roderick Jacobi because Jacobi brought a plant back from the Amazon that turned into a medicine used to treat some rare disease his sister had—Max, the photographer's sister, not Jacobi's—and it saved his sister's life. Then I went to the Athaneum where I started to rehearse but I ran into Karl Dietrich again and learned there might be a plan to keep Ellen Jacobi out of Avar Pharmaceutical's board room. But maybe not everyone is opposed to her playing an active role in the company because she has degrees in plant science—Who knew?—and she may be more in favor of plant-based pharmaceutical research, which is expensive but not as expensive as gene therapy, than gene-based pharmaceutical research, which is astronomically expensive but has the potential to earn billions. And I met a very nice, elderly lady who has great taste in suits and believes you're innocent and a not-so-nice old man who thinks you whacked Jacobi. But the nice lady put the old man in his place."

"I'm amazed," Frankie said. "I thought only a ten-year-old could pack an entire day's worth of adventure into a few run-on sentences. I stand corrected. Thirty-eight-year-old women can do it, too."

"Apologize or I won't tell you the best part. Parts."

"Are you codding me?"

She turned her back and started drying dishes.

"All right, I apologize. What else could possibly have happened today?"

She put down the dish towel. "One: someone sprayed weed killer on Roderick Jacobi's prize roses. Two: your secret admirer left a calling card in my violin case."

Sixteen

Frankie sank into a chair. "Please tell me you're codding me. Please tell me that's your attempt at a joke."

"What, about the card in my violin case?"

"No. I don't give a damn about the card. The roses. 'Lucia di Lammermoor.' Please tell me they're not really dead."

"I saw them myself, at least the ones at the theater. They looked worse than my miniature rose."

"The specimens in the show tent? Those were spared?"

"Not according to Murdoch. Someone got them all. Karl thought they'd been sprayed with a concentrated dose. So, not an accident."

"Damn. Who'd do that to a rose? What kind of monster? 'Lucia di Lammermoor' was exquisite. A masterpiece."

"'Lucia di Lammermoor' was your competition. The nice lady told me you still have a chance to win the rose show, even though your garden's been knocked out of the competition."

"Wait, what happened to my garden?"

Oops. She told him about the bloodstains, footprints, and broken stems.

"Bloody, careless wankers."

"But whatever you submitted for the rose show is okay. At least, I haven't heard otherwise. And with 'Lucia di

Lammermoor' out of the running—"

Frankie slammed a palm on the table. "That's not the way I want to win a competition."

"You weren't this upset about Jacobi's murder. Come to think of it, no one was that upset about Jacobi's murder, except Max. 'Lucia di Lammermoor's' death reduced Murdoch to tears."

"Because Jacobi was a gobshite who used people and cheated them and cast them aside. He had a mean streak longer than the River Shannon buried under that phony smile and coiffed hair. His roses never harmed anyone."

"Do you think they were really his roses?"

"I don't understand what you're asking."

"The lady in the suit—I wish I'd gotten her name— suggested, no, stated, Jacobi cheated. She doubted he actually developed any of his roses, himself. She thought his employees did the work and he took the credit. Kind of like the stunt he and Yseult pulled on you."

"Possible. Probable, even. No way to prove it. Jacobi was a master at covering his tracks."

"Maybe someone who couldn't get justice the legal way decided to get revenge the illegal way."

"By stabbing Jacobi—"

"In the back. Could be symbolic."

"—to death and pointing suspicion in my direction."

"If I've learned one thing over the past couple of days, it's that the rosarian community is as in-bred as the music community. Your feud with Jacobi isn't a secret. You're the perfect fall guy."

"Kill Jacobi, I understand. Blame me, I understand. But why kill the roses?"

"Maybe the murderer is the real developer of the 'Lucia di Lammermoor.' Maybe she preferred to destroy her creation than see Jacobi steal credit for it."

"It's operatic."

"Please don't mention opera. Things didn't go so well when the opera came to town." An opera triggered the curse that nearly killed Frankie, Niall, and half the males in the village.

"When Sutton hears about the weed killer, he'll be up here to arrest me. He'll take it as motive for killing Jacobi—to eliminate the competition. Sutton lacks anything remotely resembling a finer feeling. He'll never believe that I'd never harm a rose."

"Lucky for you, this time you have a better alibi than a secret garden near an abandoned insane asylum. You have a priest and two kids."

Frankie relaxed a little.

"Want to help me decipher this card?" Gethsemane laid it in the middle of the table.

Frankie studied it. "Euphorbia, chamomile, eucalyptus, and spirea."

Gethsemane consulted *The Language of Flowers*. "Perseverance, energy in adversity, protection, and victory."

Frankie held the card closer and traced the outline of the flowers. "This is a good drawing. Skilled I mean. Where's that other card? The one with the anemone?"

Gethsemane retrieved it from the study.

Frankie held the two side-by-side. "Both of these took some skill to execute. They're not Redouté but they're not weekend coloring classes at the local community center, either. Whoever drew these had some training in scientific drawing."

"Someone with experience in scientific illustration who buys her watercolor paper at the only art supply store in Dunmullach."

"She could be from Ballytuam or Cork or some other place nearby."

"Why would she still be in Dunmullach if she didn't live here? She must know she's a murder suspect. And if art supply stores are anything like music supply stores, you never go in without chatting about what you're working on."

"Unless you're plotting a murder."

"Okay, not that. But if you were working on scientific drawings you'd probably ask the clerk for certain types of inks or a particular paper. You might show off your portfolio. The clerk might remember that."

Frankie looked at his watch. "Too late to find out this evening. Shop's closed. Tomorrow."

"Opening ceremony tomorrow. I have to be there early for our final rehearsal."

"I hope you don't mind if I skip the hooley."

"I don't blame you. I wish they'd cancel the whole thing." A few notes from "Pathétique" played in the back of her head. "It just feels wrong."

"You'll be fine. You'll be brilliant. I just..."

"Like I said. I don't blame you. Showing up would be beyond awkward."

"May I hide out here?"

"Sure. But invite Colm and Saoirse up to work some more in the garden. Just in case you need another alibi." More Tchaikovsky. "I'm only half kidding."

"Good idea. I'm not kidding."

"I'm calling it a night." She stood and looked out the kitchen window. "I realize it's still light outside but when I said tomorrow's rehearsal was early, I meant it." She bid Frankie goodnight and climbed the stairs to her room.

She'd just pulled up the covers when Eamon appeared on the foot of her bed. An involuntary yelp escaped her lips before she could muffle her surprise with a pillow.

"Everything all right up there?" Frankie called.

"Fine," she called back. "Stubbed my toe."

"Liar," Eamon said.

"You want me to tell him he's hiding out from the law in a haunted house? Where've you been all day?"

"Happy to see you, too. I'm fine thanks. And how was your day?"

"Even if I believed you meant that and weren't just throwing snark, I wouldn't go there."

"That bad?"

"A sociopathic, almost-ex, wife turned widow, poisoned roses, and another card from the flower shop girl."

"And I thought my day was scary."

"Scary? What *did* you do? Besides freak out Frankie with your music?"

"What music? I stayed in the village all day and gained insight into the twisted mind of the adolescent."

"Just tell me."

"I hung around the computer lab in the library."

Gethsemane pulled herself up in bed. "Isn't the computer lab new?"

"The computers are new. The lab space is in the oldest part of the library and one of my favorite hangouts as a lad. It used to be the card catalog room."

"Do I want to know why you hung out in the card catalog room?"

"I used to rearrange the cards. I'd file Petersen before Parker or slip O'Malley in with the Molloys."

"No, I don't want to know. What did you do to the computers? Make all of the Google searches default to 'I'm feeling lucky?'"

"I observed. Except for a few occasions when I had to dodge one of the village's more sensitive souls—I think one of them actually saw me—I watched the little darlin's and learned what type of websites they visit when their parents and teachers aren't watching. By the way, does St. Brennan's have website filters installed? They should."

"Let me get this straight. While I spent the day running from place to place, trying to track down evidence to clear my friend of suspicion of murder, you—"

"Did the same. Climb down off your high horse. And get your mind out of the gutter. Shame on you for the assumptions you made about the websites I saw."

Gethsemane slid down under the covers and held a pillow over her face. "Please go away. You are so, so lucky my hand would pass right through you. Else, I'd—"

The pillow flew across the room. "Where's your phone?" Eamon asked.

"In my bag. On the chair."

"I see it." The bag levitated from its perch near the vanity and landed on Gethsemane's leg.

"Navigate to Murderphile dot com. Spell 'phile' with a P-H."

She woke up her phone and found the website. Her phone's screen filled with black, white, and red graphics and hyperbolic text describing various high-profile and unsolved murders in lurid detail. "The Boston Strangler, The Black Dahlia, the Unabomber, Jack the Ripper, Son of Sam...Why am I looking at this?"

"Type 'flower shop murders Dunmullach Ireland' in the search box. Don't forget the Dunmullach, Ireland. Apparently, there are lots of flower shop murders."

She followed his instructions. One of the crime scene photos Niall showed her that morning appeared on screen. "That's from the case file. It's kept locked in the evidence room. How'd they get—" Eamon's impatient turquoise aura illuminated the room. "Never mind. What am I navigating to next?"

"Scroll down to the discussion thread and read some of the user names."

"MrdrLvr979, ChopChop12, MindHntr7422, Rppr9000." She stopped with a sigh.

"Keep going."

"SrialTwin, PuzzlerX, TheFlorist—" She almost dropped her phone. "TheFlorist? Could it be? Is this our flower shop girl? TheFlorist isn't such an unusual user name for someone interested in the Flower Shop Murders."

"No one else using the site has a similar name. And I read enough of her posts to suss her out as a local. She mentions visiting some of the places connected to the crime. She also mentions a few local places like St. Dymphna's and Arcana Arcanora. She talks about being an artist and about being 'in love' with an older man."

"Now I wish you were solid so I could kiss you. That's brilliant. Think the site's owners or moderators or whatever they're called will give us her real name?"

"Is anything ever that easy?"

"What's plan B? Stake out the library as well as the art supply store?" She told Eamon about the watercolor paper.

"Why don't you and Frankie leave a message on the website and lure her to some meeting place? Then have the guards meet her?"

"Luring a teenager into a trap sounds—gross."

"TheFlorist isn't a teenager. Probably. She's younger than Frankie, sure, but twenty-one is younger than Frankie. And she's old enough to have money for out-of-season flowers and high-end art supplies. Think an allowance would cover that? Or would you need a salary? And she's a murderer. Probably."

"When you phrase it that way, not so gross. The questions now are, what message would lure her? And where do we lure her to? My previous attempts at setting traps have not always worked out as I planned." They'd often resulted in her nearly being killed.

"Did you miss the part where I said have the gardaí meet her?"

"Except the gardaí aren't going to work with me."

"O'Reilly's a garda."

"Niall to the rescue again."

"He doesn't complain. Well, he does but he doesn't mean it."

"Do you have any idea what message to send?"

"Do I have to think of everything?"

"You don't have a clue, do you?"

"Nope, not one. I admit when I don't know something even less often than I admit when I'm wrong but, this time, I'll fess up. I can't put myself in the mind of an obsessive, homicidal, young female. I've been the victim of one. If I'd seen her coming..." He partially dematerialized. The fading sun shone through his chest onto the bedspread. His aura dimmed to a sad yellow.

Gethsemane jumped in to distract her friend from painful memories. "What we need to do is read all of her posts. They'll give us an idea of how she thinks which may give us an idea of how to outwit her. But—" She yawned. "Cyberstalking the stalker will have to wait until after the rehearsal."

Seventeen

Gethsemane slept poorly. Bizarre dreams of being chased by rosebushes armed with hedge trimmers alternated with bouts of tossing and turning. Would they be able to lure TheFlorist into the open? Would Niall go along with the plan? Would Frankie? Could they pull it off without Sutton arresting them all?

She gave up on sleep before the sun rose, showered, dressed, and left the cottage without waking Frankie. She borrowed his car again. He wouldn't mind and leaving him at Carraigfaire without easy transportation would bolster his alibi in case anything happened to prompt Inspector Sutton to direct more suspicion toward him. "Pathétique" still played in the back of her mind. Something was going to happen. Hopefully, nothing more disastrous than an off-key performance or a mass panic attack by the entire strings section.

She arrived in the village in time for a caramel macchiato at Roasted before going to the Athaneum. Two or three of the other musicians had arrived before her. They had fortified themselves with cups of Roasted's brew as well. They all mingled in the parking lot and waited for the manager to unlock the theater's doors. Gethsemane suspected he'd hidden and watched them because he appeared with his keys as soon as the last coffee cup went into the bin near the Athaneum's entrance. Mr. Greevy despised food and drink in his theater. He protected the blue velvet upholstery as if state secrets were woven into the fabric.

Mr. Greevy turned on the lights, then Gethsemane and the other musicians followed him into the auditorium. Gethsemane held her breath as she waited for her eyes to adjust to the darkness, half-dreading the "ca-chunk" of the overhead lights, afraid of what she might see. She exhaled when the brightness illuminated nothing more than empty seats. No corpses propped in the back row, no bodies on stage. She peered down into the orchestra pit. No one dead there, either.

"Are you all right, Dr. Brown?" the theater manager asked.

"Yes, fine. Just, um, eager to start rehearsal."

Musicians drifted in, alone or in small groups, until the entire orchestra had assembled in their places on stage. Mr. Greevy brought Gethsemane her score and baton. The orchestra tuned to the oboe and Gethsemane ascended the podium.

She addressed the orchestra. "This is our final rehearsal before tonight's performance at the opening ceremony. You've worked hard and remained professional despite, er, certain events. Hundreds of people will fill this auditorium tonight, surrounded by the sight and smell of exquisite roses. Your task will be to give voice to those roses, to create an auditory experience every bit as exquisite as the visual and olfactory. So, we'll take the piece from the beginning and run through to the end with enthusiastic vigor, same as we'll perform it tonight."

She raised her baton. The orchestra poised in ready silence, the hush broken only by a distant car horn. She signaled the count. A flick of her baton and the notes of Strauss's waltz floated up from the strings. Barely audible at first, they rose in pitch and tempo until they crescendoed into—

An ear-splitting scream. A shouted, "Be wide!" The sound of two objects colliding. The squeal of tires.

The noises came from the street. Chairs clattered and music

stands overturned as musicians, some still clutching instruments, ran outside.

A crowd had gathered in front of the theater. Spectators stared down at something in the street.

"Get an ambulance," someone yelled.

"Call 999," yelled another.

Gethsemane, her baton still grasped, forgotten, in her hand, pushed through to the edge of the sidewalk. She looked down.

Tufts of Murdoch Collins's mouse-brown hair stuck out at odd angles. His lifeless eyes stared up at nothing. A rivulet of blood trickled from his mouth. His geometrically patterned shirt bunched up around his chest, exposing an expanse of pale, white belly. His arms, legs, and neck jutted at odd angles. A shattered flower pot lay next to him, its floral contents spread over the street like confetti from a macabre parade.

Gethsemane looked away, only to regret it. She saw something worse than Murdoch Collins's mangled body. She saw Frankie's car, front end dented and scraped, driver's door opened, abandoned by a tree.

"Frankie Grennan didn't do this, Inspector Sutton." Gethsemane sat, arms folded, on a hard plastic chair in a garda interview room. Sutton had arrived at the crash scene at the same time as the ambulance and hauled her back to the station faster than the ambulance crew had loaded up Murdoch's body.

"It's his car," Sutton said.

"Which I drove this morning."

"You're admitting you ran Collins down?"

"No!" She closed her eyes. If she recited Negro League batting averages from 1932 through 1936, it wouldn't be enough to calm her down. She clenched and unclenched her jaw a few times, then spoke. "I was on stage with more than a dozen musicians. We all heard the crash and ran out together. How could I have run Collins down?"

"Grennan could have retrieved his car from wherever you parked it while you were in the Athaneum."

"How did he get to the village from Carraigfaire? Walk? Flap his arms and fly? Hitch a ride with the pixies?"

"He could have borrowed that fancy bike of yours. Or someone could have driven him down."

She ignored the bike comment. "Driven him? So, now it's a conspiracy? Do you even hear yourself, Inspector?"

A vein throbbed in Sutton's temple. His craggy features hardened, reminding Gethsemane of the ominous cliffs above her cottage. He brought his face close to hers. "O'Reilly may put up with your nonsense, but cross the line, and I won't think twice about chucking you in a cell."

"For what? I checked the rule book. There's no law against telling a garda to—"

A uniformed garda knocked and poked her head in. "Excuse me, sir."

Sutton spun on her. "What is it?"

"Her story checks out, sir. Francis Grennan's been up at Carrick Point all morning. He's still there."

"Who'd you confirm that with?"

"Father Tim Keating. Father's with him. They took some children on a hike up the cliffs."

Sutton swore. He glared at Gethsemane, vein still pulsating. She looked down to hide a smile.

"If Grennan's tiptoeing through tulips with the wee ones," Sutton said to the garda, "and this one—" He jerked his thumb at Gethsemane. "—was on stage, who started the damned car? And how?" He put his face close to Gethsemane's again. "Did you leave the keys in it?"

"Nope. Hand me my bag and I'll prove I didn't."

"Someone wired the ignition, sir," the garda said. "It's an older model, late eighties, I'd say. A cinch to hotwire. My kid sis could do it."

"Did your kid sis run a man down in the street?"

"'Course not, sir."

"Then you're dismissed."

"Yes, sir." The garda closed the door behind her.

Sutton massaged his temples.

"Inspector O'Reilly does that, too," Gethsemane said. "Do they teach you how to do that in garda school?"

"Yeah," he said. "It's a de-escalation technique to keep us from strangling smart-mouthed busybodies."

Gethsemane stood. "Am I under arrest? May I go?"

"Sit down."

She protested.

"Sit! Down!"

She plopped back onto the chair.

Sutton sat across from her. "I don't know what version of the rule book you read but my version says there are laws against interfering in a garda investigation. So, unless you cooperate, I can and I will arrest you." He took out a notebook and pen. "You're going to tell me everything you know about the murders of Roderick Jacobi and Murdoch Collins. Leave nothing out."

Sometimes acquiescence was the better part of valor. She told him about Jacobi's affair with Yseult, she told him how much Ellen Jacobi hated her late husband and how she'd talked about killing him, and she told him about TheFlorist, who was either a love-sick young woman or a hired assassin. She started to tell him about plant-based and genetic medicine but stopped when she saw he wasn't listening. "Not boring you, am I?"

"No," Sutton said without a hint of sarcasm, "you're not. Tell me more about this florist."

"Not *this* florist. TheFlorist. All one word. It's a screen name the woman uses on a fan website."

"Fans of murder."

"They're out there."

Sutton tapped his pen against his notebook. "And you're sure the woman who almost knocked you over is the same woman who's been leaving flowers and cards for Grennan and is the same woman who uses this screen name?"

"I'm convinced it's the same woman. And I think she killed Jacobi and Collins."

"Why? Draw the line between obsession with Grennan and murder."

"Well," Gethsemane reached for his notebook and pen. "Frankie hates Jacobi for several reasons." She listed them. "Jacobi stole his wife, Jacobi stole his roses, Jacobi keeps beating him in competition. So TheFlorist kills Jacobi to eliminate Frankie's rival or to get revenge on Frankie's behalf for the loss of his roses or his wife or both. The killing was a tribute to Frankie or a token of her affection."

"The flowers weren't tribute enough? Whatever happened to asking a fella to the pub for a drink?"

"I didn't say she was rational, Inspector. She hangs out in a forum called 'Murderphile.'"

Sutton leaned back in his chair. "Maybe the secret admirer routine's bogus. Maybe Grennan knows who this woman is and put her up to getting rid of Jacobi for him."

She pushed his notebook back to him. "I don't think I want to help you anymore."

"I'll help you by pointing out a hole in your theory. Why would Grennan want Murdoch Collins dead? What's his connection to Collins? What'd he have against him?"

"Frankie wouldn't want him dead, they had no connection, and he had nothing against him. I don't think Frankie even knows who Murdoch is. Was. Frankie's beef with Jacobi was personal, over roses and women, not pharmaceuticals. Murdoch liked roses," she recalled his tears at the sight of the vandalized 'Lucia di Lammermoor,' "but he didn't compete on his own. He mostly served as an errand boy for his boss. He was no threat or concern to Frankie." She took the notebook again and wrote "Frankie" and "Collins." She drew an "X" through both names. "There's no connection."

"So why would TheFlorist kill him?"

"Because Ellen Jacobi hired her to kill everyone who stood between her and a seat on Avar Pharmaceuticals' board of directors. Murdoch was Chief Operating Officer. Karl Dietrich hinted the idea of Ellen with a controlling interest in the company didn't sit well with everyone. Maybe Murdoch wasn't on Team Ellen so Ellen wanted him gone. Maybe TheFlorist is a hitwoman and the stalker routine's a cover."

Sutton stared at the notes. "You're actually talking sense. Compensates for your being so irritating."

"Um, thanks?" she asked. Sutton's skill at the backhanded compliment rivaled her eldest sister's.

"O'Reilly told me you were a great one for coming up with plans to trap murderers. How had you planned to catch TheFlorist?"

"What makes you think—" She stopped. Sutton's expression said he wouldn't fall for any gee-officer-I-don't-know-what-you-mean stories. She could tell he knew she'd already thought of a way to bring TheFlorist out of hiding. Well, technically, Eamon had thought of a way but now wasn't the time to split hairs. "I was going to post a message on Murderphile.com. Or get Frankie to post one."

"An invitation to meet him under the old oak tree kind of post?"

"Yeah, something like that." Sutton had a romantic streak.

Who knew?

"Then what? Ambush her? Hit her over the head with a tree limb?"

"I kind of thought I'd let y'all take over at that point. I figured I could talk Inspector O'Reilly into going along."

"You probably could, at that." Sutton drummed his pen on the table and drew a few doodles in his notebook. "It pains me to say this, and damned if I ever say it again, but I like your plan, for the most part. Control of the situation will be key. If we're dealing with a professional killer instead of a love-starved co-ed—"

Gethsemane interrupted. "A professional killer's not likely to agree to a rendezvous, is she?"

Sutton allowed her a grudging smile. "Good point. Although, there are ways...If she thought you knew her true identity and you offered to sell her your silence, she might show up with her own plan to silence you permanently."

"Good point." Been there, done that. Memories of an unexpected dip in a mash tun sent a shiver down her neck.

"Are you all right?" Sutton asked.

"Fine. Just thinking about possible outcomes. Haven't lost my nerve, if that's worrying you."

"O'Reilly also said you were fearless. We need a message that will lure TheFlorist regardless of whether she's a pro or an amateur." Sutton's eyes narrowed and he fixed his gaze on a spot beyond Gethsemane. He drummed an absent-minded tattoo on the table with his pen. "The Cork garda has people who specialize in this kind of thing, luring online predators and such, but there's no time to bring them in."

The inspector's stony features gave away nothing but the tension in his posture and the set of his shoulders betrayed his excitement. Gethsemane could almost smell his eagerness for the chase.

She couldn't resist. "And we wouldn't want the Cork garda horning in on 'our' case. Big city law enforcement may underestimate the fellas in the villages but we know we can do this without them."

Sutton's face remained impassive, although his shoulders relaxed. "There's that, too."

"What about Inspector O'Reilly? He's familiar with the original Flower Shop Murders case. Maybe he can come up with a message an obsessed fan wouldn't be able to resist but a professional killer might read as a blackmail threat."

"Another good idea," Sutton said. "At this rate, I may owe you an apology before nightfall. Wait here. I'll call O'Reilly."

"May I wait in the lobby?" She looked around the pea-green room with its graffiti-covered table and dull one-way mirror. "Interview rooms aren't my waiting area of choice."

"Suit yourself." Sutton led the way out into the lobby. Chairs only slightly less uncomfortable looking than those in the interview room crowded the postage stamp-sized waiting area. A scruffy man in stained work pants and three-day stubble huddled in a chair next to the back wall. A red-eyed, well-dressed woman Gethsemane recognized as a witness from the crash scene sat in the front row, clenching and unclenching a crumpled tissue. Otherwise, the seats sat empty.

"Why don't you come up with a user name for that murder site while you're waiting?" Sutton asked. "Something cryptic yet catchy."

Gethsemane pulled her phone from her bag and took the seat at the end of the front row nearest the elevators. She glanced at the woman at the opposite end, but the woman didn't look up. She made a point of ignoring the unkempt man behind her. She navigated to Murderphile and selected "Register for an account."

"Cryptic yet catchy. What's cryptic yet catchy?" She typed:

Flower_fan.

The familiar small, blue, spinning wheel popped up on her screen and told her that the website was thinking about her request. She'd never noticed before how much the blue wheel reminded her of one of Eamon's blue orbs.

A message replaced the wheel: Sorry, that screen name is not available.

She typed: Floral_phan.

Her phone replied: Sorry, that screen name is not available.

ILuvFlorists.

Not available.

FlowerLove.

Sorry.

A bell dinged somewhere off to her left. She tried again: FlowerShopGirl.

Sorry, not available.

She swore.

"Trouble, Dr. Brown?"

She gasped and dropped her phone.

Karl Dietrich stood next to her. The elevator doors swished shut behind him. He retrieved her phone from under the chair where it landed. "I mean, Gethsemane. I apologize if I startled you."

"I was preoccupied. Good thing I sprung for the protective phone case."

He glanced at the screen before handing her the phone. "A true crime website? You never know what people are into. I would have pegged you for an aficionado of fine literature or gourmet food."

"Oh, no, I'm not—I mean, it's not—" How could she explain? "I came across this when I was reading up on an unsolved case. I think I know one of the site's users. I wanted to create an account so I could send her a message. But I can't come up with a screen name. All the good ones are taken."

"Which crime most interests your friend?"

"The Flower Shop Murders. They happened here in Dunmullach in the sixties."

"Your name is Gethsemane which is also the name of a garden. Why not try Gethsemane's Garden or something similar?"

No way she'd use her entire first name on the site. "How about g_gardener?" G could stand for Grennan as well as Gethsemane. She typed.

Another spin of the blue wheel and her phone congratulated her. "Success," the screen proclaimed with a large green checkmark next to g_gardener. She created a password then put the phone away.

"What are you doing here?" she asked Karl.

"The gardaí want to ask me some questions about poor Murdoch. I don't mind telling you, Gethsemane, I'm frightened. That could have been me run down in the street. I had agreed to bring those flowers to the theater—they were a special arrangement featuring a new rose, 'süße Rache,' Ellen Jacobi is testing, an attempt to help people forget 'Lucia di Lammermoor.' But at the last minute, the lab manager from Avar called me about a problem with an experiment. It required my immediate attention so Murdoch agreed to bring the flowers."

"Why would anyone want to kill you or Murdoch? Jacobi and his roses were both out of the competition. Killing Murdoch doesn't serve any purpose."

"Other than to cancel the opening ceremony, as well as all of the other festivities. The organizers just announced all events have been canceled and prizes will be awarded privately sometime next week. Murdoch's death also casts suspicion on your friend, Mr. Grennan. I understand his car hit Murdoch."

"His hot-wired car. Frankie has an alibi for the time of the murder, one the gardaí confirmed. Besides, he has no motive to kill Murdoch. Or you. Maybe both murders are related to the pharmaceutical company. Avar Pharmaceuticals is one thing you, Jacobi, and Murdoch have in common."

"It is possible. Jacobi's death, in particular, created turmoil. Questions swirl about leadership, future directions of research. Stock prices tumbled."

"Strange to think a company that makes medicines that save lives may have spurred someone to take lives."

"At times like this, I wish I was back in the Amazon, hunting for specimens. Plants may be as deadly as humans but they are predictable. They behave in ways you expect. They don't steal from you, stab you in the back, or ambush you in the street."

Karl broke off at the sound of elevator doors. Gethsemane turned to see the Byrnes brothers step into the waiting area. Glendon started at the sight of Gethsemane and Karl, then averted his gaze and sat near the crying woman. Gerrit, however, approached them.

"Dietrich." He greeted Karl with a nod.

Karl included his head toward Gethsemane. "You remember Dr. Brown."

"Of course." Gerrit nodded at her. "I'm sorry to run into you again under such—trying—circumstances."

"The gardaí have questions for you about Mr. Collins?" she asked.

Gerrit shrugged. "Don't know what I can tell them. Hardly knew the chap."

Knew him well enough to try to sell him on a risky, underhanded deal. Karl's cough and blush suggested he remembered the encounter at the Athaneum, too. Gerrit gave no hint he remembered as he joined his brother.

Sutton and Niall appeared around the corner.

Karl stood. "Inspector. You wished to speak to me."

"Dr. Dietrich," Sutton said, "Thank you for coming." He turned to Niall.

"I'll take Dr. Brown home," Niall said. "We'll meet you later."

Eighteen

"You told Sutton, 'we'll' meet you later." Gethsemane followed Niall out to his car.

"Because you and I both know that if I don't keep you with me, you'll run off on your own and do something with a high likelihood of getting you killed."

"And here I thought you were including me in the planning because it was my idea."

Niall gave her a half-grin and they climbed into his car. "Bill—Inspector Sutton—and I talked about where to set up a meeting. We need someplace public but not so public we can't hide some gardaí."

"We need a meeting place that seems plausible. I don't think a woman who killed two people would fall for a rendezvous at the pub. She'd suspect a set up."

"Got someplace in mind?"

St. Dymphna's popped into her head. As much as the idea of ever setting foot up there, the place where she was bludgeoned and nearly set on fire, again nauseated her, an abandoned, burned out insane asylum had flair that would appeal to a true crime fan and was isolated enough to appeal to a hired killer who thought she was being blackmailed.

Niall rejected the suggestion. "Too far out of the way, too

many ways to sneak up on someone, and too unsafe in general. I wouldn't think you'd want to be anywhere near that place."

"I don't. But if it was for the greater good...Besides, this time I'd have protection."

"I don't see why anyone who was the full shilling would go up to Carnock."

She told him about Frankie's secret rose garden. Niall sighed and shook his head.

"How about Our Lady of Perpetual Sorrows? The gardens are public but not too public on the back side of the church. And if we set up a meeting at night, there won't be many people around."

Niall thought for a minute. "The church might work. I'm sure Father Tim would cooperate with us."

"I've already set up an account on Murderphile. Screen name g_gardener. All we need is a convincing message and a bit of luck that she sees it."

"You sound like an old pro. You're getting good at this investigation business."

They pulled up in front of the cottage. They met Father Tim loading Saoirse, Colm, and Ruairi O'Brien, another one of Gethsemane's music students, into his car. Frankie stood on the porch.

"Gethsemane, Inspector," the priest greeted them. "Everything all right?"

Niall eyed the children. "Everything's fine, Father. But I need to discuss something with you later."

Father Tim and the children drove off and Gethsemane, Niall, and Frankie went inside. A trace of leather and soap lingered in the air. Eamon lurked somewhere nearby. Gethsemane risked a peek into the music room and kitchen but didn't see him.

"Looking for something?" Frankie asked when she returned

to the study.

"Just making sure you didn't destroy my house while I was gone." She winked.

"Glad you haven't lost your sense of humor." Frankie helped himself to a drink. "Is this Waddell and Dobb as good as you say it is?" He sipped the spicy-sweet bourbon. "Yes. Yes, it is."

"I'm sorry about your car, Frankie," Gethsemane said.

"It's no coincidence the killer used my car, is it?"

"No coincidence," Niall said. "Your garden, your hedge shears, your car. The killer's either trying to frame you or send you a message. Good thing you had an alibi for Murdoch's murder."

Frankie nodded at Gethsemane. "Her idea."

"Her second good one today." Niall briefed Frankie on the plan. "We need a message to lure TheFlorist to Our Lady. Any suggestions?"

"If she's a legit true crime aficionado," Gethsemane said, "she won't be able to resist something connected to the actual Flower Shop Murders case. How about offering her some of the crime scene photos?"

Niall protested. "I know the case is cold, but it's still open. I can't give away evidence."

"We're not really going to give her anything," Gethsemane reminded him.

"True. All right, we offer crime scene photos. What if she's a hired killer?"

"Phrase the message so she's not sure if the photos are of the original crime scene or one of the current ones," Frankie said. "Word it so it sounds as if someone may have taken a picture related to Jacobi's or Collins's murder that points the finger at her."

"Something like, 'Picture's worth a thousand words? When

it's from a floral crime scene, it's worth Euros. Meet Our Lady in the garden, midnight, and avoid Perpetual Sorrow.'"

"Have you blackmailed someone before?" Frankie asked. "That came easy for you."

"You've got your snark back," she said. "You must have recovered from your night at the garda station."

"If you two are finished," Niall said, "let's get back on task. We've got to hurry and post the message and hope she sees it today."

Gethsemane used her phone to log onto the site and set the trap. "Should we add another line or two? A personal message from Frankie?"

"Such as?" Niall asked.

"Wear tuberoses and forsythia, so I know it's you," Frankie said.

"Tuberoses and forsythia?"

"Dangerous pleasure and anticipation."

Gethsemane tapped the "send" icon. "Done." She displayed the post on her screen.

"Now we wait." Niall checked his watch. "Midday. I'm heading back to the village. I'll stop by Our Lady and talk to Father Tim, let him know what's going on. That'll give me a chance to stake out the gardens, figure out the best places to station our people. Then Sutton and I will coordinate getting everyone into place before our killer shows up. If she shows up."

"For the sake of the devil's advocate, what if she doesn't show up?" Frankie asked.

"Then Sutton and I will have time to prepare an explanation for the Superintendent as to why we wasted gardaí resources on a—what would you call it in Virginia?"

"A snipe hunt," Gethsemane said.

"One of those," Niall said.

"What do Frankie and I do?"

"I'm tempted to say, stay out of it and let the gardaí handle it, but I know I'll get nowhere with talk like that. You can monitor that website and call me right away if you get any response to the message."

"Since my car's out of commission until your forensics team releases it from whatever impound lot they towed it to, how about giving me a ride into the village now? That way you won't have to come back up here to get me closer to show time," Frankie said.

"You'll have to come back to get me," Gethsemane said.

Neither man answered. She repeated herself. Silence.

"What is this?" she said. "You're planning to cut me out? This was my idea."

Niall and Frankie stared at the floor.

She turned on Niall. "You said—"

"I know what I said. But I'd be irresponsible bringing a civilian along on a stake out to catch a multiple murderer."

"Frankie's a civilian."

"I need him as bait."

"Thanks," Frankie said.

"Don't complain." Gethsemane scowled at him. "At least you're not being left behind like a small child."

"This isn't a game, Gethsemane," Niall said. "I'd leave Frankie out of it if I could."

"Thanks, I think," Frankie said.

Niall continued. "This is professional law enforcement work. It's not some Agatha Christie story; it's real. And, as much as I appreciate the help you've provided up to this point, you and I both know I'm not going to willingly bring you into a situation where you might get hurt or worse when it's not necessary to expose you to risk. If I did, I should be fired for incompetence and negligence."

"So, you just told me you'd bring me along to keep me from

arguing until you got me up here with no access to a car," she said. "You lied to me."

Niall flushed. "Well, okay, if you want to put it like that, yes, I lied. For your—"

She crossed her arms. "So help me, if you say for your own good, I'll—"

Frankie stepped between them. "Enough, both of you. You know he's right, Sissy. If you were back home in Virginia, would a cop invite you to tag along to arrest a murderer?"

"No."

"And, Niall, haven't you known Sissy long enough by now to know that lying to her gets you nowhere?"

"I'm sorry. I should have been honest with you back at the station."

"I'm going to this hooley because our bure won't come out of the shadows unless she sees my charming face," Frankie said. "Unless she's an assassin, in which case, she'll probably come out shooting anyone she sees. In which case, I fully intend to hide behind Sutton. He's big and ugly and makes a much better target than I do."

"He has small daughters," Niall said.

"Well, damn it, now you're making me feel bad."

Gethsemane interrupted. "All right, I'll stay here. And I'll keep an eye on Murderphile and I'll call you if there's any response. Now both of you leave before I stop being reasonable and start being mad again."

"Sissy, I—"

"Don't say anything else." She pointed to the door. "Just go." She followed them out to Niall's car.

She called after them as Niall put the car into gear. "And, guys, be careful."

An angry blue Eamon awaited her when she returned to the study.

"What are you mad about?" she asked. "Not because they think your idea was mine? I couldn't tell them the truth about that, could I?"

"Don't be thick. I don't give a damn whose idea they think it is." Blue sparks sizzled and popped.

"Then what? I haven't seen you this, literally, fired up since—" When had she seen him this angry? "Since I accused you of killing Orla." He'd almost taken her head off with an orb then.

"I'm almost that furious. Our Lady of Perpetual Sorrows? Damn near the only place in the bloody village I can't go, and you decide to spring your trap there?"

As a suspected suicide, Eamon had been buried in unhallowed ground. As a ghost, he could travel anywhere he'd visited while he lived—except the church, its yard, and his wife's grave in the church cemetery.

"I didn't think—"

"You're right, you didn't think. What if you'd gotten into trouble? Been hurt? I wouldn't have been able to get to you."

"Eamon, I," she searched in vain for words, "I don't know what to say."

"Do you think it hasn't bothered me, all the times you were in danger and I couldn't help you? Do you think I didn't care? That I didn't feel like I'd let you down?"

She sputtered. "But, I, I mean, none of it was your fault. You were banished to limbo. Then trapped in a phone. You would've helped, I know. Anyway, I survived."

"No thanks to me."

"I never blamed you, Irish."

Eamon faded to a morose yellow. He sank into the sofa, the patterned upholstery visible through his chest.

Gethsemane sat next to him. She laid her fingers on his arm, shivering at the buzz that zipped up her arm. "What's brought this on?"

"Listening to you argue with O'Reilly and Grennan and knowing that twelve hours give you plenty of time to get to the churchyard on your own, it occurred to me I'd already let one woman important to me down and I don't think I could stand it if you became the second."

"Eamon, I'm sorry, I—" A noise outside cut her off. "Did you do that?"

"How could I do it? I'm sitting here next to you."

Another noise, louder this time.

"Sounds like gravel against a window." She stood.

Eamon glowed purple with fear. "How do you know?"

"One of my eldest sister's high school boyfriends used to signal her that way. Worked great until he cracked a window. C'mon." She started toward the rear of the cottage.

Eamon dematerialized then reappeared in front of her. The full-body buzz from passing through him made her stop. "You're not going out there."

"Of course, I am. A murderer would hardly signal by throwing rocks."

"Unless their plan is to lure you outside so they can drop something on your head. You're not the only one who watches horror movies."

Another noise—the front door handle jiggling.

"Would a killer try the door?" Eamon asked.

Why would the killer show up here at the cottage? Unless she'd seen through the Murderphile ruse, guessed Gethsemane planted the message on the website, and come to Carraigfaire to avoid the churchyard trap. "You go check," she said to Eamon. "Even if someone could see you to drop something on your head, it wouldn't hurt you."

"Things passing through me doesn't feel great. But, you're right, it's not fatal." Eamon vanished, then reappeared seconds later. "It's a woman. Young, in her twenties maybe. About your height. Dark hair, brown eyes."

"Doesn't sound like anyone I know." The doorknob jiggled again. "What should I do?" She glanced around the room. "Where's my shillelagh?"

"Beat her off with a stick? That's your plan?"

"You've got a better one? Hide under the bed while you blast her with an orb?"

A woman's voice called out. "Gethsemane Brown? Are you there?"

"I'm going to answer the door," Gethsemane said to Eamon, "and don't ask if I'm not the full shilling. I can't stand here forever, doing nothing." She started toward the entryway. "But have an orb ready, just in case."

She crept toward the door, cringing at a floorboard's creak. She held her breath and pressed her ear against the door panel.

Eamon materialized next to her. "What are you listening for? You know she's out there."

She turned to shush him and spied her shillelagh in its hiding place beneath the entryway bench. She dove to retrieve it as the doorknob jiggled again.

The woman called from the other side of the door. "Dr. Brown? Are you there?"

Gethsemane mouthed to Eamon, "What do I do?"

"You said it, you can't stand here forever doing nothing. You've got your stick. Open the door," he said.

She took a breath. William Bell, two twenty-four; Rap Dixon, three fifteen; Josh Gibson, three sixty-two. Better. Panic and reason can't coexist. *Would* a killer knock politely and call for her by name? Maybe. If, as Eamon suggested, it was a trick to get her to stick her head outside. A victim met a similar end in that Agatha Christie movie she watched a couple of years ago. She whispered to Eamon, "Stick your head out and make sure she's not armed with a rock. Or a knife. Or a gun. Or—"

Eamon cut her off with an eye roll and an impolite word. She flinched as his head disappeared through the wall. As long as she'd known him, she couldn't get use to that. He pulled his head back inside after a moment. "No guns, no knives, no blunt objects, no obvious poisons. Open the damned door."

"Do you have an orb ready?"

Eamon let off a few blue sparks. "Just in case."

Another deep breath. Satchel Paige, two-oh-nine; Double Duty Radcliffe, three ninety-six. "On three," she said to Eamon. "One." She held up a finger. "Two." She held up another. She tightened her grip on her shillelagh and grasped the doorknob. "Three!" she shouted as she yanked open the door.

The woman on the porch gasped and stumbled back, eyes wide, gaze fixed on the club Gethsemane held aloft.

"Who are you?" Gethsemane asked.

"Reston Flynn. I saw your message on Murderphile. I'm not crazy and I didn't kill anyone."

Gethsemane lowered the shillelagh but kept a tight grip. The young woman didn't look threatening in her chiffon maxi-skirt and billowy peasant blouse. Her appearance said "student" or "creative" more than "hired killer." Still...She positioned the door so she could slam it shut on Reston at the first hint of trouble. "You're TheFlorist?" she asked.

Reston nodded. "I left the flowers for Mr. Grennan. But, I swear, I didn't murder either of those men."

"Aren't you going to invite her in?" Eamon asked. "Such appalling manners. What would your Virginia granny say about your lack of hospitality?"

Gethsemane didn't have to see the ghost to know his aura radiated green with snark. She guessed from Reston's lack of reaction to his voice that the young woman couldn't hear him. Behind the door, she flipped Eamon the bird.

"Why don't we take a walk?" she suggested to Reston. Much easier to escape, or fight, out in the open than in a small cottage if she'd misjudged her. She pulled the door shut behind her as she stepped onto the porch and motioned for Reston to lead the way up to Carrick Point lighthouse. Easier to watch your back if the danger lay ahead of you. The long shillelagh doubled as a walking stick. More secure footing on the mossy slopes and a weapon, should it come to that.

Reston, a few steps ahead of Gethsemane on the clifftop path, spoke over her shoulder. "I'm not a header."

Gethsemane made no effort to catch up to her. The thump of the shillelagh on the gravel path marked cadence as they made their way toward the lighthouse. "You can see how leaving messages disguised as floral bouquets at murder scenes could lead one to doubt that assertion?"

"But I didn't know they were murder scenes, did I?" Reston halted and faced Gethsemane. "At least not the first one, in Mr. Grennan's garden."

Gethsemane waited until Reston moved again. "So why all the drama? The flowers, the ridiculous hat, the decoy? Why not just slip a note under Frankie's door? Or, hey, it's the twenty-first century. Why not just text him to meet you for a drink at the pub?"

"Where's the fun in that? I couldn't just come right out and admit my crush."

"Did you destroy Roderick's roses, the 'Lucia di Lammermoor?'"

Reston hung her head. "I did it to avenge Mr. Grennan. If Jacobi hadn't been killed, he would have destroyed the 'Sandra Sechrest'. That would have broken Mr. Grennan's heart. Besides, Jacobi's roses didn't deserve to win top prize. Mr. Grennan's deserved to win. So I sprayed weed killer on the other roses. I wanted to do something to make Mr. Grennan notice me and remember me."

"Congratulations. You succeeded."

"I wanted to intrigue Mr. Grennan. I know he helps you solve cases. I thought he'd enjoy solving the flower riddles, what with him being keen on gardening."

"How do you know Frankie? I haven't seen you around campus. Or church."

Eamon's voice sounded in her ear. "When you go."

Again, Reston betrayed no sign of having heard anything. "My nephew has him for algebra. He talks about him all the time, what a great teacher he is, how he knows all the best practical jokes. I met him when I visited my nephew on family day last year and I see him in the stationer's shop when I buy my art supplies. His jazz appreciation group meets upstairs."

Art supplies. No wonder the drawings were so good. "You're an art student."

Reston beamed. "I was. I just finished my Master's in Studio Art."

"Is that where you learned about flowers' secret meanings? In one of your classes?"

"No. My granny taught me all I know about flowers. She owned the flower shop where the Flower Shop Killer bought the bouquets for Mr. Coyne."

"Rosemary Finney was your grandmother?" Gethsemane stopped. "That's how you know details about the murders."

Reston backtracked a few steps to stand next to Gethsemane. "Granny always blamed herself. She believed she should've paid more attention, sounded an alarm, or something."

"If your grandmother told you about the murders, why'd you join Murderphile? What's a true crime discussion group got to offer you?"

"Dunno, exactly." Reston shrugged. "Help, maybe? Internet

detectives have solved cold cases. Not often, I know, but..." She shrugged again. "Mostly, it's nice to have someone to talk to. Someone who doesn't think I'm morbid. Ma wants no part of it, neither do my brother or sisters. Since Granny passed, the folks on Murderphile are the only ones who seem to understand."

The more Reston talked, the less she sounded like a killer. Gethsemane pressed her. "How did you know the message on Murderphile was phony?"

"No offense," Reston said, "but it was obvious. A new profile appeared out of nowhere and right away suggests a meetup in real life. Of course, it was a set up."

So much for a career in cybersleuthing. Eamon's disembodied laugh tickled the hair at the back of her neck. "How did you know to come to Carraigfaire?" she asked Reston.

"I knew Mr. Grennan was staying here so I figured this is where you'd come. I saw the men leave without you and guessed they were headed to the village to spring their trap. I saw my chance to talk to you so I knocked."

"After throwing pebbles at my window."

Reston blushed and scuffed her shoe in the gravel, sending a few pebbles over the cliff's edge. "That was childish. Sorry."

Gethsemane stepped closer to Reston. "If you're not involved in Roderick Jacobi's or Murdoch Collins's deaths, why haven't you come forward before now? You're a smart woman. You must have known the situation had progressed way beyond 'harmless anonymous crush.' Yet you continued leaving messages and stayed hidden."

"I left the messages because I wanted Mr. Grennan to know that I knew he was innocent, but I was afraid to come forward."

"Afraid the gardaí would think you murdered Jacobi and Collins?"

"No. I was afraid the killer would find me. I saw him kill Mr. Jacobi. That's how I knew Mr. Grennan didn't do it."

"Wait, you actually witnessed Roderick Jacobi's murder?"

Reston nodded. "It was awful. I brought a bouquet for Mr. Grennan. I tried to sneak into Erasmus Hall to leave it but the photoshoot was going on and too many people were hanging about. Mr. Grennan and Jacobi got into a dreadful row. He accused Jacobi of being a cheating gobshite and Jacobi called him a perennial loser and goaded him about his ex-wife. They said awful things to each other. I thought Mr. Grennan was going to punch Jacobi right in his mouth. Not that Jacobi wouldn't have deserved it, if half of what Mr. Grennan accused him of were true. Then that photographer intervened and cooled everybody off and Mr. Grennan went inside Erasmus Hall."

"And Jacobi?"

"He left with the photographer. I found a place to hide and waited for Mr. Grennan to leave the hall. I didn't want to risk him catching me delivering the flowers. He left about ten minutes later." Reston broke off and shuddered. She walked toward the lighthouse.

Gethsemane followed. "What then?"

"Jacobi came back before I could slip inside the building. At least, I'm pretty sure it was Jacobi. I could only see him from the knees down, from where I hid, but the pants and shoes were the same as those he'd worn at the photoshoot."

"Why would Jacobi come back to Frankie's garden?" Gethsemane spoke more to herself than to Reston.

Reston answered. "Not for anything good, I'm sure. I could see he picked up hedge shears from under a bush. He stood in one spot and banged the flat of the blades against his leg, kind of absent-minded, like he was thinking of something. Then he let the shears drop and moved where I couldn't see him." She stopped at the edge of the path and stared out over the bay. Pieces of gravel dislodged by her foot skittered over the cliff's edge.

Gethsemane put a hand on her shoulder. "Careful. Don't stand so close to the edge. It's slippery and sometimes strong winds spring up, even in summer."

Reston stepped back. "I couldn't see Mr. Jacobi anymore. Someone else came into the garden and picked up the shears. I never saw his face, only shoes and trouser legs and, for a few seconds when he grabbed the shears, a hand. He wore a gardening glove."

"You're sure it was a man? Did he speak?"

Reston shook her head. "I assumed. They were men's shoes and trousers. Different than Mr. Grennan's."

"Would you recognize them again?"

The question went unanswered. A pop, like a firecracker, sounded and a spray of gravel exploded near Reston's foot. She jumped and stumbled, nearly losing her footing on the path.

Gethsemane grabbed her in time to keep her from falling over the edge of the cliff. "What the—" She looked around. Nothing on the cliffs above and below them but moss. The cottage and lighthouse lay quiet on either side of them.

Another pop. Gravel exploded behind Reston.

"Gunshots," Eamon hissed in Gethsemane's ear.

"Someone's shooting," Reston said.

A third shot echoed off the rocks. Gravel flew up and hit Reston in the back. She screamed.

Gethsemane risked another look around. The shots had to be coming from the lighthouse. "Run!" she yelled and took off toward the cottage.

She heard another shot and a scream behind her. She turned.

Reston dropped to her knees. She tugged at her shirt sleeve where a jagged rip in the fabric exposed red-streaked skin beneath.

Gethsemane pulled her to her feet. "Keep going. We're

almost to the cottage."

The next shot struck the space where Reston had knelt a second before.

Eamon materialized between the women and the lighthouse, radiant with blue fury. Sparks sizzled and a wave of energy, like the shockwave after an atomic blast, rippled out from his core. The wave hit Gethsemane in the chest like a fist. She flew backwards, lifted into the air by the force. She sailed over the edge of the cliff and thudded onto a rocky promontory a few feet below the level of the path. Dazed, she dimly registered the sound of another shot above her. Gravel showered down on her head. Another scream snapped her out of her stupor. Her shoulder throbbed and sharp pains shot through her knee in protest as she rolled onto her side and pushed herself up into a half-seated position.

Eamon materialized beside her. "Stay down."

She ducked her head and pressed close to the cliff wall, out of the sightline from the lighthouse. She counted to five. Silence. "Has the shooting stopped?"

"I don't know. I'll check." Eamon vanished, then immediately reappeared. "For feck's sake, stay here."

About three feet of rock ledge separated her from certain death at the base of the cliff. "Where am I going to go?"

A worried saffron tinged the cerulean of Eamon's aura. "Well, just—be careful." He vanished.

Gethsemane inventoried aching muscles, flexing each sequentially to ensure it worked. She'd reached her elbows when Eamon reappeared.

"Lighthouse is empty. Saw someone running."

"Why didn't you stop them?"

His aura flared blue again. "Because I figured you'd rather I not leave you hanging about on the side of a cliff while I went off playing superhero." He softened. "I'm sorry. What I meant is, you're more important."

"I'm sorry. You save my life and instead of thanking you, I complain you didn't catch the bad guy, too. At least," she raised an eyebrow, "I assume you threw me off a cliff on purpose to get me out of the way of a bullet."

He shrugged. "Crude, but I couldn't think what else to do. The lighthouse was out of orb range."

Gethsemane remembered the scream as she forced an imagined image of a fatally wounded young woman crumpled on the gravel from her mind. She looked up toward the path-turned-shooting gallery. "Reston?"

Eamon pointed in the opposite direction. "Down there."

Gethsemane scooted as far as she dared and peered over the ledge. Reston lay, unmoving, on a similar ledge a couple of feet below her own. "Is she...?"

Eamon translocated to Reston's side. "She's breathing," he called up to Gethsemane before vanishing and reappearing next to her. "Knocked out, but alive. Bleeding like a stuck pig, though. I only see the wound on her arm but she's lying in a pool of blood. Granted, I'm no gunshot expert but I wouldn't expect a wound in a bicep to bleed so much."

Gethsemane stared down at the young woman. "Maybe she was hit more than once. Or maybe the one bullet hit more than her arm. We've got to get her some help."

"I'd lend a hand, but..." Eamon pushed his hand through the cliff face.

Gethsemane clawed at the rocks until she'd pulled herself up to standing. She winced as the jagged surfaces cut into her palms and fingertips. She wouldn't be playing any instruments for a while. She'd climbed about a foot up toward the path when she dislodged a rock and slid back down to the ledge, landing an inch from its edge. She held her breath, afraid the slightest movement might plunge her off her perch.

"Jaysus." Eamon glowed full-on terrified purple. "Be wide, would ya? I don't want you to end up like—" He broke off.

Orla. His wife had died a quarter century ago at the bottom of these same cliffs. Gethsemane pushed herself back to the wall. "Are you sure you can't levitate humans?"

"Coffee pots and bourbon bottles are about all I can manage."

"And another blast of energy is just as likely to knock me down there," she pointed to Reston, "as up top." She unleashed a few Irish swear words.

"Your gaeilge's improved," Eamon said. "You've been practicing."

Of all the times to tease her about her language skills. "Not now, Irish, I—" She smacked her forehead. "Duh. My shillelagh. I dropped it on the path when I started running. Send it down to me. I can use it as leverage to climb up."

"I'll send it up to you." Eamon pointed down at the walking stick a few feet below them. "Blast knocked it over the edge. But it won't work." The shillelagh landed at Gethsemane's feet.

She grabbed it and searched for a cranny in which to wedge it. Nothing wide enough or deep enough. She slammed the heavy stick against the rock. The vibration shot pain through her bruised and abraded hands.

"A temper tantrum won't help."

She brightened. "I know what will. My phone. I left it in my bag, back at the cottage. Can you levitate something that far?"

"Don't know. Never tried to move anything I can't see." He stared at the cottage, his frown and burnt sienna aura betrayed his degree of concentration. After a moment, his aura dissipated and he dimmed to transparent. "Sorry."

"You tried." Gethsemane looked down at Reston. Blood puddled under the young woman's arm. Eamon was right. It did look like a lot to be from a single wound in her arm. Reston needed help. Soon. She turned back to the ghost. "I've got an idea. Bunny hop the phone."

"Talk sense."

"You have to see an object to move it. Go to the cottage, find my phone, and send it as far as you can. Follow it to where ever it lands, send it a little farther. And so on and so on until you get it to me. It may take a while but," she gestured toward the waves breaking over the base of the cliffs, "like I said, I'm not going anywhere."

"Darlin'—"

Gethsemane braced for a litany of objections to her plan.

"That might work. Be back soon." Eamon vanished.

Gethsemane called down to the unconscious woman. "Reston, can you hear me? I'm trying to get you some help. Hang in there. Reston?"

No response. She sat against the wall. Nothing to do but wait. And think. Who'd shot at them? Eamon saw someone running. Male or female? Hard to imagine Ellen Jacobi doing her own dirty work. But if she was desperate...Reston saw men's pants and shoes. She hadn't seen who wore them. What if Ellen borrowed them from her lover? Or her soon-to-be-late husband's closet? Or—

"Your phone, madam." Eamon reappeared, interrupting her thoughts. Her phone floated down from the top of the cliff. She snatched it from the air and dialed 999.

The operator's voice came on the line. "What's your emergency?"

"RoderickJacobi'sandMurdochCollins'smurdershotatusa ndwefelloffacliffandRestonisn'tmovingandweneedanambulance andthegardai," tumbled out in an unintelligible torrent.

"I'm sorry, I don't understand. You've fallen off a cliff and you need the gardaí?"

Gethsemane repeated the story at an understandable speed.

"Send an ambulance and the guards. And tell Inspectors Sutton and O'Reilly their stake out at Our Lady's a bust."

Assured of imminent rescue, she sank onto the ledge and rested her head against the cool rock of the cliff wall. "They're coming, Reston," she called down to the young woman. "Help's coming." She closed her eyes.

Nineteen

"Please open your eyes."

Gethsemane squeezed them tighter. "Only if you promise to stop shining that light in them." A long-suffering sigh prompted her to open one eye for a peek at the doctor making a valiant effort to examine her. "I'm fine."

He set his pen light on the tray next to the bed on which she sat. Beeps and bells from other areas of the Accident and Emergency ward filtered through the yellow curtain surrounding them. "You fell off a cliff."

Not exactly. "I, um, jumped. To get away from bullets."

The doctor massaged the bridge of his nose. "I remember you. Your head's healed nicely, by the way."

Gethsemane touched the small scar above her eyebrow. It had been an ugly wound the last time she'd been in A and E, the result of having her head slammed into a metal shelf. This doctor had stitched it up. Just before she'd eloped from the hospital with Frankie's help.

"You were about as cooperative then as you are now," the doctor said.

"I'm fine, honest." She held up a bandaged hand. "Scrapes, nothing. Reston Flynn is the one you should be worried about."

"Miss Flynn is being attended to."

"Is she bad? How many times was she shot? Will she make it?"

Puzzlement registered on the doctor's face. "Miss Flynn suffered a single, superficial gunshot wound to her arm. The fall banged her up a bit. She broke her wrist. Nothing life-threatening. She'll 'make it,' as you say. You worried otherwise?"

"All that blood? From a superficial wound? I saw her lying in a pool—" The doctor's eye roll toned down her hyperbole. "Well, a good-sized puddle. More than you'd expect from a flesh wound." She added in response to the same you're-not-a-doctor look her brother often gave her when she weighed in on medical matters, "It was a lot of blood even by a layman's assessment."

"Ah." The doctor's skepticism dissolved into understanding. "Her bleeding disorder."

"What bleeding disorder?"

"Herbin Disease." He frowned. "You know Miss Flynn suffers from Herbin Disease?"

"Oh, that," she bluffed, afraid he'd stop talking if he thought he violated confidentiality rules by divulging information she didn't already know. "Of course I know Reston has Herbin Disease. I didn't realize it was a bleeding disorder. Not being a doctor."

"It is fairly rare. I've only seen one other case, back when I was an intern."

Gethsemane leaned forward on the exam table and lowered her voice, a tactic that always worked with her brother when she wanted him to tell her more about someone's medical condition than he'd intended to. "What causes it?"

Apparently, this doctor shared her brother's eagerness to explain medicine to an eager audience. He leaned in. "It's caused by a genetic defect that leads to the production of abnormally functioning clotting factors. Unlike von Willebrand's Disease, which affects about one percent of the population..."

A two-minute lecture on bleeding disorders followed. When the doctor finished, Gethsemane asked, "Is Herbin Disease treatable? Will Reston be okay?"

"Her wound is small. She bled a lot relative to the size of the wound but not a life-threatening amount. As I said, she'll recover. Too bad we're out of Achillervum. We'd have stopped her bleeding sooner if our pharmacy stocked it. Closest supply is at City General in Cork."

"Achillervum?"

"The drug used to treat Herbin Disease. To specifically treat it, I mean. Other treatments, blood transfusions and whatnot, are supportive, but Achillervum normalizes the functioning of the clotting factors. It's the only drug currently available that does, although rumor has it, some gene therapies are in the pipeline. Achillervum is hard to get these days, though. The only company that produced it, Avar Pharmaceuticals, stopped about six months ago."

Jacobi's company. "You know Avar's CEO and Chief Operating Officer were murdered here in Dunmullach this week."

"That Jacobi fella and, what's his name, Collins?" The doctor looked surprised. "I thought they were connected to the flower show."

"They were. But roses were an expensive hobby. Pharma was their main line of work."

"You'd think I'd recognize their names. Guess I don't get out of the hospital enough. Truth is, I don't pay much attention to the business side of pharmaceuticals—who owns which company, which companies are merging, which one is taking over another, that sort of thing. I only pay attention to manufacturers' names when I have trouble getting one of their drugs. If Avar hadn't stopped producing Achillervum, I wouldn't have known it was theirs." He held one of her hands and squeezed one of her fingertips until it turned pale.

"Ow."

"Sorry." He released the pressure on her finger and counted seconds until it flushed red again. "Two seconds. Normal capillary refill. Do you feel me touching your fingers?" He brushed the tips of each with his own. "Can you wiggle them? Make a fist?"

She performed the actions and repeated them with the other hand. "See? Fine. Why did Avar stop manufacturing Achillervum?"

"Single-minded, I remember." He scribbled in her chart before answering. "Achillervum is an orphan drug, a drug used to treat a rare condition so it's not likely to be prescribed often. It's derived from a plant that only grows in the rainforest so it's expensive to produce."

"Expensive to make, not likely to sell much. That translates to not profitable. No return on investment. But if it's the only drug that treats Achillervum and Avar's not making it anymore, what will people with Herbin Disease do when the current supply runs out?"

The doctor shrugged. "Too many late night shifts in A and E have turned me into a cynic but I don't believe the pharmaceutical companies are overly concerned with the fate of such a small number of people. Despite their claims of trying to improve lives, I think they're more concerned with improving their bank balances. At least, Avar cares more about money than patients."

"Why do you say that?"

"I had trouble getting several medications recently, so I called a druggist friend to look into it. Seems Avar's decided gene therapy is the future of pharma. They're abandoning a lot of their old medicines and selling their licenses and patents on others. They're using the profits to ramp up their gene therapy research and development."

"That sounds forward thinking, not greedy and uncaring."

"Until you find out they're selling the licenses and patents below market value to pharmaceutical companies who then quintuple the retail price of the meds. And you find out that Avar made deals for a share of the profits for the newly exorbitantly priced products. And you find out that Avar is firing a lot of their old scientists, the ones who developed these drugs, and weaseling them out of any financial stake they thought they had in the patents on drugs they developed."

"Okay, yeah, that does sound pretty Martin Shkreli."

A twitch of the curtain surrounding the exam table revealed a nurse's face. She addressed the doctor. "Excuse me, a couple of guards out here want to speak to Dr. Brown."

The doctor stood. "We're finished." He said to Gethsemane, "I know you'll refuse to stay overnight for observation, so I won't ask you to. Your discharge paperwork will contain instructions for changing your bandages." He nodded at her hands. "None of the abrasions are deep, so basically, just keep them clean and dry."

He excused himself and left with the nurse. Niall and Inspector Sutton replaced them at Gethsemane's bedside.

"Before you say anything—" Gethsemane began.

"Are you all right?" Niall interrupted.

Sutton cut them both off. "Did you get a look at the person who shot at you?"

"No," she said to Sutton. "I'm all right," she said to Niall.

Niall touched a bandage. "Your hands."

"Just scraped. And banged up. And sore. But not permanently damaged. Reston got the worst of the ordeal."

"You're up to giving a statement, then," Sutton said. Not asked.

Niall flashed his colleague a look like a gathering storm.

"Jaysus, Bill, can you not even wait 'til she's released from the hospital before you grill her?"

"A murderer's roaming the village running people down and shooting them in the street and you're worried about what? Me hurting her feelings? Wearing out her delicate constitution? I suspect Dr. Brown's made of stern enough stuff to forego a few niceties if it means getting a dangerous criminal off the streets."

"Yes, she is made of stern stuff," Gethsemane said, "and she's sitting right here so she can hear you. And there's nothing nice about the garda station, no offense, so I'm happy to forego it. I'd just as soon make a statement here than in that horrid interrogation room." A raised hand cut off Niall's protest. "But what I'd really like to do is go home, shower, and put on some clothes not covered in dirt and riddled with tears." She pointed to a rip in her blouse. "I'd also like to check on Reston. She was still unconscious when Search and Rescue pulled us off the cliff."

"You'll have to wait on that last bit, checking on Miss Flynn, I mean," Sutton said. "They just took her to surgery."

Gethsemane gasped. "Surgery? The doctor told me she wasn't seriously injured. A broken wrist was all."

"Surgery's for her wrist," Sutton said. "Needs pins, apparently. Not serious by A and E standards."

"Nor father of four standards," Niall said. "How many bones have your boys had repaired, Bill?"

"I stopped counting after the plate in Liam's collarbone." Sutton sighed and smoothed his thinning hair. "Dr. Brown, I have to go to the station and explain to the Super why I wasted garda resources on a bust of a stakeout. If I'm still employed after my tap dance, I'll be up to your cottage in an hour, hour-and-a-half. Then, you'll explain to me what happened on that cliff. No excuses."

"No excuses," Gethsemane said.

"You'll see she gets home?" he asked Niall.

"Yeah, of course."

Sutton left. His grumbling about superintendents and taking advice from civilians and making a bags of a stakeout faded away with his footsteps.

"We got Miss Flynn's version of events before they took her to surgery," Niall said, "but they'd given her something for pain, so her story didn't make much sense. Something about an invisible force lifting her up and carrying her over the edge of the cliff just in time to save her from a bullet."

Niall and Sutton would never know how much sense Reston's story made. Gethsemane looked away to hide a smile. Niall put a hand on her arm. "Are you sure you're all right? You don't have to put up a front. If you're not up to talking today, I can put Bill off."

"I appreciate the offer, Niall, but honest, I'm fine. I ache but not so much a hot shower and a couple of paracetamols won't fix it." She saw doubt flicker in his storm-gray eyes. "Honest. Sutton's right, I'm made of stern stuff. I'm not going to fall apart or breakdown or melt into tears. Besides, I'm getting used to almost being killed." His pained look prompted an added, "That was a joke."

A reluctant, dimpled grin softened the worry. "All right, all right. You've convinced me. I'll stop fussing over you like you're a hothouse flower. I forget how tough you are." He gave her a hand down from the exam table. "C'mon, I'll drive you home."

"Where's Frankie?"

"In the waiting area. Head nurse wouldn't let him back. 'Next of kin, only.' Dug her heels in. Wouldn't have let Bill and me back if we hadn't shown our garda ID. Frankie wasn't happy about it. Ate the head off the nurse. Didn't quiet down until she showed him she knew as many swear words as he did."

They joined a sulking Frankie in the waiting area. He

gestured at her bandaged hands. "What's all that? You all right?"

"I'm fine, my hands are fine, at least, they will be, and no one is blaming you so stop with that look."

"I blame me. I'm the one Reston Flynn, the header, is obsessed with. I'm the one she came after. I should've stayed at the cottage."

"And I should've stayed there with him," Niall said.

"You should both stop," Gethsemane said. "Planting the bogus message on the fan site was my idea. None of us guessed that Reston—who's overly dramatic but not crazy—would see through the ruse and show up at Carraigfaire instead of Our Lady."

"You're sure the killer came after Reston and not you?" Niall asked.

Gethsemane nodded. "The shooter fired at her. None of the shots were aimed at me, I just happened to be standing next to her. Although, I doubt whoever it was would have cared much if I'd been hit as well."

"So you're a ballistics expert, now?" Niall asked.

"Not an expert, but I do have some experience being shot at." Such as the first time she confronted a murderer.

Niall reddened. "Sorry."

"Never mind. Look, here's where we're at. We know Reston didn't kill Jacobi or Collins because the person who killed them also tried to kill her."

"We don't know that for certain," Frankie said. "Maybe Reston killed the two men and someone tried to avenge their deaths."

His remark rated hands on hips and a raised eyebrow. "Frankie..."

"I know, I know. That sounded ridiculous as soon as I said it."

"Maybe not," Niall said. "Why would the killer want Reston

dead? What's her connection to Jacobi and Collins? She doesn't work for Avar Pharmaceuticals nor Jacobi and Fortnum."

"She didn't tell you?"

"I mentioned the pain medication, didn't I?" Niall asked.

"Reston witnessed Jacobi's killing. Partly witnessed it. She saw the killer from the knees down. She also saw Frankie leave Erasmus Hall before the killing."

"Which means Reston gives me an alibi and an alibi gives Sutton a reason to go sniffing after a different suspect," Frankie said. "Which would give the real murderer a motive to kill Reston. They'd want to shut her up before she could talk to anyone about what, or who, she saw."

"Slow down," Niall said. "How would the killer, or anyone, know Reston witnessed anything?"

"Maybe they knew someone could put them in the garden at the moment Jacobi died but didn't know exactly who," Gethsemane said. "Maybe they heard someone or glimpsed—"

Frankie snapped his fingers. "The bouquets."

Niall raised an eyebrow.

"We assumed the floral messages were threats made by a killer. We read them wrong. They weren't threats, they were messages of encouragement. Perseverance, justice, resolve to win, hope, energy in adversity, innocence, protection, victory..."

"Messages of encouragement," Gethsemane said, "left by the one person who could prove you had nothing to do with Jacobi's murder. A person afraid to come forward with what she knew because she didn't know who to trust."

"An anonymous note written in plain English would've been more effective," Niall said.

"The floral messages were meant for Frankie, a rosarian."

"Floral messages left in a village overrun with plant experts," Frankie said. "Including, most likely, our murderer. Since they knew I wasn't the killer and knew Jacobi's murder had nothing to do with the Flower Shop Killer, they must've picked up on the real meaning of the bouquets straight away and figured out what Reston was trying to say."

"That Frankie needn't worry because she could clear his name."

"All right," Niall said, "I'll grant that plant people would decipher a flower code faster than a dumb guard. But how would the murderer know to go after Reston, specifically?"

"Because I led them to her," Gethsemane said. "Murderphile is a public website. You need an account to post messages but anyone can read the posts. I used Murderphile to lure a stalker into the open. The killer cyberstalked me on Murderphile to uncover a witness. Once they figured out which usernames to follow they would've known about the trap set at Our Lady. If they staked out the church and saw no one there but Frankie and gardaí, they could have made an educated guess that TheFlorist would come to me at Carrick Point. They hid out on the cliffs and waited for an opportunity to shoot. Damn."

"Don't," Niall said. "None of this is your fault. None of us had any reason to suspect the killer would head up to Carrick Point or that Reston would be in danger of anything other than being arrested. We thought Reston was the killer."

"Now that we know she didn't kill anyone," Gethsemane said, "we have to figure out who did."

"We?" Niall's turn to raise an eyebrow.

Gethsemane crossed her fingers behind her back. "I mean, Inspector Sutton has to figure out who did. Without interference from civilians."

"Uncross your fingers," Niall said. "I'm not thick. I've known you long enough to know bloody well if I try to leave you out of it, you'll start sleuthing as soon as my back's turned. The past few hours drove that message home. I won't make the same mistake twice. Not in one day at least."

Sleuthing. A step up from snooping. "To be fair, this time I didn't go looking for trouble. It found me."

"You didn't run from it when it showed up on your doorstep, though," Frankie said. "And since you know she'll—who am I kidding? I'm in this, too—we'll stay in the midst of the investigation, you may as well help us, Niall."

"It's Sutton's case."

"Don't tell him."

"I think he'll notice if we close his case for him, Frankie."

"Let him take the credit," Gethsemane said. "From his expression when he mentioned the Superintendent, I bet he'd appreciate a resolution handed to him wrapped up in a bow."

"He might, at that. The Superintendent's a wank—never mind." Niall rubbed his chin. "What were you thinking?"

She looked around at the people coming and going through the waiting area, some slumped in chairs in listless resignation, some pacing with anxiety and fear etched on their faces. "I'm thinking Carraigfaire's a better place to talk than a hospital waiting room." She led the way to the door. "Let's go."

Twenty

A quick shower, a change of clothes, and a thank you to a hovering Eamon, and Gethsemane joined Niall and Frankie in the study. Outside, the moss-covered cliffs took on a green-gold hue in the setting sun. They gave no hint of the near tragedy that had played out on their rocks a few hours earlier.

Frankie handed her a Waddell and Dobb. "The lady likes it neat."

"Thanks." She set the bourbon on the roll top desk and rummaged for pen and paper.

Eamon materialized next to her. "What're you doing?"

Frankie asked the same question.

With her back to the living, she shot Eamon a "be quiet" look. She answered Frankie. "Doing what you tell your students to do when they're stuck on a problem. Write down what you know, then work through each step of the problem until you arrive at a solution."

"A mathematical approach to crime solving," Niall said.

"Why not?" Gethsemane sat on the sofa, pen in one hand, bourbon in the other. "A puzzle's a puzzle, whether you're talking about numbers or suspects. Don't law enforcement officers write what they know on whiteboards and tape up pictures and draw arrows connecting one thing to another?"

Niall rolled his eyes.

"Unless you've got another suggestion. And I'm not being snarky. The question wasn't rhetorical."

"Get on with it, then. Start with the victims." Niall sat next to her on the sofa.

Frankie claimed the wing chair opposite. Eamon leaned against a bookcase.

Frankie checked his watch. "About three-quarters of an hour until Sutton makes good on his promise to show up here."

Gethsemane wrote, "Roderick Jacobi" and "Murdoch Collins" at the top of a sheet of paper. She thought for a moment, then wrote "Reston Flynn" off to one side.

"What do they have in common?" Niall asked.

"Jacobi owned Avar Pharmaceuticals. Collins worked for him. Jacobi entered a rose in the rose show. Collins helped him with his rose growing."

"And Reston?" asked Frankie. "You've got her name written there."

"She saw someone murder Jacobi. Other than that, I don't see a connection."

"Eyewitness to murder's enough of a connection," Niall said.

"By the way," Gethsemane said, "she is under garda protection, isn't she? Whoever tried to kill her will find out she survived soon enough, the way news travels in this village."

"Of course," Niall said. "Uniformed guards have been assigned to watch over her. Sutton wanted to assign some to you, as well, but I told him you'd have none of it."

"Gardaí to protect me or keep tabs on me?"

"Both," Niall said.

"Tell him you don't need some junior garda in his shiny uniform trotting after you like a lap dog," Eamon said. "You've got your own ghost to keep you out of trouble. Or, at least, to get you out of trouble when you get into it."

Good thing Eamon couldn't read minds. Her thoughts at that moment would have earned her an orb right in her ear. She ignored him. "Ellen Jacobi," she wrote in the center of the page.

"Jacobi's widow," Frankie said.

"She stands to inherit Jacobi's share of Avar, as well as rights to the rose patents. And she admitted she'd pay to have Jacobi killed. She hated him that much."

"Admitted to who?" Niall asked.

Gethsemane doodled in the paper's margin and avoided the rebuke she knew she'd see in his eyes. "Admitted to me."

"You didn't think to share that information with law enforcement?"

"Didn't I mention it? I'm sure I must have."

"Gethsemane Brown—"

Frankie rescued her. "Why would Ellen Jacobi kill Collins? Or pay someone to kill him?"

"I don't think Collins is thrilled with the idea of Ellen Jacobi being in charge of Avar. I overheard him talking to Karl Dietrich about control of the company. Arguing about it. Maybe Ellen decided a dead Chief Operating Officer was easier to negotiate with than a live one."

"You really think she'd have a man killed because she feared he'd do her out of a job?" Niall asked.

"Have you met Ellen Jacobi? I'm not sure she wouldn't have a man killed if he mussed her hair." She doodled a flower on the paper. "I also overheard Collins and Dietrich arguing with Gerrit Byrnes about a 'deal.'"

"Gerrit Byrnes?"

Frankie explained. "One of the Byrnes brothers. They own Belles Fleurs, the chief rivals to Ellen Jacobi's plant supply company. She's not the only plant supplier who'd kill someone they thought was trying to steal their plants."

"So," Gethsemane said, "she had double reason to want Collins dead: control of Avar Pharmaceuticals and Roderick's roses."

Niall stood. "Then we should go speak to the grieving widow. I'll text Bill and tell him where we're headed."

"We? You mean it this time?"

"As I said, I've learned my lesson. You're safer interviewing a murder suspect in the company of gardaí than you are up here on your own. If I left you behind you'd no doubt end up in a life and death battle with the killer at the top of Carrick Point Lighthouse before sunrise. Same goes for you, Frankie. You've been hanging around this one," he jerked his head toward Gethsemane, "long enough for her knack for finding danger to rub off on you. You can both consider me your unofficial garda protection."

Niall's phone played Gounod's "Funeral March" as they walked to his car.

"Alfred Hitchcock's theme," Frankie said. "A guard with a sense of humor."

Niall checked the message. "Sutton. He's located Ellen Jacobi. She's at the show grounds. He'll meet us there."

"He's cool with Frankie and me tagging along?"

"Didn't exactly tell him. He'll find out soon enough. Why court trouble?"

"A surprise attack's always much better," Frankie said.

Gethsemane snort laughed as she climbed into Niall's car.

Eamon appeared at her window. "I'll be waiting for you at the show grounds." He vanished as quickly as he'd appeared.

The evening's first stars shone over the bay. Gethsemane leaned from the window and counted them. "Isn't it late for Ellen to still be at the show grounds?"

"Nah," Frankie said from the backseat. "There's always work to do behind the scenes at a flower show. Questions from the public, complaints from contestants, inquiries from the media, making sure displays stay fresh, making sure no one vandalizes the specimens, making sure speakers show up at the proper venue at the proper time, making sure celebrities get their photo ops and their green M&M's or whatever perks they've demanded. Takes a lot of work to make a show seem effortless. Even if the festivities are canceled, there's a lot of work to do. More work. Refunds to process, complaints, protests, press statements..."

"Ellen's a sponsor, not a show organizer," Gethsemane said.

"Well," Frankie said, "that's true. She'd still have work to do after the 'Lucia di Lammermoor' disaster, though. That was an expensive loss. She's probably working triple time trying to minimize the financial losses. She'd also have to see to beefing up security to prevent any more roses from being destroyed."

"That's what Jacobi was up to in your garden the day he was killed."

"What was?"

"Reston said Jacobi brought the hedge shears. He must have found where you kept them and planned to use them to destroy the 'Sandra Sechrest'."

"Wanker," Frankie said. "Yowling gobshite. Even money whether his widow or I wanted him dead more."

"Watch it, Frankie." Niall warned. "You're not completely in the clear until the real killer's in custody."

"If it's Ellen, I'll happily contribute to her legal defense fund."

No one spoke during the remainder of the drive into the village. Niall found his attention on the road, his tight grip on the wheel the only sign of tension. Frankie hunched in the backseat, arms crossed, brow creased in a deep frown. He radiated anger as tangible as one of Eamon's blue auras. Gethsemane couldn't tell whether the anger stemmed from the idea of being suspected of murder or the idea of the unlamented Roderick Jacobi using his own garden tool to destroy his prize rosebush. A glance in the rearview mirror told her this was not the time to ask. Besides, something nagged at her. She was overlooking something important, something someone told her. What was it?

The moon had taken over the sun's position by the time they pulled into the show ground parking lot. Niall maneuvered into a space next to a car he identified as Sutton's. Sutton fiddled with a cigarette as he leaned against a tree a few feet away.

"What're they doing here?" he asked Niall when Gethsemane and Frankie approached.

"Couldn't leave them way up there on Carrick Point, unprotected," Niall said. "Killer's on the loose. Your words, remember?"

Sutton grunted and aimed the cigarette at his lips. Gethsemane stared. He grunted again and ground it into the dirt beneath the tree. "Kids made me quit. Are making me quit."

Gethsemane pointed at the sponsors' tent area. "Jacobi and Fortnum are set up over there, inside the big one." Lights inside the tent illuminated it like a luminaria.

"You two stay behind Niall and me." Sutton led the way to the entrance.

Eamon's disembodied voice spoke in Gethsemane's ear. "He's just going to march through the front door? Full-on frontal assault? As much subtlety as an erupting volcano?"

She hung back so she could whisper a response. "No one's expecting us. Maybe he's counting on the element of surprise. You know, like the Spanish Inquisition. No one expects the Spanish Inquisition."

"This is no time for Monty Python jokes," Eamon said.

"What's that?" Frankie asked over his shoulder. He slowed

his pace to match hers.

"I was just wondering if someone—we—shouldn't watch the back door to make sure Ellen doesn't slip out." Someone like a ghost with the power to blast people off of cliffs. "In case she sees Sutton and Niall coming in the front."

"Sutton did order us to stay behind them," Frankie said. "Behind the tent is 'behind' them."

She hoped Eamon took hints as well as Frankie. "On my signal."

Music teacher and math teacher slowed until the distance between them and the gardaí widened to a few yards. Niall and Sutton veered left toward the tent's main entrance. Gethsemane jerked her head toward the rear, where she'd seen Ellen and Glendon in a clinch. She and Frankie veered right. A whiff of leather and soap told her Eamon had, too.

She and Frankie crouched in the darkness. The faint sounds of Niall and Sutton debating their entrance strategy drifted from the other side of the tent. The voices stopped. Seconds passed: five, ten, twenty. They felt like a million. Her knees ached. Hiding in bushes wasn't a game for anyone over thirty.

At last, Sutton announced at a decibel level that could be overheard in Cork, "Garda!"

The sounds of a commotion arose in the tent. Something heavy—furniture?—hit the floor. Angry shouts increased the cacophony.

Ellen's irate voice reverberated above the others. "What the bloody hell do you think you're bloody doing, you bloody wankers?"

"Stop! Wait!" Niall and Sutton shouted simultaneously.

Footsteps ran toward the back door. Another crash and Glendon Byrnes tumbled outside. He clutched his belt in one hand and his suit jacket in the other.

"Stop!" Sutton's voice sounded after him.

"Stop!" Frankie yelled. He jumped from his hiding place and launched himself at the fleeing Byrnes brother.

Glendon threw his jacket over Frankie's head and pushed him backward into a potted shrub.

Gethsemane tensed, ready to run, as Glendon neared her. Before she could move, Eamon materialized in a blaze of blue and hurled an orb at Glendon's knee. Glendon howled in pain and clutched his patella. Eamon snapped a low-hanging branch at Glendon's head. Glendon went down and stayed down.

"Did you kill him?" Gethsemane peered down at the motionless form.

A muffled, "You mean did he kill me?" came from under the suit jacket as Frankie fought to disentangle himself.

"Nah," Eamon said, "Just knocked him a good one." A zap of energy to Glendon's foot elicited a moan.

Ellen, her hair loosed from its usual bun and her tailored blouse untucked and buttoned wrong, spilled out of the tent. Niall and Sutton stumbled out after her. Their hair awry and their ties askew gave them the appearance of having battled a round with a wildcat and lost.

Ellen screamed when she saw her lover. "Glen!" she shouted. "What have you done to him?" She evaded the gardaí's grasp and flew at Gethsemane.

Gethsemane flashed back to her days as a state champion high school softball player standing behind the plate with an opponent running straight at her. She held her ground until the last second before collision, then stepped aside. Ellen's momentum carried her forward, past Gethsemane. Her heel caught on a vine that crossed her path with the aid of a finger wag from Eamon. She landed face-down a foot away from Gethsemane and the now-conscious Glendon.

Sutton bellowed, "Enough!" He hoisted Ellen by an arm while Niall helped Glendon to his feet. "Inside."

Gethsemane and Frankie trooped into the tent after Sutton, Niall, and the two heads of plant supply empires. She and Frankie leaned against Ellen's desk as Sutton and Niall righted chairs and pushed Ellen and Glendon into them.

"You've no right—" Ellen began.

"Shut it," Sutton said. "This is a criminal investigation which gives me the right to ask questions. You have the right not to answer them but not answering won't do you any favors. If you've got any sense, you'll talk."

"Which is it, Inspector?" Glendon tugged at his shirt cuffs and swiped his silver hair back into place. Dignity somewhat restored, he straightened up tall in the chair and looked down his nose as best he could from a seated position. "Shut it or answer your questions? She can't do both."

Sutton stepped forward. Niall put a hand on his arm. Gethsemane suspected Glendon Byrnes would have learned exactly what the Dunmullach Garda thought of smart-mouthed suspects if Sutton hadn't had any witnesses. The smack in the face from Eamon's tree branch would have felt like a love pat. Time for a distraction.

She stepped in front of Ellen. "Why'd you kill your husband, Mrs. Jacobi? For control of the pharmaceutical company or control of the rose patents?" She looked back and forth between Ellen and Glendon. "Or for true love?"

Ellen snorted. "Don't be daft. You think I'd risk life in prison for him?" She gestured toward a wounded-looking Glendon. "For anyone? True love's for suckers. Isn't that right?" She turned to face Frankie. "How's Yseult these days?"

Frankie shrugged. "Last I heard she was running around with a London billionaire selling fake documents to smugglers trading looted artifacts out of Syria. We don't really keep in touch."

Sutton edged Gethsemane aside and glared down at Ellen.

"So you killed him for his company? Or for his flowers?"

"I didn't kill my husband, Inspector." The ice in Ellen's voice made Gethsemane shiver. "Nor did I have him killed, to anticipate your next question. I'm not sorry he's dead but I had nothing to do with him ending up that way."

"Can anyone," Sutton glanced at Glendon, "vouch for your whereabouts at the time of your husband's murder, Mrs. Jacobi?"

"More likely than not," Ellen said. "Tell me precisely when he was killed and I'll have my assistant check my schedule."

Nice dodge. Don't say where you were because you don't know when the murder occurred. Gethsemane didn't envy any prosecutor who ended up questioning Ellen Jacobi on the witness stand.

"What about Murdoch Colllins?" Sutton asked.

"Wasn't poor Murdoch run over in front of the Athaneum this morning? I haven't been anywhere near the theater today." Ellen smirked. "I don't need my assistant to check my schedule to know that."

"What reason would she have to kill Collins?" Glendon asked.

"What reason would your brother have to offer Collins a deal?" Gethsemane asked him.

Glendon stared, slack-jawed and wide-eyed.

Ellen reddened and turned on her lover. She spoke through clenched teeth, each staccato word an accusation. "Yes, Glen, darling, why would your brother Gerry offer Murdoch a deal?"

"What kind of deal?" Sutton asked.

Everyone looked at Gethsemane.

"I don't know all the details," she said. "I overheard Gerrit Byrnes, Murdoch Collins, and Karl Dietrich talking in the hallway at the Athaneum. Gerrit tried to convince Karl and Murdoch to accept some sort of deal, telling them it was the best they'd get. Murdoch complained it wasn't worth the risk for what he offered."

Ellen swung her legs around ninety degrees in her chair to face Glendon. She leaned forward, almost touching him, and glared through narrowed slits of eyes.

He shrank back and looked up at Niall and Sutton as though begging for rescue. "I, I swear, Ellen," he said without looking at her, "I don't know anything about any deals. I have no idea what Gerrit might have been talking about, nor why he'd be talking to Collins or Dietrich. The only deal I know about is the one I made with you." He glanced at her, then quickly looked away, as though he'd looked directly at a solar eclipse. "I swear I'd never cross you."

Niall stepped between the lovers. Ellen swung back around in her chair to face forward. She crossed her arms and fixed her gaze on the far wall of the tent. Her pursed lips suggested she intended to heed Sutton's advice about exercising her right to remain silent.

"What deal did you and Mrs. Jacobi make, Mr. Byrnes?" Niall asked.

Glendon kept his gaze on the floor. "I planned to sell Ellen a controlling interest in Belles Fleurs."

"Did your brother agree to this?"

Glendon shook his head.

"Did your brother know about this?"

Glendon shook his head again.

"You were going to cut your brother out of the business? Make Mrs. Jacobi the senior partner?"

"No," Glendon said, "I was going to cut myself out of the business, go out on my own, start my own garden design company. Belles Fleurs is an emotional and financial drag. Jacobi and Fortnum is a much larger company and can manage Belles Fleurs' assets much more ably than I can."

"Meaning Gerrit would either have to sell his part of the business to Jacobi and Fortnum or live with his rival being his new boss."

Glendon nodded.

"What was Mrs. Jacobi's part of the deal?" Sutton asked. "What was she going to give you?"

"Patent rights to 'Lucia di Lammermoor.'"

Her husband's rose. "All the more reason to want your husband out of the way," Gethsemane said. And dead was certainly out of the way.

"I told you, I had nothing to do with his murder. The idea of selling the patent didn't even occur to me until after Roderick's death."

"Why should we believe you?" Sutton asked.

"You can talk to my solicitor in the morning. She'll tell you that Roderick faced a lawsuit, one he was probably going to lose, over the rights to 'Lucia di Lammermoor.' He'd stolen the rose, like nearly every other rose, or medicine, he took credit for developing. You can speak to that, can't you Mr. Grennan?"

Frankie grunted.

Ellen continued. "Anyway, the daughter of the rose grower Roderick stole 'Lucia di Lammermoor' from makes me look as timid as a dormouse. She tracked down her father's former garden assistant at an ashram in Borneo. The assistant gave the daughter copies of plant journals and correspondence with her father that proved he'd developed the hybrid. In addition to suing Roderick for everything he's worth and, quite possibly, everything I'm worth as well, the daughter interested a blogger or journalist or some such person in the story. They intended to make a podcast or documentary about Roderick's intellectual thievery and broadcast the premier at next year's Chelsea Flower Show. No one would believe I wasn't involved in the theft. Jacobi and Fortnum would have been ruined. We'd never have recovered from the scandal."

"And you saw your husband's death as an opportune time to rid yourself of a liability—'Lucia di Lammermoo.'"

"You are as smart as you look, Dr. Brown," Ellen said.

"You didn't mention a lawsuit, Ellen," Glendon said.

"Of course I didn't, you horny gobshite. You'd never have agreed to the deal if you'd known it was encumbered."

Tears formed in Glendon's eyes and his lip quivered. "You mean you planned to take control of Belles Fleurs and leave me holding the bag with a ruinous lawsuit?"

Ellen shrugged.

No honor among thieves even when the thieves were lovers. Or brothers. "Gerrit didn't know about the lawsuit, did he?" Gethsemane asked. "I bet the deal he tried to make with Murdoch and Gerrit was for 'Lucia di Lammermoor.' He tried to steal the rose for Belles Fleurs, not realizing you were about to sell Belles Fleurs out from under him."

"Gerrit and I haven't seen eye to eye on the business, or anything else, for any number of years," Glendon said. "I'm sure if he'd gotten his hands on 'Lucia di Lammermoor,' he'd have found a way to exclude me from any benefit gained from the acquisition."

"None of this proves you didn't kill your husband, Mrs. Jacobi," Sutton said. "Get rid of him and his tainted rose all at the same time, why not?"

"I rather think it's up to the prosecution counsel to prove I killed Roderick, not to me to prove I didn't, Inspector."

A shouted expletive interrupted the interrogation. A large orchid in a delicate celadon pot teetered on a stand near Frankie's elbow. He fumbled with the exotic flower balanced on the edge of its perch and managed to right it before it crashed to the floor.

"Be careful with that," Ellen said. "It was a gift. One not

209 FATALITY IN F

easily replaced."

Something nagged Gethsemane She turned to Ellen. "Mrs. Jacobi, how involved are you with Avar Pharmaceuticals?"

"I'm not involved in the day-to-day operations. My work with Jacobi and Fortnum occupies most of my time. But, I keep abreast of what's going on at Avar."

"You'll become more involved now that your husband's gone."

"Yes, of course. I'll be the majority shareholder. But I'll rely on Avar's board of directors to keep things operating."

"You have plans for the future of Avar?"

"Plans? What do you mean?"

"I understand Avar shifted production away from the manufacture of many of its older medicines in favor of the development of new gene therapies."

"The company's in the process of transitioning, yes. Many pharmaceutical firms are making the shift. Gene therapy holds great promise for the future of curing disease and ending suffering."

"You sound almost sincere, Mrs. Jacobi," Sutton said.

Ellen glared at the garda. "I am sincere, Inspector. I make no claims to sainthood but I'm not a sociopath. We're talking about human lives, not plants. I'm proud of Avar's contributions to the improvement of health and well-being."

"Who orchestrated the shift from old therapeutics to new?" Gethsemane asked.

"Lots of people," Ellen said. "Gene therapy is a major undertaking."

"The future of pharma. Was Murdoch Collins involved in the transition?"

"Of course Murdoch was involved. He championed new technologies. He envisioned Avar as the leader in gene therapeutics."

"What about Avar's scientists? How did they feel? Were they as much in favor of the company's new direction as Murdoch?"

"Most of them, yes" Ellen said. "After all, they are scientists. They're at the forefront of progress."

"Most of them. Not all."

"Where are you going with this?" Sutton interjected.

"I heard rumors, Inspector, that not all of Avar's scientists were enthusiastic about the company's new focus. Some were unhappy their drugs were being abandoned or sold to other manufacturers."

"Change is difficult," Ellen said. "More difficult for some than others."

"More difficult for those who had developed non-profitable, orphan drugs? Drugs expensive to produce because their base compounds are hard to come by? Who decided which drugs got the ax from the Avar formulary?"

"Several people were involved in those decisions. The board, scientists—"

"Accountants?"

Ellen shrugged.

"Your husband and Murdoch Collins?"

"Of course the Chief Executive and Chief Operating Officers would have input."

Gethsemane walked over to the orchid and ran a finger along one of its fleshy leaves. "Orchids are tropical plants, aren't they?"

"Some varieties, yes. Not all of them."

"How about this one?"

"Yes. That particular variety is found in the tropical rainforest. The Amazon Basin, specifically."

"You brought it back from the Amazon yourself?"

"No, as I said, it was a gift. From Karl Dietrich. He found it on one of his ethnobotanical expeditions. Why the interest in my houseplant?"

"Karl's a botanist. He developed plant-based pharmaceuticals for Avar. He's been with the company for a long time, hasn't he?"

"Decades."

"How does Karl feel about change?"

Ellen hesitated. "Karl is old school. Skeptical about gene therapy. He'll remind anyone who will listen that plants have been used to improve human existence almost since human existence began. Gene therapy lacks plant therapy's track record."

"How many of the drugs Karl developed over his decades with Avar were slated to be sold?"

"A few of them." Another hesitation. "Many of them."

"Your husband was fond of cheating people out of their rights. Did he try to cheat Karl out of his rights to royalties on the drugs he devoted most of his career developing for Avar?"

Ellen protested. "I had nothing to do with that. Karl's work, and the work of the other scientists, saved lives. They deserved their share of the profits."

So Ellen had limits. She'd cheat someone out of profit for a rose but not for a medication. Roderick, apparently, had no such scruples. "Roderick was cheating Karl."

"Wait," Niall asked, "are you saying Roderick Jacobi and Murdoch Collins were selling off Avar Pharmaceuticals' assets, including those developed by Karl Dietrich, but were cutting Karl out of the deal?"

"Dietrich would have lost a fortune," Sutton said.

"But with someone new in charge of Avar, someone more sympathetic," Gethsemane touched the orchid's leaf again, "Karl's fortune might have reversed."

"Are you suggesting Karl Dietrich killed my husband and

Murdoch Collins?"

"Not suggesting, Mrs. Jacobi, stating. Roderick stabbed Karl in the back, figuratively, so Karl stabbed him in the back literally."

"Then used my car to kill Murdoch?" Frankie asked.

"You were already the prime suspect in Roderick's murder. Why not frame you for Murdoch's? He didn't know you had an alibi. With both Roderick and Murdoch out of the way, and someone sympathetic to his work in control of Avar, he must've figured he'd be fairly compensated, even if he couldn't save his drugs from being sold."

"What about Reston?" Frankie asked. "Karl shot at her?"

Gethsemane nodded. "He must have known he'd been witnessed killing Roderick. He just couldn't track down who'd seen him. Until the garda station when I showed him the Murderphile website and told him about the set up."

"You weren't to know," Eamon said. Which didn't make her feel better.

"Where is Dietrich?" Sutton asked. No one answered. "When's the last time anyone saw him? Mrs. Jacobi?"

"I'm not his mother, his wife, nor his secretary," Ellen said. "I don't keep track of his comings and goings. I don't remember when I last saw him."

"The garda station was the last time I saw him," Gethsemane said.

"Has he tried to contact you, Mrs. Jacobi?" Sutton asked.

"No." She looked at the other faces in the room and repeated her statement. "No, he hasn't."

"You'll tell us if he does," Sutton said. "Right away."

"I'm sure he won't," Ellen said. "But, yes, if by some unlikely chance he contacts me, I'll let you know right away."

"Does this mean we aren't under arrest?" Glendon asked. "We're free to go?"

"For now," Sutton said. "Some gardaí from the Fraud Squad may want words with you in the near future but that's not my department." He allowed Ellen and Glendon to go after extracting their promises not to leave the village then turned his attention to Gethsemane and Frankie. "As for you two..."

"You've no reason to hold us," Gethsemane said.

"There's always protective custody," Sutton said, "for your own protection."

"Please tell me he's kidding," she said to Niall.

"Karl's not likely to go after Sissy or Frankie," Niall said. "He's more likely to try to flee the village."

"You have a point. I'd better put some guards at the train and bus stations and along the road between here and Cork. He'll probably try for the airport." Sutton ran both hands over his hair. "The Super's going to love this. Why'd I quit smoking?"

"For your kids," Gethsemane offered. She earned a scowl in return.

"Don't tease him," Eamon said. "He's having a rough night."

"I'll drive them back up to the cottage, Bill," Niall said.

Sutton thanked him. He pulled out his phone and began making calls on his way out of the tent.

"C'mon, you two." Niall headed in the same direction.

"You may as well drop me off at Erasmus Hall," Frankie said. "I don't need to hide out at Carraigfaire with Reston in the hospital and Karl in Sutton's sights."

"Because being brought home by the garda at night won't require any explanations in the morning," Gethsemane said.

"When you put it that way," Frankie said, "one more night at the cottage won't hurt." He and Gethsemane followed Niall out to his car.

Twenty-One

Silence filled the car on the ride back to Carraigfaire. Gethsemane leaned her head against the cool glass of the window and stared into the darkness. Where was Karl? Was he lurking out there somewhere, hiding, waiting for—what? Another chance to get rid of Reston? She was the only real witness against him. His motive for killing Roderick and Murdoch was clear—money—but what evidence was there? She kicked herself for showing Karl the true crime website. She even let him help her choose a screen name. How stupid.

"Are you all right?" Niall asked her.

"Yeah," she answered without looking away from the window. "Just wondering if he's out there. Karl, I mean."

"If he's smart, he headed to Cork for the airport as soon as he ran from the lighthouse after shooting at you," Frankie chimed in from the back seat.

"No train until day after tomorrow," Niall reminded him, "and bus service stopped before noon today. Won't start again until nine in the morning."

"He could drive to Cork."

"If he stole a car," Gethsemane said. "I doubt he'd risk calling a taxi."

"No stolen cars and we're watching the road."

"Did you check with the taxi dispatch?" Frankie asked. "Criminals aren't always smart."

"We've alerted the taxi company," Niall said.

"Ellen's smart. If she'd killed her husband and Murdoch, the prosecutor never would have proved it." Gethsemane kept her fears about the likelihood of the prosecutor's success in proving Karl guilty to herself. "I assume someone's guarding Reston at the hospital."

"Of course," Niall said.

"Do you really think he'd go after her again?" Frankie asked. "Why risk it?"

"She's the only witness against him," Gethsemane said. "Karl's well-known, a respected scientist. Where could he hide if he ran? There's no statute of limitations on murder. He'd spend the rest of his life looking over his shoulder. As long as Reston lived, she could give evidence against him."

"Think Ellen and Karl could be in it together?" Frankie asked. "They both benefitted from the deaths. Maybe Ellen put Karl up to it."

"We'll ask him when we find him," Niall said.

The opening notes of Beethoven's "Fifth Symphony" rang from Gethsemane's bag. "My push notification tone," she explained as she fished in her bag.

She pulled the phone out and read the notice: *g_gardener has a Murderphile clue.*

"Who's it from?" Frankie asked.

"Someone on Murderphile dot com." She logged into the site.

"You should delete your profile," Niall said. "Do you really want a bunch of murder fanatics posting messages to your wall?"

"Murderphile has mailboxes."

"Whatever. Mailbox or wall, you're courting trouble by

inviting crime-obsessed misfits into your life."

"Maybe it's a message from Reston, telling us how her surgery went."

"She's typing messages with one arm in a cast?"

"Or, maybe not." She opened her mailbox.

Garish red font, all caps, danced across her screen: *I HAVE ELLEN.*

She stared at her phone, trying to process what she saw. She re-read the words. I. Have. Ellen. Was this a joke? Her finger shook as she tapped the screen, trying to reveal the sender's name.

Niall looked over at her and pulled off to the side of the road. "What is it? What's happened?"

She showed him and Frankie the message.

"Someone's codding you," Frankie said. He looked less convinced than he sounded.

"By using Ellen's name? How would anyone on this site, except Reston, know that I know Ellen?"

"Can you tell who sent it?" Niall asked.

"I'm trying to..." She held up the sender's screen name: "Rosen aus dem Suden."

Niall read the name aloud. "Is that German?"

She nodded. "It translates to 'Roses of the South,' the Strauss piece I was conducting for the rose show's opening ceremony. You know who this is? Who it must be?"

The men shook their heads.

"It's Karl. Karl Dietrich. He's German. He knows 'Roses of the South' was the scheduled performance. He knows my screen name on this site is 'g_gardener.' He helped me come up with it. Karl has Ellen Jacobi."

Niall gripped the steering wheel and stared straight ahead. "Answer him."

Gethsemane stared at her phone for a moment, her finger

hovered over the screen. She typed: *What do U want?*

A moment, then the response: *Safe passage.*

She typed: *How can I help?*

Response: *Your garda beau.*

She ignored the error. This was no time to point out the inaccuracy of Karl's assumption about her relationship status. *Where's Ellen?* she typed.

No message appeared.

Where's Ellen?

Safe passage, was the only reply.

Gethsemane asked Niall, "What do I do?"

"Tell him 'yes.' Find out where he is."

She typed: *Where can we meet?*

Carnock. Old asylum. Rose garden. You and O'Reilly.

Frankie leaned over Gethsemane's shoulder. "He must have found my roses."

"You've been up there recently, Frankie," Niall said. "You know the layout well?"

Frankie said he did.

"So do I," Gethsemane said. "I'm pretty sure I left the door unlocked last time I was there." She'd pried the door open. And neither she nor her rescuer bothered to tidy up as they escaped the flames.

"Not much of any doors left after the fire," Frankie said.

"Are you up to this, Sissy?" Niall asked. "You don't have to go."

"I'm going. Karl is expecting both of us. Ellen's life depends on him thinking we're cooperating. I may not like Ellen but I don't want her dead."

"He didn't actually say he'd kill her," Frankie said. "It's possible she's in it with him. That's the kind of stunt Yseult would pull."

"You want to take that chance? If she's a real hostage, her

life's in danger. That's how hostage-taking works. No one would give in to your demands if you only threatened to give your hostages a stern talking to."

"All right, then." Niall keyed the ignition and turned the car back the way they'd come. "Off to Gologtha."

Twenty-Two

Gethsemane checked her phone again. No new messages. Karl was a killer of few words.

Visions of her first and, until now, last trip to the abandoned St. Dymphna's Insane Asylum flashed into her mind. Reciting the batting average of every Negro League baseball player for the entire 1932 season failed to keep the memories away. The lonely bike ride up the desolate hill, oblivious to the person following her. The overgrown brush. The boarded-up doors. Her heart beat faster as Niall's car drove through the darkness, bringing her closer to the place where real danger first invaded her orderly world. She traced a finger along her scar. She'd led an ambitious, high-achieving, controlled, upper-middle class life until the moment someone slammed her head against a metal shelf and left her to die in the fire they started in the hospital file room. Until her lungs filled with the acrid smoke that nearly killed her, setbacks and obstacles she'd encountered had only been problems to fix, puzzles to solve with the single-minded determination passed down through generations of strong women. Women who suffered untold indignities with class and grace and who sacrificed every day to spare their children and their children's children the grief they bore and to give them an easier, safer existence. Until that day at

Carnock—Golgotha—it hadn't occurred to her she might land in a dark place from which there was no escape to the light on the other side.

"Snap out of it." Eamon's voice spoke in her ear. Niall had stopped the car at the foot of the isolated hill south of the village proper. Eamon materialized outside the window. "You've faced worse than Karl Dietrich and you've faced it alone. This time, I'm here."

Her heart slowed a few beats. She relaxed fists she hadn't realized she clenched. Eamon had once committed himself to St. Dymphna's which meant he'd be able to go inside. She opened the car door.

Niall reached across her and pulled it shut. "You don't have to do this. Change your mind. I can go alone."

"With Karl God-knows-where up there in the dark and possibly armed? You'd never see him coming. You need me to watch your back. I don't want you dead even more than I don't want Ellen dead. And Karl specified both of us."

Frankie put a hand on her shoulder. "I've got faith in you, Fearless Brown. And I've got both your backs."

"Where's your rose garden, Frankie?"

He pointed into the night. "South side of the building in the clearing near the edge of the woods." He leaned out a car window. "There's enough moonlight to make it out."

Niall handed Frankie his phone. "I texted Sutton. He's on his way. Wait here for him. I'll yell when Sissy and Mrs. Jacobi are safe. Then come running to lead Sutton up to your garden. Ready?"

Frankie pulled his head back in the car. "Ready."

"Ready." Gethsemane opened the car door and stepped out.

"Ready." Eamon juggled a handful of blue orbs.

She allowed herself a small grin. As competent a garda as Niall was and as intrepid a friend as Frankie was, you couldn't beat supernatural back up.

Gethsemane crept single file behind Niall toward the Carnock's summit, keeping the asylum in sight the entire time. Even in the dark she could see the crumbling, burned remains of the gothic edifice that had once housed Dunmullach's mentally ill. The grim had become grimmer. Edgar Allan Poe would have had a literary field day out here.

Niall stopped without warning. Gethsemane bumped into him. She yelped as Eamon bumped into her, sending an electric thrill through her shoulders.

"Ssh." Niall stepped off the path and crouched behind a tree. He scanned the inky horizon. "I don't see anyone."

Gethsemane pulled out her phone and opened the browser to Murderphile. *We're here*, she typed.

The reply came a moment later: *Rose garden*. She showed the phone to Niall.

"Frankie said south side of the building. That way." He pointed to the left at an area of darkness that seemed less dense than those surrounding it. He crept forward.

"Be right back," Eamon said. He vanished.

Gethsemane hurried to catch up with Niall.

"Stay close," he said. "Karl could be anywhere."

Eamon reappeared beside her. "Actually, he's hiding on the steps leading down into the laundry room at the back edge of Frankie's garden."

"Where's Ellen?" she whispered to Eamon.

Niall answered her. "She could be anywhere, too. If she's his hostage, not his accomplice, he's probably stashed her somewhere inside the ruins."

"You don't think he'd..." She couldn't make herself say it.

"Kill her? Not if he didn't have to. So far, the only people he's killed were two men who tried to cheat him out of his life's work. He injured Reston but she's alive. And we know who he is now. He doesn't need to keep his identity secret."

"So it doesn't matter if Ellen can identify him. Which improves her chances of survival."

"This way." Niall veered off the path.

"No," Gethsemane said, "this way." She started in a direction to the right of the one Niall had taken. "There's a hillock that will put us on higher ground. We'll be able to look down on Karl instead of Karl being able to look down on us."

"You sound as if you know where he's hiding."

"I, um, I remember a stairwell at the back edge of the clearing where it meets the building. Perfect place to hide and watch someone come up the path. That's where I would be if I was Karl." She took the lead.

Niall followed. "So, you think like a murderer now?"

"No," she said over her shoulder.

Eamon shushed her. "Do ya want Karl to hear ya?"

She lowered her voice to a whisper and repeated her answer. "No."

"You needn't whisper," Niall said. "I don't think Karl can hear us up here."

They climbed. Gethsemane looked back toward the asylum and squinted into the darkness, trying to glimpse any movement in the shadows surrounding the abandoned, overgrown building. Or glimpse the moonlight glinting off a gun barrel. Or did that only happen in movies?

Without warning, the rocky ground shifted beneath her foot. She swore and stumbled as pebbles skittered.

Niall grabbed her arm. "Careful," he and Eamon said in unison. "Are you all right?"

Gethsemane regained her balance. "I'm fine. Embarrassed, but fine." Maybe moonlight gleaming off gun metal only happened in the movies but the heroine tripping as she crept through the woods trying to evade the bad guy apparently happened for real.

"You've not twisted your ankle?" Niall squatted and reached for her foot.

"No, I'm fine. Seriously." She looked around. Nothing but hulking shapes distinguished from their surroundings only by gradient of blackness. Every bramble and vine seemed to be a monster looming in the night, ready to grab her and drag her away. "Where's Karl?" she asked, intending the question for Eamon.

Niall answered as he stood. "Probably not hiding on the laundry stairs anymore. He must have heard us by now and know we're here. I think we should—" Niall stepped forward— And went down with a yelp as a large rock shifted loose under his foot. Niall and the rock tumbled down the hill and out of sight.

"Niall!" Gethsemane yelled.

"O'Reilly!" Eamon yelled. Then he swore. "Damn, he can't hear me."

Gethsemane yelled louder, to hell with Karl. The inspector didn't answer.

Eamon vanished. Gethsemane scrambled down after Niall, thoughts of Karl's whereabouts replaced by visions of her friend with a broken leg, a cracked skull, lying unconscious, or, or...She sucked in her breath and froze at the foot of the hillock. Niall lay prone. Not moving. She stepped toward him. "Niall?" she whispered.

Eamon materialized beside her, making her jump. She lost her balance for the second time that night. She gasped as a blast of energy from a tiny blue orb hit her in the side and pushed her back the other way. She steadied herself and rubbed the spot where the orb had hit. It stung.

Niall stirred and moaned. Gethsemane rushed to help him stand. "Are you all right?"

"I'm fine." Niall worked a shoulder and massaged his neck. "Embarrassed." The moon cast enough light to see his dimpled grin. "But fine."

Gethsemane flinched as a light a hundred times brighter than the moon flashed in her face.

A man's voice sounded from behind the light. "Thank you for your promptness."

Karl. Gethsemane shielded her eyes with her hand. The light dipped toward the ground. Karl held a flashlight. A large one. The kind bad guys in movies used to club people over the head. Time to stop watching movies.

"Where's Mrs. Jacobi?" Niall asked.

"First things first, Inspector," Karl said. "How are you going to get me safely to the Cork airport and onto a plane out of the country?"

"First, you show me Mrs. Jacobi's okay," Niall countered.

Leather and soap teased Gethsemane's nose, followed by Eamon's, "I'll find her. Keep him talking," in her ear.

"You're not in charge, Inspector O'Reilly," Karl said. "I'll thank you to remember that and not try my patience."

Gethsemane stepped forward. "I'll swap places with Mrs. Jacobi."

"The bloody hell you will." She didn't need daylight to see the storm clouds in Niall's eyes. "Have you effing lost your mind?"

"How gallant, Dr. Brown," Karl said. "Why would I accept your offer?"

Gethsemane swept an arm in a grand gesture to take in the garden, the woods, and the remains of the asylum. "Because Ellen Jacobi is trussed up like a Christmas goose somewhere inside or tied to a tree in the woods or down a hole someplace and it'll take time to retrieve her. Time you don't have because you know damn well at least three-quarters of the gardaí in Dunmullach are waiting for a cue signaling the civilians are safe so they can rush in and arrest you for enough crimes to fill a library shelf-worth of legal books. You know you need a hostage if you have any hope of getting out of here. You don't want him," she jerked her head toward Niall, "because he's younger than you and taller than you and stronger than you and more trouble than he's worth. I, on the other hand, am about your height and only a third of your size and I'm a girl."

"What you're not is the full shilling," Niall said. "Will you please shut it and let me handle this?"

"What is it with men, Karl? A woman makes a perfectly logical suggestion but, because she's a woman, the men in the room think she's crazy or annoying or not very smart or all of the above. They tell her to sit down and be quiet. Why do you men do that?"

Niall's jaw tightened and a vein popped out on his temple. "Now is not the time for a feminist screed." His voice rose a few decibels. "This has nothing to do with you being a woman. This is about you being a civilian, regardless of how clever and fearless and well-meaning, and me being an actual fecking garda who is trained to—"

Eamon materialized. "Found her. Up there." He pointed to the asylum roof. The moon shone on a figure, just visible from the hillock, perched in a gap in a crumbling parapet, dangerously close to a fatal plunge to the ground. "Tied to a chair. Gagged. Mercifully."

"About time," she said aloud.

"Thank you, Eamon," the ghost mimicked her Virginia accent, "for finding the hostage." He winked out.

Niall stopped mid-rant and frowned down at her. "About time for what?"

"About time for both of you to be silent. I warned you about trying my patience," Karl said. "I accept Dr. Brown's generous offer to take Mrs. Jacobi's place. You will please come with me, Dr. Brown."

Niall grabbed her arm. "No, she won't."

"I'm afraid I must insist." A small pistol appeared in Karl's free hand. The moonlight did not glint off the dull metal.

Gethsemane forced herself not to think about the previous time a murderer pointed a gun at her. "Is that what you used to shoot Reston?"

Karl raised the flashlight and shone the beam in Niall's face. He held the gun steady in his other hand. "This? Of course not. It doesn't have the range to shoot someone on the ground from the top of the lighthouse." He aimed the gun at Niall. "In case you're wondering, Inspector, you are, however, quite within its range."

Niall raised his hands. "Don't do anything you can't take back, Dietrich."

Gethsemane scanned the area for something to use as a weapon while Niall tried to talk Karl into putting down his gun. She spied it near the stairs—a hoe, its blade up and facing Karl. Never again would she scold Frankie for not putting up his garden tools.

She rushed forward and stomped the blade. The handle flew up and smacked Karl hard in the face. He staggered. Gethsemane grabbed the hoe and slammed the head down on Karl's forearm. He cried out and dropped the gun. Niall rushed forward and tackled him.

"Garda!" The shout rose from behind them. Sutton came into view from the woods, followed by a half-dozen uniformed gardaí and Frankie.

"Sorry I didn't wait for your cue, Niall." The math teacher helped his friend up as the other gardaí took control of Karl. "As soon as Sutton and crew arrived I took them the long way 'round the back."

"Sometimes, Frankie," Niall brushed himself off, "I'm glad no one listens to me."

Gethsemane approached the two men. "Someone please listen to me." She pointed to the roof. "Ellen Jacobi needs help."

"Hey, Bill," Niall said, "It's your case. You want to handle that?"

Sutton looked where Gethsemane pointed. He alternated swear words with names of uniformed gardaí. Some ran to aid Ellen while one called for an ambulance.

Niall squinted at Gethsemane. "That holy show you put on about men telling women to go sit the corner..."

"A classic American amateur sleuthing technique, Niall—stalling." She picked up the hoe and handed it to Frankie. "Your garden tool, sir."

Sutton snatched it. "That's evidence."

"I want a receipt," Frankie said.

Sutton grunted.

Hints of sunrise glimmered on the horizon. Details of Frankie's roses began to emerge from the lessening gloom. Bushes and vines and tree-forms filled a space Gethsemane remembered as a patch of snarled brambles.

"Hey, Frankie," she said, "maybe later today when the sun's up you can show me around the garden. It's hard to tell in this light but I think it might be beautiful."

"How's this afternoon sound? There's one in particular I want to show you. It's a hearty rambler, quite strong. It repeat flowers, even in poor soil, no matter how rough you treat it. It has gorgeous fully double blooms so deep red they're almost black. It refuses to be tamed and is taking over the side wall. I dubbed it, 'Fearless Brown.'"

The aroma of coffee greeted her when she stumbled into Carraigfaire a couple of hours later. "Where's my favorite ghost?" she called out as she followed the fragrance to the kitchen.

"Where I always am." Eamon sent a steaming mug of caffeinated goodness sliding across the table. "At your service."

"Irish, have I told you lately how—"

"How much I aggravate you?"

"How happy I am that I was cheated out of a dream gig, had my bags stolen, accepted a make-ends-meet job, moved into a haunted house, and ended up with you as a roommate?"

Eamon's aura glowed pink with embarrassment. "Aw, shucks, Ma'am," he said in his best American cowboy accent.

Gethsemane saluted him with her coffee mug. "Cheers."

Twenty-Three

Two weeks after the Director of Public Prosecutions agreed to prosecute Karl Dietrich for murder, attempted murder, and kidnapping, Gethsemane walked into the Mad Rabbit. She ordered a Bushmills 21 at the bar and made her way through the early evening crowd toward the tables at the back.

"Gethsemane, hi!" A cheerful voice stopped her halfway there. Reston waved her cast-free arm.

"How are you?" Gethsemane asked. "Glad to see you've been freed from your plaster prison. Or do they only use fiberglass now? How's the wrist?"

"Great. No pain, a wee bit of stiffness. But Brian says if I complete my rehab, that will go away. This is Brian." She introduced Gethsemane to the tall, handsome, red-head who stood with his arm around Reston's waist.

"Pleased to meet you Brian," Gethsemane said. "Why do you look familiar?"

"You probably saw me at the hospital."

"Brian is one of the fierce orthopedists who put my wrist back together."

The young man blushed. "Not full-fledged yet. Doing my internship."

"He's already brilliant, though." Reston kissed him on the

cheek. "Oh, guess what? I've got an art show opening in Dublin in three months.

"That's wonderful, Reston. Your own show. How exciting. That's such an honor."

"Well, not just mine. It's a group show with two other women. 'Floral Illusions.' Abstract still lifes, mostly. You're invited, of course."

"A group show in Dublin's still a big deal. I look forward to it." She spied Frankie and Niall at a rear table. "Found my party. Excuse me."

Frankie sat next to Verna Cunningham, the Latin teacher, who laughed at something he said. Niall sat across from them, his arm draped over the back of the chair of a pretty blonde who looked very much like Verna, minus a few years.

"Room for one more?" Gethsemane asked. The others slid over to make room for her chair. "Good to see you off desk duty, Niall."

"Good to be back in the Superintendent's good graces. And Sutton's back on speaking terms. And I beat them both at last night's poker game."

She high-fived Frankie. "Congratulations. I just heard the news. The International Rose Hybridizers awarded 'Sandra Sechrest' best in show. A well-deserved gold medal, my friend."

"I just wish there had been a show," Verna said. "They should have handed Frankie that gold medal up on stage in front of the whole village. And they should have let you play your solo, Gethsemane."

The blonde next to Niall spoke up. "Vern, after what happened, they could hardly have gone through with the garden show. That would have been…" She waved her hand in the air.

"Gethsemane," Verna said, "have you met my sister, Vivian?"

The women shook hands.

"Vivi's just enrolled at University College Cork, in the PhD program in performance. She's a savage flutist, aren't you Vivi?"

"Not nearly as talented as you, Dr. Brown. When Vern told me you were in Dunmullach, so close to Cork, of course I had to get myself invited down to meet you."

"Please," Gethsemane said, "call me—"

"Sissy," Frankie interjected. "We all do."

She made a face. She'd have kicked him under the table if she could have been certain of not kicking Verna.

Verna elbowed Frankie in the ribs. "Stop it. You know she hates that name."

"Let me make it up to you." Frankie reached under the table and brought up a small pot containing a miniature rose full of tiny pink blooms and lush green leaves.

"My rose." Gethsemane pulled the pot to her and buried her nose in a blossom. The delicate sweet scent filled her nostrils. "You resurrected it. You're deadly, Frankie. An effing genius."

"Ten points for decent use of Irish slang," Niall said.

A gasp from Verna cut off the table's laughter. She stared toward the Rabbit's front door, a pained expression on her face.

"Vern?" Vivian laid her hand over her sister's.

Verna, her gaze fixed on the pub's entrance, stifled a sob.

Gethsemane and the others turned to see what had upset the Latin teacher.

Three men, a thin brunet with a square jaw and unkind eyes, flanked by a tall, burly blond with a florid scar down his cheek and a handsome Asian wearing trousers so well-cut they looked as if they'd been sewn directly onto him and Italian leather Oxfords Niall must have envied, had entered the pub. The three stood in the doorway, surveying the crowd.

Vivian rose from her chair. "I'll get rid of him."

Verna grabbed her sister's wrist and pulled her back down. "No, don't. Don't cause a scene."

"You know those fellas?" Frankie asked.

"Not the two on the ends," Verna said. "But I know the one in the middle, the brunet. I'd hoped he was dead." She gave in to the sobs and fled the table.

ALEXIA GORDON

A writer since childhood, Alexia Gordon won her first writing prize in the 6th grade. She continued writing through college but put literary endeavors on hold to finish medical school and Family Medicine residency training. She established her medical career then returned to writing fiction.

Raised in the southeast, schooled in the northeast, she relocated to the west where she completed Southern Methodist University's Writer's Path program. She admits Texas brisket is as good as Carolina pulled pork. She practices medicine in North Chicago, IL. She enjoys the symphony, art collecting, embroidery, and ghost stories.

The Gethsemane Brown Mystery Series
by Alexia Gordon

MURDER IN G MAJOR (#1)
DEATH IN D MINOR (#2)
KILLING IN C SHARP (#3)
FATALITY IN F (#4)

Henery Press Mystery Books

And finally, before you go...
Here are a few other mysteries
you might enjoy:

COUNTERFEIT CONSPIRACIES

Ritter Ames

A Bodies of Art Mystery (#1)

Laurel Beacham may have been born with a silver spoon in her mouth, but she has long since lost it digging herself out of trouble. Her father gambled and womanized his way through the family fortune before skiing off an Alp, leaving her with more tarnish than trust fund. Quick wits and connections have gained her a reputation as one of the world's premier art recovery experts. The police may catch the thief, but she reclaims the missing masterpieces.

The latest assignment, however, may be her undoing. Using every ounce of luck and larceny she possesses, Laurel must locate a priceless art icon and rescue a co-worker (and ex-lover) from a master criminal, all the while matching wits with a charming new nemesis. Unfortunately, he seems to know where the bodies are buried—and she prefers hers isn't next.

Available at booksellers nationwide and online

Visit www.henerypress.com for details

FATAL BRUSHSTROKE

Sybil Johnson

An Aurora Anderson Mystery (#1)

A dead body in her garden and a homicide detective on her doorstep...Computer programmer and tole-painting enthusiast Aurora (Rory) Anderson doesn't envision finding either when she steps outside to investigate the frenzied yipping coming from her own back yard. After all, she lives in a quiet California beach community where violent crime is rare and murder even rarer.

Suspicion falls on Rory when the body buried in her flowerbed turns out to be someone she knows—her tole-painting teacher, Hester Bouquet. Just two weeks before, Rory attended one of Hester's weekend seminars, an unpleasant experience she vowed never to repeat. As evidence piles up against Rory, she embarks on a quest to identify the killer and clear her name. Can Rory unearth the truth before she encounters her own brush with death?

Available at booksellers nationwide and online

Visit www.henerypress.com for details

CIRCLE OF INFLUENCE
Annette Dashofy

A Zoe Chambers Mystery (#1)

Zoe Chambers, paramedic and deputy coroner in rural Pennsylvania's tight-knit Vance Township, has been privy to a number of local secrets over the years, some of them her own. But secrets become explosive when a dead body is found in the Township Board President's abandoned car.

As a January blizzard rages, Zoe and Police Chief Pete Adams launch a desperate search for the killer, even if it means uncovering secrets that could not only destroy Zoe and Pete, but also those closest to them.

Available at booksellers nationwide and online

Visit www.henerypress.com for details

MURDER AT THE PALACE

Margaret Dumas

A Movie Palace Mystery (#1)

Welcome to the Palace movie theater! Now Showing: Philandering husbands, ghostly sidekicks, and a murder or two.

When Nora Paige's movie-star husband leaves her for his latest co-star, she flees Hollywood to take refuge in San Francisco at the Palace, a historic movie theater that shows the classic films she loves. There she finds a band of misfit film buffs who care about movies (almost) as much as she does.

She also finds some shady financial dealings and the body of a murdered stranger. Oh, and then there's Trixie, the lively ghost of a 1930's usherette who appears only to Nora and has a lot to catch up on. With the help of her new ghostly friend, can Nora catch the killer before there's another murder at the Palace?

Available at booksellers nationwide and online

Visit www.henerypress.com for details

CPSIA information can be obtained
at www.ICGtesting.com
Printed in the USA
LVHW081608150219
607700LV00014B/304/P